At That Moment She Knew She Was Totally His . . .

The silence was velvet. It was as though he were reading her mind and heart, seeing the thoughts behind her eyes, as he slowly leaned forward to move his lips against hers. And through that warm, impassioned kiss that seemed to part her soul, she could hear him murmur, "It is I who need you, Sarita. Don't ever think it's the other way around. You are my strength more than I am yours."

And then Morgan's lips coaxed and caressed hers. His tongue glided searchingly, sensuously, inside her mouth. Involuntarily she pushed herself back against the wall, but his hands caught and held her face motionless for his lips to savor. He took away and he gave, and Sarita, her eyes closed, felt herself sway against him . . . the victim and the victor.

Dear Reader:

We trust you will enjoy this Richard Gallen romance. We plan to bring you more of the best in both contemporary and historical romantic fiction with four exciting new titles each month.

We'd like your help.

We value your suggestions and opinions. They will help us to publish the kind of romances you want to read. Please send us your comments, or just let us know which Richard Gallen romances you have especially enjoyed. Write to the address below. We're looking forward to hearing from you!

Happy reading!

Richard Gallen Books
330 Steelcase Road East,
Markham, Ontario L3R 2M1

Flowers In Winter

MURIEL BRADLEY

PUBLISHED BY RICHARD GALLEN BOOKS
Distributed by POCKET BOOKS

Distributed in Canada by PaperJacks Ltd., a Licensee
of the trademarks of Simon & Schuster, a division of
Gulf+Western Corporation.

Books by Muriel Bradley

Tanya
The Sudden Summer
Destiny's Star
Flowers in Winter

This novel is a work of fiction. Names, characters, places and incidents
are either the product of the author's imagination or are used fictitiously.
Any resemblance to actual events or locales or persons, living or dead,
is entirely coincidental.

 A RICHARD GALLEN BOOKS *Original* publication

Distributed by
POCKET BOOKS, a Simon & Schuster division of
GULF & WESTERN CORPORATION
1230 Avenue of the Americas, New York, N.Y. 10020
In Canada distributed by PaperJacks Ltd.,
330 Steelcase Road, Markham, Ontario.

ISBN: 0-671-45142-1

First Pocket Books printing August, 1982

10 9 8 7 6 5 4 3 2 1

RICHARD GALLEN and colophon are trademarks
of Simon & Schuster and Richard Gallen & Co., Inc.

Printed in Canada

FOR STAR HELMER—
who looked over my shoulder
from three thousand miles away

Flowers In Winter

Chapter One

THE TWO WOMEN HAD ALWAYS WORKED WELL together. Until today. Sarita was the first to sense trouble approaching. It was something in the brusque tone of the senior vice-president's voice when she stuck her head into the younger woman's office and invited her to share lunch out of a couple of brown deli bags in the conference room.

"Okay, on my way." Sarita began putting folders into her top drawer. Then she looked up, but Meg Kirby hadn't waited. She'd already disappeared down the hall. Sarita shrugged. She wondered what was crackling in the wind at Dome Advertising. Even Peter Dome, who was usually easygoing, had been testy these last few days. Sarita recognized his attitude as the big-deal-about-to-be-made syndrome.

Sarita Miller, head of Dome's research department, was aware of her own touchiness but realized it had its roots in events occurring in her personal life. No one knew about her breakup with Ross Bailey. Yet. Of course, with Peter Dome and Ross, Peter's eminent lawyer friend, it wouldn't be long before the news flew around the office like Tinker Bell. She could see the gossip, like tracings of light, flashing from the water cooler to the men's room to the Xerox machine and on into the annex where the computer stood.

Everyone had expected her to marry Ross and live happily ever after. High excitement would hit when her office mates learned this wasn't going to happen. Did she care?

Sarita stood up. She was a tall young woman, slim-hipped and supple, and the sudden alertness of her movement sent her short blond hair spinning out like the abrupt unfurling of a yellow fan. One thing she would never do, and that was to confide the real reason for her split with her fiancé. It had come to her gradually, the knowledge that Ross had serious character flaws she couldn't overlook, that he was serpentine in his dealings with clients, devious in his various financial operations. She wondered if Peter Dome knew the extent of Ross Bailey's conniving sharp practices. She doubted it. Peter was such an honest man himself. At any rate, Sarita wouldn't be the one to tell tales. Unless it became truly necessary.

So the answer to whether she cared was no, not now.

Well, let's have at it, she thought, and started down the hall toward a brown bag business lunch.

Seated at the conference room table, Sarita glanced at Meg, unwrapped the tinfoil around the stuffed pita bread, then stared out the window. To lighten the mood, she talked about the weather. "Meg, it's sleeting again. You love winter, don't you?"

Not answering Sarita, but talking to herself, Meg inspected the watercress in her sandwich. She grumbled, "They got it right this time. What do you know!" She looked up at Sarita. "Of course I love winter. I have to. This is Chicago, the world's winter garden spot. Yesterday we had eight inches of snow on top of six inches the day before. It's icing up now. Don't look complacent because you have an apartment in town while we commuters live dangerously trying to get home. Yeah, sure I like winter . . . I have to accept the inevitable." Suddenly Meg looked dreamy. "Sarita . . . Dome has that Caribbean account. Think we could work out a trade deal with one of the hotels down there?"

"You could, but you won't. I tell you, you love this weather. Remember the time you asked me out to your Glen Ellyn suburb and we rode the snowplows?"

Meg Kirby nodded and then ran an index finger up the bridge of her short nose to push back the black-rimmed specs that gave her proper focus. The red-haired executive had a wonderful smile, so most people considered her to be a very pretty woman. All of a sudden she stopped being irritable and turned on the smile. She was softening up Sarita for reasons of her own.

Bemused at Meg's change of manner, Sarita grinned back. "You were a real chum to cover for me while I had to be away at that convention these last few days."

Meg opened a half-pint carton of nonfat milk. "Sar, you're very good at what you do. When you're good, you make me look good. So when I cover for you, I'm just looking out for myself. You'd do the same for me. We have to have a life support system around here. Now, what about Coombs Corp? Should we be nervous handling their bigger account buys since they're putting some of their real estate holdings on the market?"

Sarita helped herself to a handful of Meg's sunflower seeds before saying, "There's nothing to worry about with them. They're solid, with an okay cash flow. I've researched the whole deal and sent the report to Peter, so he knows about it."

"You sure?"

"Sure I'm sure. You remember when General Motors put its mid-Manhattan headquarters building up for sale last year? Same thing here. Most of Coombs Corp's real estate is undervalued on their books because they've owned it so long. That looks bad, even though the price they can get for it today is astronomical. Their move simply indicates that commercial real estate is a hot market and they're going to take advantage of it."

"That sounds fine. They'll probably pump the new money they get into acquisitions, which will mean more account goodies for us." Meg pushed at her specs again and murmured curiously, "Did Ross Bailey fill you in on the Coombs Corp matter? I know, as a lawyer holding hands with City Hall, he has a scan on every deal in town."

"I told you, I researched Coombs myself. The only person that helped me was the computer. I didn't even turn Coombs over to the staff."

"Sorry. Forget I asked. I have never been known for my sensitivities." Meg crumpled her paper bag, glanced at the chit from Murray's Deli and absentmindedly tossed both in the direction of the woven wood basket beneath the conference table. She was thinking to herself that another woman might have been incensed by her suggestion that Ross Bailey had been an information source. But Sarita, though she'd tensed visibly at the mention of Ross's name, was reasonable and non-neurotic. She was not the kind to look for insults where none were intended. How rare that was! And Sarita wasn't a meek mouse either. Meg darted a close look at her lunch companion, intrigued by the sudden stubborn set of Sarita's jaw.

Something was wrong. The nature of her job made Meg Kirby perceptive, if not especially sensitive, to the feelings of others. There was a riptide of unease flowing in the air of the room. The way Sarita looked at this moment indicated that trouble was afoot. Meg studied the expression, or lack of it, on the face of the other woman. Behind Sarita's fine-boned features and her straight-searching blue eyes that seemed to change color to match her moods, there was turmoil.

Meg frowned. Then it happened.

Sarita bowed her head, laced both hands across her eyes and bit at her lips in a struggle for composure. She was trembling, an involuntary tremor she couldn't hide. Horrified, she thought, I didn't know it was going to hit me this hard!

Meg started to her feet. Before she could reach her colleague's side, Sarita stopped Meg with a shaky smile. The vice-president sank back into her chair, letting Sarita choke, swallow and pull herself together. Then she reached across the conference table to touch the tips of Sarita's fingers in a warm gesture of sympathy. "If you want to talk, talk. If you don't, it's okay, I understand. Whatever is the matter, Sar, don't be too hard on yourself."

Sarita had thought she couldn't talk about Ross Bailey and the broken engagement. But she told Meg enough. Meg nodded sagely. "You're a nice woman. Ross is an attractive man. You were thrown together because of his and our boss's friendship. Now you've told him you don't want to marry him. That part is what I don't quite get. Ross isn't just another pretty face, you know. He's brainy, rich, eligible. Knows everyone worth knowing. So why not keep on being involved? Have you anything against power and money and good looks, even if the man has to be forty years old to earn his stripes?"

"I can't love him. I'm glad he doesn't really love me." Meg started to protest, but Sarita shook her head firmly. "No, he doesn't, Meg. He just thinks he does. I can tell."

Sarita knew she'd said enough. She would never tell Meg the truth, because it really wasn't Meg's business to know that Ross had shared confidences with Sarita that she wished he hadn't. He'd seemed so proud of certain duplicitous dealings, but she was embarrassed by them and by his pride in them.

Inevitably, if she told Meg even half of this, Meg would hoot and say, "Who's totally clean? From presidents to pipe fitters, we all make deals!"

But Meg surprised Sarita. "All right, Dr. Kirby will listen to you for fifty minutes. I won't charge you—it's all too interesting." She was playacting but sincere. The two discussed Ross Bailey and Sarita's upset at what had occurred between them for a rather intensive fifteen-minute span. Sarita looked at her wristwatch. She'd been very careful not to

5

destroy whatever reputation Meg might believe Ross had. As for Meg, she believed she had Sarita smiling again. Now might be the right time to bring up the new project.

Earlier, getting ready to make her pitch as she'd been instructed to do by Peter Dome, Meg had expected failure with Sarita Miller, who was Chicago born and bred. Any good native of this wonderful skyline city with its superb lakefront views would look with disdain on a venture that might take him or her to the outlands—Los Angeles and perhaps beyond. Still, Peter had asked his vice-president to give Sarita a chance at first refusal, since the concept of what was in the wind might be vastly important to Dome Advertising.

Now Meg wasn't so sure that Sarita's reaction to her proposal would be negative. Sarita might want to get away for a while. "Let's go into my office and talk," she suggested.

Back at her desk, with Sarita sitting opposite her, Meg opened a folder she brought out of the drawer. "In our little world of Dome, what I have here takes priority over anything else." She paused portentously. "Will you do background on a man named Morgan Wycoff as soon as possible—like yesterday? He maintains a low profile, but I'm certain you've heard of him. He's involved in major construction projects around the world and has headquarters in New York with offices in Houston and Los Angeles. He also has a base in banking, shopping centers, iron ore mines, strategic materials, antique art, coins, et cetera."

Sarita looked thoughtful. "I've heard of him, yes. I read about him in a *Time* mag article while I was doing that antinuclear report for our Utah account. You seem to know all about the man. What's there for me to do?"

"We might have a very interesting situation here. A terrific client. Not Morgan himself, but his wife—his former wife."

Sarita's eyes widened in surprise, and she leaned forward intently. "I do remember. Patrice Wycoff."

6

"Exactement."

"There was a rumored scandal—almost a lawsuit, I think. She retired, gave up that successful Patrice line of cosmetics, sold out. I can't recall the actual details, but they'll come to me. Where is she now? What is she doing?"

Meg was pleased to see the hunter's gleam in Sarita's eye. "That's for you to find out and tell us. An associate of Wycoff's contacted Peter very hush-hush. Peter asked me to discuss it with you. After you do homework on Wycoff, would you be willing to fly to the West Coast and see his representative there?"

"When do you want me to leave?"

"We can have you on a flight on Thursday."

"Three days from now. How long will I be there?"

Meg Kirby looked out her office window toward the chill, wind-driven February sleet that was creating dangerously slick ice conditions in the streets forty stories below. "Maybe only for a long weekend. It depends on you and what you find out—whether this is a project for us to undertake." Meg peered into the folder. "You'll have to see this Los Angeles attorney in Century City. If you like the deal, feel comfortable with it and make the proper impression yourself . . . you may go off our payroll."

An astonished Sarita rose from her chair.

Meg put out a detaining hand and quipped, "Oh, we'll continue to pay into your profit sharing and retirement, don't you worry about *that* detail. It's just that Wycoff and Patrice may want it that way."

"They're together?"

"In a sense."

"But if we discover there's potential in this for Dome Advertising, why can't we handle whatever it is from here?"

Meg's smile was wide and beautiful. "Because the tycoon and the ex-wife live on some kind of fabulous estate, and the problem for which they need an expert in marketing survey techniques—as well as savvy in cosmetics research—is under wraps there."

"Meg, where is *there?*"

"Hawaii. To pinpoint it more precisely—an island called Maui." As she stared out at the lashing sleet, Meg's smile was beatific. "No one ever promised that life would be fair, you know."

Sarita walked to the closed door of the office. Her back turned to Meg, she looked down pensively at the doorknob under her hand. "You said—now let me get this straight— you said an associate of Wycoff's contacted Peter in a hush-hush manner." Sarita swung around to face the vice-president.

In profile, the delicacy of Sarita's forehead, nose and throat was misleading, projecting a defenseless cameo. Full-face, however, Sarita's dark brows above large and muti-nous sea-color eyes, and her firm red lips, presented a far more formidable picture. "That associate wouldn't be Ross, would it?"

"Why should it be Bailey? Peter himself knows all the important people around, and our firm has a fine reputation worldwide."

"And Ross knows everyone too. No doubt including Wycoff. And Ross is into everything . . . worldwide." Sar-ita's smile was crisp.

Heatedly, Meg said, "Take my word for it—" She broke off quickly.

Sarita's gaze was searchlight bright. "Peter didn't tell you who it was who initially approached him about this, did he?"

Meg finally admitted, "No, he didn't. It could've been Bailey, I suppose. Why would it make a difference?"

"Because I don't intend to be manipulated. Or deceived. If this all works out, where does my allegiance lie—with Dome, with Wycoff or with Patrice?"

Meg Kirby's response was pragmatic. "With all three, of course. You can manage that, can't you?"

Sarita gave Meg a long look and didn't respond.

"How old are you, Sar?" Meg asked dryly.

"Twenty-five. You know that very well."

"For your age, you've come a long way. You're an exec here at Dome and you head up your own department, which will have to mark time until we see what's going on out there in the Pacific. You have a blazing, bright future in front of you." Meg slapped her hand on the desk. "Sarita Miller, I want you to think about that."

The 747 taking Sarita to Los Angeles lifted off from Chicago's O'Hare International Airport at the start of a blizzard that was to be remembered as the most severe in that city's weather history. The plane landed hours late in a downpour of rain that had brought its fifth day of disaster to Southern California.

The storm had undermined hillside houses and sluiced them down the narrow canyons. Small cars were buried to their rooftops in mud. Larger cars stalled in the middle of flooded intersections, with a twenty-four-hour wait for the tow trucks. Public transit was prohibited from running, but independent cabs couldn't be prevented from operating if their drivers were willing to face the worst. Pedestrians were nowhere. Muck spilled against the barred doors of fashionable shops. The westside streets were transformed from normally dry gullies into rushing flood waters.

The tough airport taxi with its equally tough driver deposited Sarita, her one piece of luggage and bulging briefcase at the main entrance to her hotel. Its doorman, once a dazzle of uniformed chic, now stood in hard hat and slicker with moisture puddling down the brim of his nose. He held an umbrella over Sarita's head and handed her to a slippery position inside the marbled entryway. She was wearing a sensible Midwest raincoat, a soggy nylon rain hat and rubber boots; nothing helped and everything leaked. Part of her job was to be aware of weather reports for clients, so she had expected this curtain of Southern California rain that obscured palm trees, hibiscus hedges and traffic lights. Even the tall buildings on the Avenue of the Stars, across the way from her hotel, seemed to weave drunkenly behind the watery veil.

Sarita's bellhop extracted the key from the registration desk and led her to an elevator that shot them skyward. They walked down a cushily carpeted corridor and into a handsome room with an expanse of sliding glass doors opening onto a rain-drenched balcony. The bellhop put down the bags, checked the room, folded Sarita's tip into his palm and departed.

Tugging off her coat and cloche hat, Sarita stepped out of clammy boots and leaned forward to read the words printed on a discreet wall plaque: *For your protection, please read this notice NOW! While in your room, the door must be kept double-locked at all times. Place valuables in the lobby safe. Otherwise this hotel is not responsible. Identify all callers through the one-way door viewer before opening door.*

Sarita was familiar with precautions like these in New York and Chicago, but she hadn't expected the same directive in the City of the Angels. She shrugged and began to strip off her damp jacket and skirt. Underneath she was wearing a lace teddy, and remembering the expected intimate occasion for which she'd bought this piece of trousseau lingerie, she turned away from her tall, slender image in the full-length mirror. So much for the past, and a recently retired engagement. It had been silly of her to wear this bit of satin luxury just because she was on her first trip to Southern California.

Sarita moved to the table next to the king-sized bed and peered curiously into an ornate basket of fruit. Could these pears and grapes and giant strawberries be real? She touched them, and they were. In the basket's center was a split of California champagne, a fancy green bow decorating its gold-foiled neck. Next to the fruit basket, a Lalique crystal bowl held a florist's arrangement of hothouse tulips and daffodils. Sarita noted with amusement that the bowl was carefully lacquered to the top of the table. So much for trust. The attached card stated: *To our guest. We hope you enjoy your stay with us. Please continue to maintain security regulations for your personal safety. Again . . . welcome!*

This formidable greeting tickled Sarita's sense of the ridiculous, and she started to laugh. As she sank down onto the bed's green velvet cover, the bedside phone rang. She reached over to answer it and heard the long-distance sound rushing across half a continent.

A familiar voice chirped, "Sarita! See you got in safely! How was your trip?"

One panicked moment snapped by before Sarita answered coolly, "Ross, hello. How did you know where to find me? I only got into this hotel at the last minute because there was a cancellation." She tried not to sound surprised that Ross had called her.

"*I* got you in there, little one. Reservations are impossible in California this time of year. Everyone's ducking out on the cold weather back East and traveling to the Coast."

"I don't know why. They're having a deluge here. If you have a spare ark, send it on. I could use it." Laughter started to well up again. It was so ridiculous to be talking to Ross as if they were still intimates and he had a right to see that she was well taken care of. She tried to hold back the giggles. They must be brought on by jet lag, because the situation wasn't funny.

Ross was saying, "They're masochists out there, so they don't mind their climate. Tell me, are you comfortable? Did the management send up champagne, flowers, the works? Are you glad to talk to me?"

Her former fiancé was the last person in the world she wanted to talk to. In an attempt to be civil, she heard herself mutter, "Everything is fine here. There's a bar and a fridge in my room, and I'll stick the champagne into it for the next person." She added, "I'd bring you a genuine Lalique bowl as a souvenir, but these trusting people have stapled it to the table." Laughter rocked her once more at this thought.

"What's the matter with you? You sound overtired."

"I'm very tired. I swam up here from the airport."

"Sarita! Not funny!"

She stopped her nervous chatter and ran an impatient hand through her bright hair. Why the hell had Peter Dome used Ross Bailey's travel agency connections to get her into this hotel anyway?

Ross's patronizing voice ordered, "Sarita, do as I say. Have room service bring dinner up, and after that you get a good night's sleep. I'll see you in Chicago the early part of next week."

"Yes, yes, yes." Sarita hung up abruptly. Ross appeared confident they would go on as before, though she'd certainly been forthright in telling him why she couldn't marry him. Sarita hadn't been able to buffer herself against the realization that Ross Bailey was an unscrupulous and manipulative man. He was legitimate, but barely so, and too clever to be honest.

The flight to California seemed to have lost some of its adventure. Ross knew where to find her, and he probably also knew why she was here. Which was more than she did. She glanced over at her briefcase. Earlier, she had believed that it held all the answers she needed concerning the Wycoffs. Now she had some doubts.

After room service had brought her dinner and the empty cart had been wheeled into the outer hallway, she thought about that last night in Chicago. Before her departure, she and Ross had met once in her apartment. She had refused his invitation to dine with him when he had appeared unexpectedly at her door and petulantly said, "You weren't planning to leave town without at least a goodbye, were you? Sar, why must you be so self-destructive?"

What exactly did he mean by that? she had wondered. Ross had brought out all the old arguments, along with the velvet box containing the diamond she'd returned to him. He did not plead. That wasn't his style. His self-esteem wouldn't permit it. He was wonderful with words when he wanted to be, and she had seen herself as a court case that he intended to win. Finally he'd worn her down to the extent that she had resorted to subterfuge.

"I'll be back in Chicago on Monday. We'll talk then." Instinct had told her that if she didn't allow him to believe he had won, he might attack her in a more intrinsic way. He could detour her career or destroy her personal reputation by innuendo. He was a dangerous opponent, and he had the ear of everyone in town who counted. She'd been too naive in the beginning to understand this. She should have known that Ross Bailey had the sensual pride of Lucifer.

Before he had left her apartment that last night, he'd made a move to take her by force. She'd squirmed awkwardly away from his grasp, ripping her velvet lounging robe with the gymnastics of her action. His eyes had burned angrily at her for her refusal of sex, but he'd walked out of her apartment without slamming the door. She'd defeated him again.

After Sarita had heard the hum of the descending elevator, she'd opened the apartment door once more and slammed it shut, hard. She had done this for Ross Bailey, and it had made her feel better.

Now, as she turned off the bedside lamp, the dull glow of the brass wall plaque by the room door caught her eye. She could double-lock a door. To bar Ross from her life might be more difficult. The clock radio by the bed was set at an FM station. In the darkness she clicked it on and let the music flow softly into the room while the rain rattled the sliding glass doors to the balcony. Sarita made herself concentrate on tomorrow and the meeting with the attorney who represented the Morgan Wycoff interests. Almost immediately, she fell asleep.

Chapter Two

THE NEXT MORNING IT WAS STILL RAINING WHEN Sarita stepped off the elevator onto the thirtieth floor of the Century City high-rise. Her hotel was nearby, and normally she would have walked the distance, but today she'd taken a cab. Sarita's wristwatch told her it was half-past nine on Friday and gave the date. She was exactly on time.

The receptionist in the office suite of Morgan Wycoff's representative was a glossy youngster with a great tan and Malibu-blond hair whitened by the sun that shone most of the year. She took Sarita into a functional waiting room, brought her a cup of tea, hesitated, then produced a fresh Danish on its own saucer. Her accent was a curious blend of North Dakota and some Sunset Boulevard school of drama. "Will you wait momentarily, please? Mrs. Adams is here, of course."

"Of course."

After a fifteen-minute wait, Phoebe Adams appeared. As the elegantly tailored, black-haired attorney led Sarita into her private office suite, she apologized. "I had to shower, and something was wrong with the showerhead. I tinkered it right again, but it put me off schedule." Sarita's eyes widened. Phoebe went on. "I suppose I should explain. I didn't go home last night. I slept here, and I always keep an extra wardrobe." While Phoebe Adams talked, Sarita was aware that she was being scrutinized from beneath those long black eyelashes. "I was at it until three this morning, reviewing depositions. I have to be in court later today." The attorney gestured to a chair opposite hers. "Did Sylvia bring you tea?"

"It was very good."

"Probably clover blossom. Syl's big on natural foods. Still, we all have our transgressions. Syl's is health tea and junk Danish. I'm sure you got the Danish?" Sarita nodded. "Now that we've put domestic details behind us, let's get to it."

Phoebe Adams had been studying Sarita, taking in every detail of her manner, attitude and appearance while talking about inconsequential matters. Sarita understood the procedure; she'd done it herself on research interviews. As she sat there, she wondered whether she particularly cared about being put under a magnifying glass, or even whether this project would turn out to be the appealing blockbuster at which Meg Kirby had hinted. Would the impression Sarita made on this lawyer really matter as far as Dome Advertising was concerned?

From habit, Sarita straightened her shoulders and smoothed the skirt of her gray wool suit, then became uneasily aware that her hair had reached the shaggy stage. She hadn't had time for her usual just-below-the-ears trim before the hurried flight to the West Coast. The hem of her skirt was mud-splashed. But the rest of her was all right, she hoped—including her brain and the responses she was making.

Why did she hope? If the deal was offered, did she really want to leave Chicago and research this mysterious account for Dome? She'd be leaving behind her good friend, the huge main-frame computer, which dominated the space down the hall from her office. However, she had come prepared with other tools of her trade—graphs, charts, tape recorder, notebooks. In case. In case what? She'd better listen to Phoebe Adams.

"Patrice needs someone who's completely discreet, who will be loyal and will be on her side—in everything. But not a yes person. Are you a yes person, Sarita Miller?"

"Not at all," Sarita replied evenly. Her level tone reassured Phoebe Adams. The attorney did not feel comfortable with women whose delicate feelings bruised easily. Sarita herself was impressed by the attractive black-eyed lawyer, who didn't seem to think it at all unusual that she should work alone on a case presentation for most of the night, shower in her office bathroom and be ready for a nine-thirty appointment in the morning. She was human, though. Phoebe had kept Sarita waiting fifteen minutes.

The two women talked for more than an hour. Questions were asked and answered. Credibilities were tested. At the end of that time, each felt she knew the other fairly well. Both were accustomed to making quick, perceptive judgments. As they stood and shook hands, Sarita realized no hint had been given as to the nature of Patrice Wycoff's personal project and its seemingly urgent need for a consumer analyst to run a product survey.

She was about to bring this up when Phoebe Adams said briskly, "As far as your contract with the Wycoffs is concerned, I'd say go. But mine isn't the final commitment to make. Would you be willing to fly to Maui—at our expense, of course—and talk to Patrice? Or rather, to Morgan Wycoff? If they both meet with you, I can say the project belongs to Dome Advertising. The budget will be sizable. There's an interesting potential for you personally. You'll be working independently." Sarita sensed that doing research on her own was being dangled in front of her as a tantalizing offer. Ready for the query on Sarita's tongue, the attorney shook her head. "The Wycoffs prefer that I say nothing further about their project until they talk to you."

Sarita's mouth snapped shut. "May I let you know my decision this afternoon?" she asked finally.

"I'll be in court, as I said. But I'll be back in my office around seven tonight."

"I'll call then."

Phoebe smiled. "I'll be here."

Sarita knew what her own answer would be, but experience and her one-time mentor, Ross, had taught her never to be precipitous. Out in the corridor, Sarita consulted her watch. According to Chicago time, Peter Dome would have returned from a late lunch. She'd call him from her hotel and inform him of the odd fact that she was prepared to leave the next day to fly twenty-five hundred miles across the Pacific to be interviewed for a project about which she knew very little.

Phoebe Adams had hinted at independent research. Sarita knew she had the ability to do a good job. She didn't have to qualify this in her own mind with the added caution, "depending on what was required." If everything went well and hung together, this time it could be something of her own. It was *her* time. She was sure of it.

Sarita took the express elevator down and walked out into the scudding rain. And there was a cab. She looked skyward. Chalk up an ace for Sarita Miller.

United Airlines Flight 101, destination Hilo Airport on the big island of Hawaii, took off from Los Angeles at noon in the slashing storm. Within minutes the giant plane sped above the coastal islands of Santa Catalina and San Nicolas, leaving behind the last of the rain as it flew upward into brilliant sunshine.

Sarita's assigned coach seat was opposite the front bulkhead in the nonsmoking section. If no one claimed the vacant window seat next to hers, she'd move into it. In the meantime, there were background details to review on the Wycoffs. Opening her briefcase to take out a folder of data, Sarita pushed aside the extra bag of toilet articles she'd jammed into it.

The suitcase she'd brought from Chicago was being checked through to Maui, along with a new piece of luggage. Thanks to her Visa credit card, it contained last-minute clothing purchases from one of the shops in the hotel. Phoebe Adams had helped with these, advising Sarita what she'd need in the islands' temperate winter climate. The fact that the temperatures would be in the eighties had sounded unreal to Sarita. Fingering a halter top cotton dress that the lawyer had suggested she buy, even though the price tag had appalled them both, Sarita had protested, "I may be over there only forty-eight hours."

Phoebe had smiled enigmatically. "Wait till you step off the plane at Hilo and see what happens."

A hired limo had taken both women to the airport, and Phoebe had suggested that Sarita could pick up anything else she might need in the boutiques on Maui. Sarita had repeated her doubts about how long she would stay. This was only an interview she was flying to, not a firm commitment.

Phoebe hadn't replied. Discretion had told her to withhold her own assurance that Sarita Miller would soon be shopping in Lahaina, Maui's historic town. As for that unsightly raincoat and nylon hat that the Chicagoan was wearing, Phoebe had been certain Sarita would dispose of that unchic, though sensible, attire before she was fifty miles over the Pacific. Phoebe knew the lure. When the flight attendants murmured their welcoming *aloha,* when they thanked their passengers with a soft *mahalo,* when the corks popped and the complimentary champagne was poured— one quickly shed all mainland hangups.

Sarita might have a Midwestern attachment to that practical raincoat of hers, but she'd soon shuck it. It rained in the islands, but there it was more a form of liquid sunlight that misted one's hair and caressed one's skin. Phoebe Adams knew Hawaii, and her keen black eyes had gentled with her memories as she'd said goodbye to Sarita Miller.

Sarita had already stuffed raincoat and hat into the overhead compartment. Now, in a skirt and blouse, her golden hair tucked behind her ears, she looked over the summary she'd made up of newspaper and magazine pieces on Patrice.

The information had come from periodicals dating back through the years. Some of them featured Patrice on the cover. In several of the more recent photographs, Scavullo had worked his cover art magic. Though Patrice looked gorgeous in her elfin fashion, one couldn't tell much about her as a person. One saw merely a petite and perfect body, a delicately featured face and a bang of dark hair hiding what might be enormous eyes.

The articles themselves were mostly puff pieces extolling the empress of the cosmetics industry who happened to be her own best model. There was no year given in which to bracket Patrice's age. She appeared to have arrived in the United States from Belgium during the Korean War, but Belgium was not her birthplace. She had worked first as a laboratory assistant to an American chemist. In some undefined manner her career had soared from that point. She had expanded into her own business and finally into her own handsome multistoried building in Manhattan. That address had since been supplanted by a high-rise condominium. Patrice and Morgan Wycoff had been married for nearly ten years before their quiet divorce a few years ago.

Sarita shuffled her papers to those about Morgan Wycoff. Here again, nothing had been written, even in *Fortune* magazine, that Sarita could consider to be "in depth."

As Meg Kirby had suggested, Morgan Wycoff had kept a low profile. Oddly, there were no pictures available of this man. He seemed to have bowed out behind Patrice's image. Sarita knew, however, that he was now thirty-seven years old, had been born in Webster Grove, Missouri, had been graduated from the Missouri School of Mines at Rolla and had gone on to an advanced degree in engineering at MIT. Aptitude guided by knowledge, opportunity and luck had landed him in the heart of several expanding industries, and he too, like Patrice, had skyrocketed into the stratosphere of richness and power. Sarita was sure that the two of them must have worked sixteen-hour days at a minimum.

The Korean War had ended in 1953. Morgan would have

been about eight years old. Patrice herself had probably been close to age twenty when she arrived in the States. Was this interesting thirteen-year difference between them significant? It might have been at one time, but certainly not now.

The drawl of the captain's voice came over the loud-speaker. "For those of you interested in figures, flight time from Los Angeles to Hilo is five hours. Right now the temperature in Hilo is seventy-eight degrees." Applause erupted from the passengers traveling in a tour group. This was what they'd left their frigid East Coast homes to hear. The soothing Texas accent continued. "Total distance from the mainland to the Big Island of Hawaii is twenty-five hundred miles. We'll be cruising at thirty-five thousand feet initially. Speed will be approximately five hundred and thirty miles per hour the first half of the trip, five hundred and ten miles the second half. Touchdown at Hilo is scheduled for three twenty-six, Hawaiian time."

Sarita set back her watch to conform to the time difference between the mainland and Hawaii. She was preparing to move into the vacant window seat when a man stopped in the aisle beside her. She looked up at him and he looked down at her. In that moment without speech, their eyes met. His were brown, amber-flecked, unreadable. Sarita's were very blue and slightly puzzled. The charged instant sped by.

The man excused himself and swung six feet of compactly built, well-tailored masculinity into the seat beside her. He settled down with a sigh and muttered, "Best location in the plane, plenty of leg room. Did I disturb you? I've been at the bar back there in the middle of the plane, but I kept an eye on my seat here."

Chatting it up with the pretty bar hostess, I'll bet, Sarita thought dryly. So this was her assigned seatmate. For all his no-nonsense appearance, she hoped he wasn't drunk.

"I missed out on the champagne they served earlier. How was it?"

"Intoxicating." Sarita's smile was sweetly cool.

There was a silence. Sarita wondered why she felt an instant prickling resistance to this fellow passenger. The most obvious reason was that he was now settled into "her" window seat. Another reason might be the man's remarkably smooth expression. He seemed almost bland, until one looked beneath the surface. Sarita suspected an intentional mask, but he hadn't fooled her. She was already aware of the lurking strength in the deeply tanned face with its broad cheekbones, strong nose, sensual yet firm lips and forceful outline of jaw.

Sarita sat up straighter. Why was she feeling shy and unequal to the occasion with this stranger? She was even reacting in a slightly hostile manner. She glanced down and saw that he was wearing pointed-toed stockman's boots. Showoff, she thought critically. Probably a Hollywood type. Yet she knew she was wrong about that. There was too much substance to him. Trying not to seem too obvious, she took in the immaculate fit of his beige pants, the custom-made tan shirt, the expensive tweed jacket, all of which almost too cleverly matched his eyes, his russet-brown hair and his sun-bronzed skin. She sneaked another surreptitious look at him. He wasn't wearing a wedding band, but that didn't mean a thing. He appeared to be in his mid-thirties and was probably spoken for. Weren't they all? But why should she care?

In his turn, the man beside Sarita let his tawny gaze flick quickly toward her. Taking his time, he summed her up physically and approved of the total he received. Beneath a rather lovely face was a creamy throat, and the unfettered swell of bosom told him she never wore a bra because she didn't need to. The firm breasts were upstanding above a slender rib cage that tapered to the delicate in-curve of waist, a flat stomach and trim hips.

"Are you one of those who are interested in the pilot's figures?" he asked, obviously interested, but not in flight statistics.

"Figures are my business," Sarita replied stiffly. She deplored the crisp sound of her voice. Why was she feeling uptight? She knew why. It was because she simply couldn't believe her luck. After all the talented, creative too-fats, too-thins, too-youngs and too-olds in her business, here was someone different and appealing. Best of all, she was certain he wasn't interested in graphs and charts and marketing procedures. He just didn't look as if he were. Not a terribly astute reason, but one she could live with.

It was only now, in this vast Pacific sky, that she was beginning to realize a facet of her life that she hadn't admitted to before. The truth had been clamoring to come out, and finally it had broken through. Four years at Northwestern University, a master's degree in business administration, then Dome Advertising and then . . . No more "and thens." She suddenly felt released from the necessity of trying to be superbright and was amazed that she'd never before recognized what had caused the edginess hidden deep within her.

No one in the office had known, not even Meg. To her colleagues, she was always even-tempered Sarita Miller. Give her a directive, and she would do it. Others could be abrasive and vent their frustrations, but Sarita was wonderful; she never took anything personally. One could count on Sarita. Up here in the sky, no one could count on her. She might do something totally fantastic and out of character. Whether or not she really would, it was nice to think about anyway.

The carts with the midday meal arrived. Trays with tiny purple vanda orchids on the side of each plate were placed in front of Sarita and her seatmate. She'd chosen Paradise Salad from the menu card and looked down now at a combination of shrimp and diced celery, tomatoes, mushrooms, water chestnuts and onions, served with fresh Hawaiian pineapple spears.

The hostess glided by. "More champagne?"

Sarita agreed, sipped and glanced past her companion's

profile to the view beyond the plane window of a cerulean sky scattered with white meringue clouds.

The two of them ate in comfortable silence. At least Sarita hoped it seemed that way to him. The next course was Chicken Teriyaki, marinated in soy sauce, baked and topped with pineapple chunks and served with rice and Oriental vegetables. Later came Carrot Cake Monte Carlo and excellent black coffee. Everything tasted unbelievably delicious.

She was about to turn to the man beside her and speak when the pilot's voice came on again. "Are you ready— those of you who like figures? We're now cruising at thirty-seven thousand feet. Head winds, twenty-five knots. We're on schedule. That's it for now. Enjoy the film coming up."

The showing of films was a part of the many flights Sarita had taken that she disliked. To be encapsulated in silver and floating high above the earth was a surreal experience, not to be profaned by either a movie screen or earphones dispensing classical or country music.

Sarita's seatmate pulled down the window shade, shutting out clouds, light and sky. When Sarita protested, the man shrugged. "I don't like it either, but others want to watch the film." He punched a seat button, and a spear of overhead light beamed down.

Since neither of them intended to be entertained by canned sight or sound, there was no reason to conduct a liaison in silence. Sarita cleared her throat and said, "I'm Sarita Miller. Destination Maui."

"I'll be going right along with you." His eyes, their admiring expression momentarily unguarded, watched her lips.

"You're on vacation?"

"Not quite that." There was a pause before he resumed speaking. "A little earlier you said figures were your business. Are you a CPA on your way to get a client out of some tax trouble?"

"Wrong guess."

23

"I didn't think I was right." His lips quirked in amusement. Then he completely startled Sarita by his next action. Leaning forward, he took her face between his hands and with a quick flick released the hair she'd tucked primly behind each ear. Golden strands fell in loose curves against her cheeks. "That's better," he said. "You don't scare me now."

"I . . . scare you?" She was astounded. "When did that happen?"

"Because you were sitting in the seat next to the one assigned to me, I watched you from the bar back there. You looked so damned serious, going through all those papers. Career woman type, I said to myself. What will I talk to her about, even if she wants to talk to me? Then you looked over at the hostess during the wine pouring, I saw that profile of yours and here I am."

Sarita flushed. "You are—as we used to say—putting me on."

His tawny eyes twinkling, he agreed pleasantly. "I am."

Just then the flight attendant passed, heading into the first-class compartment with a tray of after-dinner drinks. She glanced at the two of them and smiled widely. Her playful look lingered on Sarita's male companion.

"Polly . . ." he said.

The attendant paused, bending over seductively. "And what can I do for you?" It was obvious they knew each other from the bar.

He indicated the tray of drinks intended for first-class consumption only and started to take out his wallet. Polly stopped him with a flutter of her fingers. She winked and handed over a couple of drambuies. "Don't tell," she cautioned, and departed with a swish of her abbreviated muumuu.

For the remainder of the flight, while the other passengers watched the film, Sarita and her seatmate traded conversation. Sarita told him about the work she did in the advertising agency on Michigan Avenue. As to why she was going to Maui, she merely said that she was researching a project for her company.

He didn't volunteer any information about himself, but by this time Sarita didn't expect it, since he hadn't even told her his name. Instead, he shared with her all that he'd learned about the islands' history. A half hour before landing, they felt the plane's engines begin to slow. The film screen rolled up, and so did most of the window shades. The two of them looked out to see the green surface of the sea moving in slow motion beneath them.

The long, downward glide began. They switched seats, and Sarita sat at the window while he pointed out the outline of the Big Island with its awe-inspiring Kilauea Crater, crowned with heavy clouds. "Since you're an expert with figures, Sarita, you should know that Hawaii is the largest of the island group. You can put two Oahus, two Mauis and two Molokais into its four thousand square miles. I've been on the ranchland slopes of both of the other volcanoes. Mauna Kea is probably dormant, but Mauna Loa and Kilauea are very much alive, active enough at times to fire up and spill that black lava flow you can see even from here." He paused. "It's the sweet life, the good life. Sometimes I think I've been branded like the up-country cattle on Maui . . . by a special magic."

She looked at him, at his amber-dark eyes brooding toward the island that seemed to move upward to meet them. She thought she knew something about him now. He probably was in cattle ranching. He had removed his jacket sometime earlier, and the pure cotton of his shirt stretched tautly across his chest and wide shoulders. An unexpected ripple of wild attraction stirred within her. Carefully she turned her gaze away from the bronze of his skin glimpsed through the thin tan shirt.

"These islands own me," he concluded as though speaking to himself.

He looked so serious, she became a little uncomfortable and tried to keep her tone light. "I have to leave in a few days. I hope the islands don't put their mark on me."

"Maui will."

"Why are you so sure?" Sarita challenged.

"I'll see to it. I'll show you the real Maui after you have that interview you told me about. When is it set up for?"

"Later today or tomorrow. I'm to take the interisland plane from Hilo to Maui's Kahului Airport. Someone will meet me there, and from then on . . ." Sarita shrugged. "It's in the hands of those ancient Hawaiian gods you told me about. I really don't know how long I'm going to be here."

The man regarded her beneath half-closed lids. "I will visit the goddess Pele in her fiery palace at Kilauea and make her an irresistible offering so that she cannot refuse my request."

"And that is?"

"That you will remain here in the islands as long as your heart desires."

Chapter Three

SARITA DESCENDED THE RAMP INTO HILO AIRport, her jacket and briefcase slung over one arm. Her raincoat and nylon cloche hat were left behind—forgotten in the compartment above her plane seat. It was a starting point unrealized at the time.

Sarita's companion moved ahead of her through the crowd to negotiate a plumeria blossom lei from a pretty young Hawaiian girl. The girl's smile was pearly white as she handed it over. Oh, he was a charmer, all right, Sarita thought, amused, as she watched the transaction. The man came back to place the lei over Sarita's head, then bent and kissed her lightly on the cheek. "Welcome to the islands."

He adjusted the yellow and white petals around her neck, holding the garland toward him as he guided it down her shirtfront. Sarita shivered as the back of his sun-bronzed hands slid over her pointing breasts. The thin silk of her blouse wasn't a barrier, but enhanced the provocativeness of his touch. With his head down close to hers, he appeared absorbed in his task. She could feel the warmth of his breath, the emanation of his physical power and protectiveness.

A strong urge seized her to slide her fingers up his solid chest, to let her hands move slowly sideways to caress the spread of his shoulders. Was it witchery in the air, the exotic

27

pulse of this place? She didn't know. For all his promises of showing her Maui, she might not see him again. She didn't even know his name!

His brown eyes were steady and intent as he finished arranging the lei. Then he quickly, wickedly, glanced at her and grinned. Their gaze held, building a marvelously intimate bridge. His proximity made her heart do a little spangling dance. The bare six inches between them chased all rational thought from Sarita's mind, and the tremor in her body extended into a rush of tenderness she'd never known before.

An influx of passengers from behind them knocked the two rudely against each other. His arms braced her against the invasion. They remained close, creating their own small island as the crowd flowed forward. Finally he released her, his hand lingering on her wrist, then closing over her fingers.

Sarita tingled to the touch of his hand, but he said nothing more. She decided that when they made the connecting flight to Maui, she'd take a peek at the cover of his trip ticket. It would have his name on it. She should come right out and ask him, but for some reason she was shy . . . or was simply allowing him his privacy, if that was what he wanted. For all her flight of independence in the Pacific air, she was still being that nice, even-tempered Sarita Miller.

At any rate, she told herself to enjoy the *now*. She was enchanted by the welcome of the flower lei, by the scent of ginger in the air and by this island's gentle magic.

She looked up at her companion. "The flower lei is beautiful, the perfume delicious. Thank you." Her smile was mischievous as she glanced down at her blouse front. "And how cleverly you arranged it." He laughed, understanding her meaning, and tucked her arm inside his. She glanced around. "This isn't like any airport I've ever seen."

He agreed. "It's an experience. Come on, I'll walk you to your flight. Down this way."

Carved wooden columns soared to support a latticed sky

roof. Ropes of broad-leafed tropical vines entwined themselves around the overhead rafters, their green webwork sending down spirals of emerald light. Since there were no walls to obstruct the humid air, it flowed, warm and sensuous, into Sarita's throat, filling her body with a stunning sense of total relaxation. All of her seemed limp, serene, drenched in languor. Now she understood Phoebe Adams's remark, "Wait till you step off the plane at Hilo and see what happens."

They walked to the interisland line at the far end of the colonnade, though Sarita was sure she could have opened her arms and floated there—past giant ferns in stone grottoes, past tiny quicksilver bright waterfalls splashing into hollowed-out pools, past the delicate orange of dwarf poincianas, past elegant bird of paradise plants. Rose-red anthurium bushes and torch gingers were inset within squares of earth to bloom along the open-air corridor. An archway was decorated with cattleya orchids, their petals lavender, their hearts violet. In a far corner gleamed the pale gold of a candle bush.

At the next ticket counter there was more bustle. Sarita's trip ticket book was opened, the interisland ticket extracted. She waited for the man's ticket to follow her own, but his hand at her elbow pushed her in line with the other passengers at the security gate. Her handbag and briefcase were inspected. When his hand abruptly left her arm, Sarita looked over her shoulder in surprise. Weren't they going through together?

He answered the question in her eyes by momentarily pulling her back to him. "I'll be on a later flight."

She was astounded. Was that all? He could have said he had business in Hilo that would delay him, or that he would see her in Maui, or that she should wait for him. He could have said any one of those things. He didn't. He let her go. Perhaps, she thought wryly, he would remember her name. He hadn't asked for her address on Maui, and she was too proud to give it to him.

She smiled brightly and turned quickly so that he couldn't see the hurt in her eyes. She followed her briefcase to the end of the conveyor belt, picked it up and started off. She didn't once look over her shoulder to see if he was watching. Why should he be?

"Sarita!"

She spun around so fast, she bumped her nose and chin into the fronts of three hurrying tourists. Everyone apologized, and then Sarita found herself thrust into a pair of supporting arms. They were his—and the man at the gate was shouting at him! His hair was tumbled and his eyes were laughing as he flipped his hand at the guard to keep him quiet. He was accustomed to having his own way, and Sarita quickly discovered why.

"Take this card," he told her. "Call me from wherever you'll be, when you get settled. I want to see you again. Remember, I'm your Maui guide."

As he walked back to the irate guard with apologies, Sarita stared at the business card. Then, like a proper zombie, she turned away, went up the ladder platform to the small orange and gold plane and found a seat. Only when the plane was airborne and flying in a northwesterly direction toward Maui did she look once more at the card in her hand.

Morgan Wycoff. That was what it said. She took off her dark glasses to make sure. Yes, there was that name again, an address she didn't recognize and a telephone number.

Sarita accepted a plastic cup of guava juice from the attendant. The flight was to be a twenty-five-minute journey through a sapphire sky over blue waters color-traced with cobalt and turquoise—a sight to thrill to after a snowy Midwest February. She would have twenty-five minutes to absorb all this beauty around her, but she knew very well that she would spend the entire time gaping at the card in her hand.

The usual announcement began. The flight hostess told her passengers that ground temperature was eighty-one degrees. With this, Sarita's attention was jogged and reality intruded. She carefully put away the card, got out her notebook and began to write determinedly: "The island of Maui contains an area of seven hundred and twenty square miles supporting its permanent population of sixty thousand. Its major industries are sugar cane and pineapples."

Morgan Wycoff!

She raised her hand to the lei around her neck, her fingers tangled helplessly in its soft, clinging petals. The scent of plumerias dissolved all sensible intentions. She'd keep her Hawaiian lei until it faded. She'd probably keep it forever. Thinking this, she smiled to herself. She was really up in the air in more ways than one.

The Airport terminal at Kahului was filled with sunburned tourists wearing slogan T-shirts and carrying mesh bags labeled "Maui Onions." Most of the travelers were rushing to board DC8s that would take them to Honolulu and then home to the mainland. The luckier ones were going on to Lihue, on the island of Kauai, to prolong their holiday. Sarita hurried along, toting briefcase, handbag and jacket. The Los Angeles attorney's instructions had been that she was to be met here by a man named Alex Firman.

Alex Firman found Sarita Miller with no difficulty. His station wagon waited in a special parking area, watched over by a security guard. He had already assembled Sarita's two bags that had been checked through from Los Angeles to Maui's main airport. There was no mystery as to how he had managed to retrieve them without her luggage stubs. Alex Firman was an invaluable aide to the Wycoffs. He got things done effortlessly, speedily and without going through the regular channels. He was indispensable and self-assured. Not even the Wycoffs were completely aware of the keyboard of strange moods that this suave, expressionless man kept carefully contained within himself.

He immediately picked Sarita out of the deplaning passengers from Hilo and watched her for a few minutes, taking his time, enjoying the appearance of her irresolution as she peered about, apparently seeking the person she was to meet. After inspecting Sarita carefully, Alex Firman approved of the tall, blond young woman with a flower lei around her neck, her fine-boned face misted with perspiration. The humidity-induced sweat was beginning to soak through her shirt in a manner that displayed interesting-looking breasts. He liked the lithe hips, the sway in her walk as she paced while anxiously gazing about her. Above all, he liked the anxiety she showed. To most people, Sarita would appear to be poised. But Alex Firman, like a trapper, could smell anxiety. It pleased him because it seemed to personify female helplessness, a quality he enjoyed exploiting.

He threw away his cigarette and walked forward. "Miss Miller?"

Sarita turned to see a man slightly taller than herself, clad in trim-fitting white slacks and a white shirt. His sharp features were deeply tanned, his hair sun-bleached. She was grateful to be recognized. "You're Alex Firman."

"That I am. Did you have a good trip?" He didn't wait for her answer. "This way."

"My luggage . . ."

"I have everything." He reached for her heavy briefcase.

"How did you do it?" Sarita glanced down at her ticket folder with its stapled-in baggage stubs.

"My secret. Like the islands?"

"So far . . . heaven."

"That's what we like to hear."

They got into the station wagon, and the security guard waved them off. Sarita was quick to detect that they'd been in a VIP parking zone. Wycoff clout, she decided, smiling to herself. That was probably the reason why her luggage was lying on the back seat while the rest of the passengers were still waiting at the baggage counter.

She lifted up the sticky front of her blouse from her glistening skin. "It's humid here, more so than in Hilo."

"Not for long. Just a lull in the trades."

"Trades?"

"The trade winds . . . our air-conditioning system. They blow most of the time. Hang on!" The station wagon swerved to a hard right. Alex kept a firm hand on the wheel, pushing his vehicle ahead of a long line of halted cars. Sarita muffled a startled exclamation and glanced at the driver beside her.

Alex's face was impassive. It showed no concern that he'd just illegally erased a ten-minute traffic bottleneck in order to get them quickly on the highway leading to Lahaina.

They sped swiftly past fields of red earth and swaying sugar cane, reaching the coast within fifteen minutes. Alex Firman waited for Sarita's gasp of pleasure. It came, as he had expected, as a picture-perfect beach dazzled her with its flawless crescent of white sand. Beyond the combers curling onto the shore lay the blue-green swell of the sea. The far horizon was crayoned with a line of deeper marine blue. Above this eerie reach curved a boundless sky. Infinitude. Sarita was awed.

"If you look back, you'll see Haleakala, our ten-thousand-foot volcano. That's part of the up-country region— nearly thirty thousand acres of cattle rangeland." Rare for him, and not quite understanding why he did it, Alex Firman disclosed information. "Wycoff owns a ranch there."

Wycoff! In her turn, Sarita wondered why she had said nothing of having met Morgan on the flight from California. Perhaps because she wanted to hug the surprise of it all inside her for a little longer.

"Is the volcano dormant, I hope?" she asked Alex.

"A sleeping giant, they say, but not to worry." Firman looked closely at Sarita. "You tired? Want to get to Napili Bay and sack out, or how about seeing the sunset from Lahaina? We're almost there. I'll buy you a *mai tai*, best rum drink you ever had."

"I think not, thanks. I am pretty tired. Another time?"

"Sure."

Sarita kept her eyes straight ahead, conscious of Firman's

scrutiny whenever his gaze wasn't needed on the road ahead. Instinct told her she should deflect this man's interest in her, which went a little deeper than mere hospitality to a newcomer to the islands. She wasn't sure about Alex Firman. Was he an employee, a friend or a business associate? She didn't quite trust him, despite their brief acquaintance. She sensed he was a predator, even though his scene of action happened to be the lovely island of Maui.

Alex's pale eyes remained blank much of the time, but malice lurked beneath their controlled expression. His fingers on the car's steering wheel were bony-thin, yet Sarita had seen their strength when he'd spun the station wagon ahead of the stalled traffic on the airport road. A red lantern signifying danger warned her to go slow, to back away from this man.

The car swept on past Lahaina. The town lay fronting the ocean, its shops and main street hidden by fan palms and thick tropical undergrowth.

When Firman spoke again, he nodded his head toward the sea and said, "Coming up . . . Kaanapali." A few moments later Sarita saw the span of luxury high-rise hotels and the monumental towers of concrete condominiums that seemed a strange contrast to the tropical shore. Alex explained. "Three miles of the best beach in the world, but it's got its concrete curtain, as you can see. Kaanapali's hubba-hubba, but it's fun. You'll want to go there sometime to shop, dance and see the sights."

Sarita opened her mouth to say that she expected to be here a couple of days only. Even if the Wycoff interview turned out well, it would be necessary for her to fly back to the mainland to make further in-person arrangements with her employer. She changed her mind about speaking and kept silent.

The traffic turning left into the Kaanapali resort area and golf course slowed the station wagon to a crawl. A multicolored rainbow appeared against a distant cloud cover above the West Maui Mountains to their right. Sarita watched as the perfect arch glimmered in pastel splendor. Where did that rainbow end? she wondered. It had not yet faded above the misty valleys that grooved into green hills when the station wagon picked up speed, turning once more toward the sea, which lay polished and silver in the late afternoon light.

They were soon off the main highway, twisting along a narrow coast road through a bramble of picturesque fern-leafed kiawe trees. Guavas and papayas grew thick among palms and eucalyptuses. It was a fanciful jungle strung with pods, vines and fragrant yellow blooms that seemed to honey the air. Exactly one hour after leaving the Kahului airport, Sarita saw the sign for Napili. The definition of "estate" would seem to indicate a high gate, manicured gardens, graveled paths, stretches of rolling lawns. There was nothing like this to be seen at the Wycoffs'. Instead, the station wagon made an abrupt left jog off the tortuous coast road and jounced down a turnoff lane. Sarita felt as if she were lost in a strange jungle, a place of half light, half shadow, swimming with masses of brilliant orange and red hibiscus flowers as large and decorative as those in a Gauguin canvas. Golden light filtered through feathery bamboo. The sea ahead was obscured by an impenetrable growth of tiger's-claw trees, their branch tips ending in scarlet, claw-shaped blooms.

The car dipped precariously into a steep gully, then strained upward to a high knoll. Again it plunged through a curving gorge. Alex didn't speak. Sarita glanced sideways at him in surprise. He seemed to be deliberately driving with careless speed. Like a madman, was more like it, she thought uncomfortably.

Alex was aware of his passenger's consternation. He saw her hand tighten on the edge of the car door, but she didn't utter a sound. She kept her balance by bracing those graceful legs of hers straight out against the upward slant of the floorboard.

He swerved the car intentionally, sending her body slipping across the seat against his. Her shoulder was soft, the garland of blossoms she wore fragrant. Sarita quickly righted herself, not glancing at him. Alex relished the alarm which he knew this woman must be suppressing. She was a tenderfoot from the Midwestern part of the States. He'd learned that much from Patrice the night before over the special drink he'd mixed for her. Against orders.

The station wagon climbed once more to shoot forward and come to a breathtaking stop. There was Napili Bay with its fantastic colors of blue, green and lavender, its currents and its coral reef. In the distance rose the lonely outline of another island.

Sarita slowly turned her head and looked Alex Firman in the eye. Her gaze was as green as the ice-sheathed waters of her native Lake Michigan in February. Anger trembled within her. She thought she understood the implication of this man's dangerous handling of the car on its rough drive up from the coast road. For his own reasons, which she had yet to understand, Alex Firman was testing her mettle. It might even be that he didn't want her here at all.

Alex was the first to look away, his curious gaze falling beneath Sarita's. He was beginning to suspect that, despite her sensitive lips and delicate profile, she was a lot tougher than he had supposed. Those eyes of hers could turn to blue ice.

He nodded toward the spectacular view of the ocean and the black rocks that tumbled directly downward to some unseen point. "Well, what do you think?"

"What I think is that you'd better take me to the Wycoff house right now. No more fancy stuff." She looked around her at the emptiness and repressed a shiver.

Alex's pale eyes narrowed. "Our roads aren't the best."

Sarita's glare was sweet. "I should think you'd have had plenty of experience driving them."

Alex didn't reply. He put the station wagon in reverse, backed away from the crest of the Napili cliff and swung down another roller-coaster road, but at a more moderate speed this time. Soon they were into a clearing which widened to a small meadow of roughened sea grass. A large house came into view.

"You'll be staying at the guest house. That's Wycoff's place you see there." Alex made an attempt to sound amiable.

In the lengthening twilight they drove past the main house. Two-storied, with wide balconies and natural wood siding, it appeared to blend into the environment. The landscaping was native and tropical. Surrounding the house were graceful coco palms, bending with the trade winds which had started up and were cooling the air.

Alex halted the station wagon in front of a small structure whose architecture matched the outlines of the Wycoff residence. Carrying Sarita's bags, he led the way along a winding path to the porch. The front door was unlocked. Alex glanced at Sarita and explained, "It's the custom here. You'll be perfectly safe."

Sarita entered the guest house first, then turned quickly. The eyes of the two met again as Alex put her luggage by the bedroom door.

Sarita spoke stiffly. "Thank you for meeting me at the airport."

The man's light eyes flickered. "It was my pleasure . . . Sarita." He added, "Dinner will be at eight. Mrs. Wycoff will be on the terrace earlier than that if you want drinks."

Sarita was eager to meet the famous Patrice, but the Los Angeles attorney had made it clear that it would be Morgan Wycoff who would make the final decision about Sarita's staying or leaving. So, smiling inwardly, she asked, "And Mr. Wycoff?"

"Morgan's been on the mainland on business. I believe he's due back in Hilo today." Alex eased out of the doorway and across the porch on sandaled feet.

He left Sarita staring thoughtfully after him.

Chapter Four

SARITA SETTLED HER GEAR INTO THE BEDROOM, then hurried out to the porch to look at her surroundings. Luminous stars hung like lanterns in the night sky. The tide surged in the distance, reminding Sarita that centuries of water had pounded these shores. She heard the crackle of the palm fronds bending under the pressure of the constantly blowing trade winds. Again the sense of her own freedom, which she had first perceived on the flight from California, grew tangible. She could really do what she wanted to when she wanted to—as long, of course, as she performed creditably for Dome. But here she was free of Dome's umbrella. She was no longer sweet Sarita, accommodating and even-tempered. She could even begin to think about going out on her own. It wouldn't be that impossible to form her own company, in a small way, certainly, but now she could plan.

Sarita walked back through the sitting room. Intricately woven straw mats dotted the bleached wood floor. The sunny tone of the walls and ceiling blended with handsome rattan furniture. Louvered shutters constructed of native wood folded back from open windows. Seashells of graduated sizes spilled across a saffron-colored tray set on a low glass table. The colors of the shells—foam pink and palest silver—were repeated in the silk of a bamboo screen near the front door. An artist had used these same shells as the subject for the unframed watercolors that hung on the walls.

The bedroom itself was pale-toned and restful, except for the covering on the wide bed. The spread was a mélange of riotous colors—violet, crimson, tints of ruby and garnet, even a Goya red that was yellower and deeper than geranium. Its edge was embroidered with yarns of twisting green vines. The overall effect was that of an artful painting created by a sensual brush. The bed was ripe for ardor, for lovemaking.

Sarita's brows arched at the absurdity of her thought. This wanton impression must have been aroused by the fading fragrance of the flower lei that still clung to her breasts. Slowly she unslung the necklace of blossoms and carried it into the small kitchen, where she placed it on a shelf inside the refrigerator, a reminder of the interesting man she'd met on the plane. Recalling Morgan's hand against her breasts as he'd arranged the flowers, she became amused. He was a bit of a flirt too!

Sarita unpacked, hung her clothes in the closet and walked naked into an Italian-tiled modern bathroom. Stepping into the shower, she saw above her head a glass-roofed skylight. Very luxurious indeed, she thought as she turned on both water taps and began to soap away the sweat of the journey and the distracting memory of Morgan Wycoff. Quit thinking about him, she told herself severely, and attend to business!

A half hour later she was wearing one of her newly purchased outfits—a chalk-white, sleeveless tunic and emerald-green silk pants, both expensive enough to pass for casual chic. She added a pair of small but genuine emerald ear clips. Too dressy, perhaps, but they complemented her costume and were her only family heirloom.

The sky was dark and starry, yet the afterglow from the rosy Maui sunset still seemed to touch the white pebbles on the path that took her to the main house. Tropical ferns grew like tender green lace high above her head. The sudden raucous scream of a night bird catapulted her into a fast run up the terrace steps of the Wycoff home.

The terrace appeared to wrap itself around the entire lower floor of the house. Hurricane lamps, placed at intervals along a wooden railing, guided Sarita to double doors thrown open to the night. She stepped across the threshold into a large, square room whose walls, ceiling and furniture were glamorously tinted in ivory and white. Overhead, a wooden paddle fan revolved slowly, sending down a draft of lazy breezes to cool her face and throat. The flow of gentle air fingered into the cleavage of her tunic and swirled her bright hair across her cheeks. Sarita's senses reacted to the romantic ambience of this room. It reminded her of the film *Casablanca*, her favorite late-night television outing on those nights when she couldn't sleep. She hummed a bar or two of the signature tune, raised an arm as though to rest it on an invisible partner's shoulder and glided across the floor to a musical strain only she could hear.

A voice spoke. "Very pretty."

Sarita jumped and whirled around. From a staircase the length of the room away, Alex Firman stood watching her. "How about the next dance?" He ran lightly down the remaining steps, crossed the room and came to a halt so close to Sarita that he almost touched her breasts. To his fresh white shirt and slacks he had added a white silk jacket. Scent from some men's cologne wafted into Sarita's nostrils.

Alex's tone was sardonic. "Has the orchestra gone home? Too bad." He looked her up and down appreciatively. "We're pretty fancy, aren't we? Patrice doesn't usually come downstairs to dine. When she does, she likes her peasants to dress for the occasion." His voice lowered confidentially. "In your honor she'll make an appearance tonight."

Sarita moved backward, putting a careful distance between herself and Alex Firman. It was awkward enough for him to have surprised her just now in her bit of playacting, but she certainly didn't want to become a confederate of his. "I walked over here early because you said Mrs. Wycoff would be on the terrace," she explained.

"Yes, I did say that. But she changes her mind sometimes. Come on outside with me. I'll fix us a drink."

Again Sarita didn't like the manner in which he seemed to be linking the two of them. She hoped Alex Firman wasn't a permanent object around here, but recalling the casual way he'd come loping down the stairs, she thought otherwise. Deciding to be straightforward, she asked, "Are you staying here?"

Alex gave Sarita his off-target smile, took her arm and led her outside. She was an appealing woman, the type whose independence he liked to assault. In her turn, Sarita disliked Alex's hand guiding her. As they reached the lanai, she halted and abruptly seated herself in a high-backed peacock chair.

While he began to mix drinks at the lanai bar, Alex answered her question. "It's a little more complicated than simply saying I'm staying here, Sarita. I'm here all the time. Just . . . here. Not a guest. Not really an employee."

"And not a friend?" Sarita concluded smartly, then wondered why she'd said that at all.

At Sarita's terse comment, Alex's hand stopped their movements at the bar. With a peculiar stillness those hands hung suspended over the tall glasses. "Did you just jab a spur into my rear . . . or throw a whip at me?" he asked curtly. When she didn't respond immediately, his fingers went back to what they'd been doing. This time they twisted and squeezed and tortured a lime until its green juice spilled into a glass. His eyes continued to watch hers. She saw now that they were avid as well as pale. Oddly, Sarita was reminded of Ross Bailey, that busy civic eminence thousands of miles away in Chicago.

Her reply was bland. "I might not have put it in exactly that fashion—whips and spurs, for instance—but the answer is yes."

Sarita rested her head against the chair's fan-shaped back, not moving her gaze from Alex's. Taking her time about it, she crossed her legs. Momentarily she glanced down at the graceful flow of emerald silk along her limbs. The man's glare couldn't help itself. It followed her gesture, as she knew it would. She looked up quickly to see his eyes linger on the outline of her legs. Whatever the reason for the duel between herself and Alex Firman, Sarita intended to win it. When Alex glanced back at her, a sullen silence lengthened between them.

In an intransigent situation, mothers teach daughters to use honeyed words and the wiles known as feminine. Not this daughter, Sarita thought. She spoke coolly. "When we turned off the Napili road, it was quite a wild ride you took me on. Was that trip really necessary?" Sarita knew that Alex's precarious braking of the station wagon so close to the cliff edge had been deliberate and cruel, and she wasn't going to let him get away with it.

A smile like a scar spread across Alex Firman's sharp face. His expression predatory, he crossed his arms on the bar top and leaned toward Sarita. This woman was turning out not to be small, tender game after all. He flexed fingers that resembled talons. He had wanted to see Sarita squirm, be self-consciously polite to him, even blush with discomfort and avert her eyes. It had happened this way with other women, and he liked the feeling of mastery it gave him. But this woman wasn't going to assume those attitudes which he regarded as female and weak. Instead, she remained cool and assured. Sarita had a smart mouth, but he would take care of that.

Testing the sound of each syllable before attack, he uttered her name slowly. "Sarita . . . Miller." Whatever he intended to say next was smothered. His gaze shifted toward someone who had approached silently in the shadows behind Sarita's chair. Alex's glowering look, which had been intended for Sarita, changed to one of deference.

"We've been waiting for you," he mumbled gallantly.

A whispery voice replied, "No, you haven't. You started without me."

Dutifully Alex chuckled.

A small and elegant figure, clad in a cotton frock lacy with antique detailing, came around the fan shape of the peacock chair. Sarita rose and looked down as the tiny woman extended her hand. The handshake was surprisingly vigorous.

"I'm Patrice. Welcome, Sarita Miller. It is you, isn't it? It seems I heard Alex hissing your name a moment ago."

Sarita felt a surge of relief. The unexplained clash between herself and Alex Firman was to be postponed. Not that she couldn't handle anything he threw her way, but, if possible, she first wanted to discover the reason for the dissension between them.

Patrice Wycoff's entrance had changed Alex into the man who had met Sarita at Kahului Airport. Then he had appeared suave, pleasant enough, eager to please. Now he seated Patrice in a small chair, in which she looked doll-like but regal.

Sarita quickly found herself beguiled by the older woman. Patrice was a stunning exotic, certainly worthy of her press, even though it had been several years since the media had focused their attention on her. A film of fine bangs accented lucent, almond-shaped black eyes. Medium-length brown hair was swept back to frame flawless features. The sun had touched her skin, delicately bronzing it, yet her complexion had the creamy smoothness of a dark gardenia petal. Had Patrice discovered a formula to enable her to remain ageless under a tropical sun? It was probably nothing as dramatic as that. Sarita was beginning to suspect that her being summoned here might be part of a plan to reestablish Patrice's former flourishing career. She was even more curious as to how that career had been sidetracked.

Patrice waved a hand at Alex. "The usual for me. What are you having, Sarita?"

As she was meant to do, Sarita's gaze followed the gesture of those supple fingers, which were inordinately long for so small a person. The hand itself was an undulation of grace—suntanned and slender, with no distracting jewelry. Those magic fingers had successfully contoured clients' cheeks, throats and jowls, with startling results—firming muscles, toning skin, restoring youth to tired faces. All of that had happened at the very beginning of Patrice's career.

Amusedly aware of Sarita's scrutiny, Patrice prodded, "Well, Sarita, what will it be?"

Sarita hesitated. Alex's teeth glittered. "Let me make you a specialty of the house," he said.

Patrice looked sharply at the man behind the bar. "Not a *wainani*."

"No one does it better than I."

"I'll say no for Sarita."

Sarita carefully pronounced the unfamiliar word. "What is a *wainani*? You've made me curious."

Patrice turned to the younger woman. "It's a dubious concoction. The juice of passion fruit is blended with tequila, cointreau, and curaçao. Sometimes Alex puts it together to help us get rid of boring after-dinner guests. We don't want to lose you, Sarita. Not yet anyway." Patrice sipped her imported mineral water and ordered brusquely, "Add a twist of lime to this, will you?" Alex did so. Patrice's eyes shimmered in Sarita's direction. "You and I must have a talk." Pointedly she glanced at Alex. "In private. After dinner."

"I'll look forward to it." Sarita understood this was to be the first of her interviews with the Wycoffs. She accepted the tall glass Alex handed her, not trusting his sudden choir boy's smile. She tasted the drink and discovered it was a very sour lemonade. He'd left out the sugar syrup.

Patrice thumped her glass on the stand next to her chair. "By the way, Alex, I was upstairs looking out of my window when you arrived with Sarita. You came from the direction of the cliffs. Why did you bring her the long way around on that rotten road?"

"To show her the view of Napili Bay. I pointed out Lanai, Molokai—"

Sarita interrupted. "Molokai?"

Patrice's black eyes narrowed. "Molokai is an island to

the northwest of us. Sarita seems to have missed an important part of your purported view, Alex. What kind of a guided tour did you give our guest? Were you busy in other ways?"

Hastily Alex raised his glass to his lips and mumbled through the ice in his drink. Whatever he said was indistinguishable.

Sarita was chagrined at the implication in Patrice's words. Was she hinting that some kind of intimacy had taken place between Alex and herself? Sarita decided that her first evaluation of Patrice might have been too simple. It was evident that Alex Firman was being intentionally harassed.

The situation in this house might be a more complicated one than Sarita had supposed. Perhaps all of Patrice's associates became whipping posts. She was a woman no longer young but still vigorous, who had stepped down prematurely from the summit of an exciting career. Leading a quiet life in this indolent paradise might not be Patrice's cup of Eden. The fast lane of success could still beckon to her. Once a familiar of the world's most stimulating city, Patrice might find it difficult to get New York out of her system.

Since Alex Firman had behaved unpleasantly toward Sarita, she should be glad to see him getting back his. Instead, she felt a tug of sympathy. Then, for a reason she again couldn't fathom, Alex threw her a spiteful look. After that, the little shred of compassion vanished.

A strikingly handsome young man in a white jacket appeared with a tray bearing sashimi and a soy sauce to which fresh ginger and mustard had been added. If Sarita hadn't been introduced to this delicacy in one of Chicago's Japanese restaurants, she might have blanched at having to eat raw fish, sliced thin and chilled.

Conversation became desultory. It was obvious that Patrice's thoughts were floating off in some bubble of memory.

At any rate, she was exquisite to look at. At times those great dark eyes of hers were so dreamily mournful that Sarita found herself anxious to please.

When Patrice rose and drifted from the lanai toward the direction of the dining room, Sarita and Alex followed obediently. Patrice's body moved with a lithe, athletic grace inside the loose cotton frock she was wearing. She halted and looked back at Sarita. "I swim every day with the dolphins in my private pool. It's carved out of a natural rock basin—the sea waves wash in over the sides. The dolphins leap into my world from their own. What do you think of that?"

"It sounds fantastic. I'd love to see it."

"You very nearly did. My pool is at the foot of the cliff where you were today." She turned away. "No one visits my pool."

Sarita glanced swiftly at Alex. Was this the real reason he shouldn't have driven her the long way around? Though she had been unaware of it at the time, the station wagon had come to a precipitous halt just above Patrice's private pool.

Dinner was announced by the same handsome young man who had appeared with the sashimi earlier on the terrace. Patrice gave him a quick, warm smile. "Ah, yes, Nils—we're ready for you."

Once inside the dining room, however, instead of directing social traffic around the table, Patrice again appeared to be off in a world of her own. Alex Firman lapsed into preoccupation with the Hawaiian prawns on his plate. Sarita nibbled at them. They were delicious, threaded on skewers and dipped in a sauce of lemon butter, anchovy fillets, wine and parsley. Since she was trying to turn herself into a gourmet cook in her small Chicago apartment, this sort of food interested her.

Even though the Wycoff household seemed a bit on the dizzy side, Sarita was fascinated by Patrice and her background. The woman had been a world-bender in her time.

Whatever plan for their association Patrice wanted to discuss, Sarita was eager to hear it. For the first time she was truly excited about the project—whatever it might turn out to be. She hoped it would work, for herself as well as for Dome Advertising. Her own ambitions tantalizing her, she remained silent through the serving of mango ice and sliced exotic fruits. She tasted the dessert, and it was even better than the Floating Island delight of her Illinois youth.

Over black coffee, Patrice seemed to come back from the absorption of her thoughts. Behaving once again as a hostess, she smiled whimsically and explained to Sarita, "This Kona coffee we're drinking is absolutely the best in the world. It's made with beans from the plantations on the Big Island. Your plane set down there this afternoon, didn't it?"

"I was in Hilo briefly, but I did notice the volcanic soil from the air." No purpose in saying that a nameless someone had pointed out the fertile earth to her.

As though by rote, Patrice mimicked, "The rich soil there lends the coffee beans their special character." She whipped an acid look in Alex's direction. "Food, drink and real estate values are all we ever talk about on Maui. Have you seen any good condominium buys lately?"

Alex had no time to think up a tactful reply to this querulous remark. The sound of tire wheels crunching on the driveway gravel sent Patrice shooting upright in her chair. "He's here! And I haven't had my talk with Sarita yet."

Who was here? Sarita wondered.

There were sounds of steps on the terrace and a door opening and closing. Patrice's tone was sarcastic, yet at the same time her voice seemed to purr sensuously when she said, "Get set for the master."

And then Sarita knew. She felt amused and excited as she awaited Morgan Wycoff's arrival.

Chapter Five

SARITA FOCUSED EXPECTANTLY ON THE FIGURE in the doorway. Would Morgan be as she remembered him, just as intriguing, just as kind? His strongly built physique was clad in the same beige drill he'd worn on the plane. Her vision narrowed to hone in sharply on his broad cheekbones, sun-darkened skin and splendidly formed lips, on the face she'd watched with interest while he'd told her those magic tales of the islands. He was really quite overwhelming.

Morgan's amber eyes fixed on her in startled bewilderment. Then she remembered that he had had no way of knowing that her "project" was an interview with the Wycoffs of Napili Bay. She'd been so discreet that he hadn't connected the Sarita Miller who worked for an anonymous Chicago ad agency with the young woman Patrice was expecting. Her name had meant nothing to him, as he'd had more important matters on his mind.

Patrice, tiny and potent, stood up and walked forward. Or did she swim forward? Her movement was as lithe and slippery as her supple friends the dolphins. Because this idea was so absurd, Sarita fought the shimmer of nervous laughter that rose to her lips.

"Morgan, this is our house guest from Chicago, Sarita

Miller. She's with Dome Advertising. Phoebe phoned from the mainland that we were to expect her. I'm glad you're back in time to have a talk with Sarita."

"I am too," he acknowledged gravely. "How do you do, Miss Miller." Then, chuckling, he glanced at Patrice. "We were seatmates on the same flight over from California."

Morgan Wycoff and Sarita Miller shook hands officially, both of them grinning broadly.

Patrice remained standing with a catlike smile curling her lips. "I am surprised," was all she said. She raised one slender hand to waft the bangs from her brow. But the film of fine hair settled stubbornly back into place, veiling the expression in Patrice's luminous eyes.

As Morgan released Sarita's hand, she felt a thrilling tingle in the fingers that were freed from his. He left her and walked toward his former wife. Sarita was relieved to see them greet each other casually.

He smiled impartially at both Patrice and Sarita. "You two go ahead and finish your coffee. Don't wait for me. I had dinner in Lahaina."

Alex Firman had been observing the scene before him, nonplussed, because he also had been unaware that Morgan and Sarita had flown to Hilo not only on the same plane but in the same tourist section. He wondered, as usual, why Morgan refused to travel first-class like any other rich man. Then he jumped to attention as Morgan spoke.

"I'd like to see you in the office, Alex." Firman nodded and preceded Morgan to the door. Morgan paused in the doorway, his amused glance sweeping back to Sarita. "Welcome to Maui, Sarita Miller."

Sarita heard herself murmur an uninspired "Thank you" in reply to Morgan's welcome. Actually, for some reason, she felt incredibly exhilarated.

When the two men had left the room, Patrice remarked languidly, "Quite a coincidence, your being on the same plane with Morgan." She paused. Sarita merely looked brightly expectant, so Patrice went on. "You must be tired,

49

Sarita. Time change and all. We'll have our preliminary talk tomorrow. I'll have our houseman, Nils, walk you to the guest house with a flashlight, since the path is new to you. Everything comfy there?"

The word "comfy" didn't sound like Patrice, who had averted her head while she adjusted the antique lace on her bosom. Unexpectedly, she looked over at Sarita, her black gaze burning a direct challenge, and concluded brusquely, "Tomorrow we'll make up our minds whether you stay." The harshness of the sentence caught Sarita by surprise— as it was meant to do.

Sarita hoped her answering smile wasn't too forced or insincere. She knew that nothing short of a tidal wave would move her from this spot as long as Morgan Wycoff was here. She had to find out what he was all about, and what this attraction was that she felt for him. He was easy to talk to, full of island knowledge, and she suspected herself of being a bit of an opportunist. She had made up her mind that she wanted freedom. He, as a successful entrepreneur, might be able to show her the key to attaining that independence. She could learn from him as well.

Patrice tinkled a hand bell on the table. The white-jacketed young man who had served dinner reentered the dining room. Patrice waved one undulating hand at him. "Nils, will you take Miss Miller to the guest house?"

Sarita really noticed Nils for the first time. He was an extraordinarily handsome man in his early twenties, with gray-green eyes and soot-black hair. Sarita guessed that an exotic blend of both Nordic seafarers' and islanders' blood ran in Nils's veins. Sarita smiled at him, bade her hostess good night and thought, I'll be damned if I'm going to call her Mrs. Morgan Wycoff. She's had her chance. He's no longer a part of her life. Patrice and Morgan don't belong together any more.

"Sleep well, Sarita." It was a dismissal.

Sarita followed the handsome Nils out of the house. She

didn't think she could sleep at all. Even with those waves booming out there on the beach, she felt overexcited, over-stimulated. Thus preoccupied, she stumbled behind Nils and his flashlight. Nils turned quickly, caught her, then bent down and flicked the light across the path. He handed her a glittering green object. It was her emerald earring.

"Thanks, Nils. That was awkward of me."

She held the earring in her hand as they went up the steps of the guest house. Nils opened the front door and reached inside to turn on the light. His action was almost a replay of Alex Firman's earlier one that afternoon.

"Could you possibly find me a key to this house?" she asked.

Nils smiled pleasantly as he stepped out onto the porch. "There should be an extra one at the main house. I'll get it for you. Do you have everything you need down here?" Sarita nodded. "Then, good night." He disappeared quickly into the darkness.

Sarita closed the door briskly and crossed the bleached wood floor to her bedroom. Before undressing, she carefully closed the tilt rods on all the louvered shutters. After living in a city, she couldn't readily adjust to the lack of security on this island estate.

She was in bed, thinking about Morgan Wycoff and all the possibilities therein, when she heard the clattering ping of metal hitting against the outside of the shutters. Abruptly she sat up in bed. Her heart did a nervous tattoo. She was wearing her cotton slip, which was cooler than the night-gown still packed in her bag of winter clothing. She tugged a sheet off the bed and wrapped it around herself, toga-style. Then she ran over to the closed bedroom shutters. "Who's out there?" she called.

The male voice was close. The man must be standing in the ferns and speaking through the chink in the wood. "If I don't see you, neither one of us will sleep tonight."

Sarita recognized that voice. "Morgan Wycoff, what makes you think I won't sleep? You go have your own insomnia." She was half laughing, but still totally surprised.

"Come on, Sarita. Before I leave here and go home, I want to talk to you," he pleaded.

Sarita was curious. Didn't Morgan live on the estate, then? This was something she would have to find out. "Wait a minute. I'll meet you on the porch."

Sarita hastily brushed her hair, brushed her teeth, put on the white tunic and green pants and went out barefoot into the tropical night to meet Morgan Wycoff. They came face to face in the darkness, and he said, "Let's go inside. Better than standing here on the porch."

Once they were in the living room, she couldn't keep her curiosity in check. "Don't you live here?" she asked.

"I have my own condo over on the other side of Napili Bay, about five miles up the road from here. You wouldn't have passed it today."

Sarita's expression didn't change, but for some reason she was pleased to hear that Morgan didn't live on the estate, as she had assumed. He and Patrice weren't all that friendly, then. Morgan had his own separate establishment, even though he kept office space here.

Sarita reflected to herself, we hardly know each other. It was a nice flight today, a nice conversation, and we both were attracted to each other. And then there was that business with the lei, which was a bit fresh of him. But why are we being so serious now? As if we're going around a corner and can't let go.

"May I sit down? I'll be on my best behavior." Morgan grinned suddenly. "I think I will be."

Sarita immediately felt more comfortable with him. As they moved toward the cushioned rattan couch, they were smiling at each other.

"By the way, why are you wearing only one earring?" Morgan's hand touched the side of her face. She'd put away the loose earring she'd dropped on the path, but she'd forgotten to remove the other one from her ear. Morgan's hand felt good on her cheek. His thumb moved up and down, caressing the sensitive tendon along her throat. This seemingly innocent motion sent unexpected stabs of desire ricocheting through her body. She found herself wanting to snuggle against his hand, to lean against his shoulder. Instead, she sat very straight.

"I like wearing one earring to bed," she replied.

"It's nice to know these things about you." With a humorous expression on his face, he tilted her head and observed her closely. "I can't tell you how surprised I am to learn that it's you . . . the girl on the plane. The goddess Pele must have had something to do with it, I swear."

Sarita looked a little shy. "Personally, I think it's a very neat coincidence." That remark was simple and direct, but she felt embarrassed saying it.

Morgan chuckled as though he approved of her words. His next comment really astonished her. "That golden hair of yours is growing out. Don't have it cut again." Sarita knew her hair was a shaggy mess, all different lengths. But instead of telling him that her hair was really none of his business, she foolishly asked, "Why not?"

"I see you as Rapunzel . . ."

Sarita knew the fairy tale. But *she* wasn't incarcerated in a tower, nor was she going to let down her golden hair for him to climb upon. She wasn't an idle princess, she was a businesswoman. She spoke more sternly than she had intended. "Morgan—what's going on here with you?" His smile widened. Annoyed by what she considered to be his cavalier attitude, she stood up and walked away from the couch, leaving him sitting there alone. It was difficult to walk with dignity when one was doing it on bare feet, but Sarita managed to move fairly gracefully across the room. Perhaps it would be better if she put this situation into a businesslike framework.

"It's getting late. We'll have to settle a few things. Until I hear what the Wycoff project involves, I can't say whether I'll be able to stay or not."

Morgan chose to be evasive. "We'll talk about that tomorrow. Will you sleep tonight?"

"Of course I'll sleep. Won't you?"

"I'm not so sure." Morgan leaned back, stretching his arms. He almost yawned, then indicated the cushion beside him. "Come back here."

"I don't think so."

He leered. "You have a headache?"

"You're impertinent . . . I think. I *am* tired. See you tomorrow?" It took all her willpower to assume an air of dismissal when she was actually enchanted by his presence but trying not to show it.

Slowly Morgan got to his feet. "I know when I'm being kicked out. I had to get another look at you. I'm still surprised it *is* you. Well, we'll do the obligatory interview in the morning. As far as I'm concerned, I'll only be going through the motions."

"What if Patrice doesn't want me?"

"She will." His words were matter-of-fact.

"Morgan, I really haven't had time to construct a concrete opinion about anyone as yet. I think I'd kind of like to take it easy. But there are a few things I'm curious about. Who is Alex Firman? He appears to detest me. Why is that? Am I a threat to him in some way?"

"All women are a threat to Alex."

"Why is he here at all?"

"I could say I don't keep guard dogs on the place, so I keep Alex. The truth is, I inherited him from a business partner I had at one time. He's useful in a number of ways. He's loyal and discreet, sort of a watchman and general foreman. He runs errands for Patrice. She doesn't like to leave the property. For some reason, she's never been too fond of Maui. She doesn't want to socialize. She doesn't want to explore. She works in her laboratory."

Sarita wanted to ask Morgan about himself and Patrice, but she knew that would be stepping out of bounds. From what she'd seen, they appeared to have a casual, almost businesslike arrangement, yet she sensed that Patrice still felt a kind of ownership toward the man who had once been her husband. Sarita sighed. She really wished she weren't so attracted to him.

Morgan was near the door. Sarita, standing by the bamboo screen, was suddenly conscious that he was staring at her full lips. And she knew those lips of hers were ripe and waiting. . . .

"We understand each other," Morgan said at last. In one lithe movement he moved toward her and caught her in his arms. As his lips closed lingeringly over hers, Sarita shuddered at the warm, sensual tracing within the sensitive inner rim of her mouth. The fiery and urgent desire flowing through her was a sensation she'd never known before. The sun seemed to be beating on her, reflecting great waves of heat from the earth into her body. And Morgan was that sun.

Sarita didn't believe in love at first sight, or even at second sight like this. Yet Morgan's touch, his presence, seemed right and timeless. She recognized that this wasn't a hope, or a fake, or a maybe. She'd never experienced such sweet responsiveness within her own body.

Morgan gently released Sarita. "Forgive me for that. I'm a thoughtless bastard. You must be tired, and I come along and do what I want to do without a thought for how you must feel. Here." He took a key out of his pocket. Earlier he'd thrown it at Sarita's closed shutters as if he were a kid, then had gotten down on his hands and knees and scrambled for it among the ferns. He didn't know what had prompted such a foolish act. It would have been more civilized to have left the key and a note hanging on the front door. But his reason was simple—he'd wanted to see Sarita again.

Morgan tried to keep his tone light. "No one's been in this guest house for so long that we've kept its key on a peg up at the main house. Considering you're a somewhat permanent resident, I think you should have it now."

Sarita was still remembering their kiss. She gulped as she took the key. "Well, thanks—but how do either of us know how permanent I'll be?"

"We know. We both know. Sarita, I believe we do understand each other. I don't want you to leave here, or me. It's important that you stay. I feel that way, and I don't know exactly why."

The force and urgency in his words—even his need to say them at all—left Sarita bewildered. "But of course I want to stay." She tried to reassure him, not comprehending why he needed to hear her say so.

Morgan appeared almost stern. "We'll talk tomorrow."

Sarita followed him to the porch and tried to sound casual as she said good night. He ran down the shallow wooden steps, looked back at her once, then vanished into the night.

Sarita remained staring after Morgan. He had disappeared, but imprinted on her vision was the outline of his head with its mahogany-dark hair roughened by the not-always-gentle winds that blew continuously. The tropical night was fragrant with the earth aura of growth and pulsating life.

As though her body were shaped from the same clay as this teeming earth, Sarita's senses responded to the exotic fertility. She could feel the points of her breasts tense into hard little buds. Her body ached, not with weariness but with longing. She wanted to call out to Morgan to come back to her, but that would be madness. What kind of person was she turning into?

The crackling sway of palm fronds had masked all sounds until the trades diminished temporarily. It was during such a lull that she grew aware of a sound that was human and not one of nature's. It was definitely someone's footsteps in the dark . . . departing, hiding?

Too late, Sarita realized she was silhouetted against the light fanning across the porch from the partially open front door. Putting one hand behind her, she nudged the door closed and stood against it, listening. Her own body seemed to be vibrating noisily with her quickened breathing and nervous heartbeat. Swiftly she opened the door, slipped inside the sitting room and doused the light. The key Morgan had given her was still clutched in her hand. She locked the door, relieved to be safe, but uncomfortable with the knowledge that she had been observed.

For how long and by whom? She and Morgan together? At least on the porch she had acted the role of poised house guest, and Morgan had walked up the path to the main house with a nonchalance that gave no clue to the emotional scene that had taken place in this room.

Could some passerby have spied on her? The estate was too isolated to attract wanderers. A curious servant, perhaps? She had seen no domestic tonight other than Nils, though Patrice had mentioned that the staff consisted of a cook and two helpers. There was no security watchdog. There was only Alex Firman.

Sarita shot the bar on every wooden shutter. Without the trade winds' natural air conditioning blowing into her bedroom, the heat was oppressive. She stepped out of her tunic and green pants and lay nude on top of the still-cool sheets. She hadn't realized her exhaustion. Not even fear, suspicion or what was far more attractive, the memory of Morgan Wycoff's mouth consuming hers, could keep her awake. She fell into a deep sleep accompanied by the echo of Morgan's voice murmuring, "Rapunzel . . ."

Chapter Six

SARITA WOKE UP THE NEXT MORNING WEARING one green earring and nothing else.

What had happened last night?

She rolled over onto her back and lay staring at the ceiling, still tasting the sensual warmth of Morgan's surprising kiss. His possession of her mouth had soared and comforted and teased. She did remember. Everything.

First there was the sight of Morgan standing on the porch in the darkness. Then came the picture of the easy strength of his solidly knit body as he'd entered the sitting room, seeming to conquer the space he moved in. All of this she saw, but then visual perception ceased, and a high tide of emotion came flooding in with its delicious rhythm, pounding and almost unendurable. Her sexual response to this man startled her with its power to strangle the breath and increase the heart's tempo. What should a normal rate be— seventy-six beats per minute? Hers had accelerated to at least one hundred and ten!

Sarita turned restlessly onto her side, digging her elbow into the pillow, propping her chin on one hand. She hadn't needed her tape recorder for their conversation. She could recall every word spoken between them, as well as each pause and nuance. A tight little smile curved her lips. Morgan had handed over the key to her front door.

Her front door? Was she claiming possession and assuming she'd stay here on Maui and do a job for the Wycoffs? Sarita sat upright on the edge of the bed, bare toes tapping the floor. There were two Wycoffs to be considered. Morgan had said he wanted Sarita to remain here. But what did Patrice want? Her closing remarks to Sarita the night before had indicated a cool indifference. Sarita had been quick to pick that up. Who could tell what the enigmatic Patrice Wycoff was really thinking?

Staring at the closed wooden shutters reminded Sarita there was something less pleasant to think about than Morgan's kiss—the crackle of that human footstep in the foliage. It could have been the sound of a prowling cat, but Sarita knew this was sheer rationalization on her part.

She crossed the room, unbolted the shutters and threw them open. The air felt good on her unclothed body, and it was easy to forget last night's alarms. Hands on the sill, she leaned forward, sure that no one could see her. The expanse of ocean was much nearer than she had thought. Sunlight glinted on its surface, while the waves pounded the black rocks beneath the slope of meadow. The sandy beach itself was invisible from here.

Morgan . . . twice she breathed his name.

Sarita's blue eyes changed to an intensity that matched the darker shade of this morning's sea. She looked down at her naked self, glad that she was lithe-figured, that her waist was narrow, that her full, deep breasts arched upward with a rare kind of impudence. Because she was unashamed of her body didn't mean that Morgan was ever going to see it—except, of course, when she was wearing a bikini. Phoebe Adams had insisted that she buy those two expensive scraps of cloth that were supposed to cover strategic areas, but the reality only served to delineate her body's intimate curves. If she remained here, she'd buy herself a tank suit, one-piece and practical, a silky second skin that wouldn't exactly flaunt her sex.

Breathing in the salt air, Sarita stood away from the

windowsill and made a feint at doing some minimum calisthenics. She touched her toes, flailed her arms and slapped her bottom. Then she raced toward the shower, hungry for breakfast, but more hungry for the sight of Morgan Wycoff. She passed the bathroom mirror and saw her reflection, a rosy nude still wearing the single emerald earring. Laughing out loud, she shook her head, unscrewed the jewel and stored it away with its mate.

Sarita plunged into the shower and let the water swirl down on her while she looked up through the skylight's glass roof. The sky was a periwinkle blue, frilled with white cloud ribbons that appeared to be strung along by racing winds. A mass of purple bougainvillea blossoms broke loose from its vine and blew across the skylight. She could hardly wait to get outside and see this new Maui world.

Sarita dressed herself for this morning's expected interview in a green cotton blouse and matching skirt. She slid bare feet into beige sandals and went out to the porch, locking the front door behind her with the key she considered hers. She held it up and looked at it intently. She really mustn't assume that she was taking possession of anything. There was Dome Advertising to consider; she was its representative. To concentrate on handling the Wycoff assignment, she'd have to relegate Morgan and Patrice to an impersonal status.

As she walked along the path, she couldn't resist the temptation of thinking that if everything worked out, it could be a first step toward an independent Sarita Miller, creative and marketing strategist. Mentally, she was already designing her own logo. A scarlet hibiscus brushed against her throat, its yellow stamen drifting a trail of gold dust inside the bodice of her blouse. A scented fern caught and traveled along her lips, caressing her cheek. The ocean boomed, sunlight streaked through the thin-sketched lines of bamboo. It wasn't a career she was hurrying toward . . . it was Morgan.

Sarita ate breakfast alone on the lanai. It wasn't the

stunning Nils who served her, but a pleasant-faced young woman with an exotic cast of feature, enhanced by eyes that slanted slightly above perfect cheekbones. When the girl turned around, Sarita was intrigued by the sight of blue-black hair that fell waterfall straight to the curve of her buttocks. An orange headband held the thick mass of hair in place.

While she poured coffee, the girl's doelike brown eyes were closely observing Sarita. "My name is Maile," the young woman murmured.

Sarita pronounced the unfamiliar syllables. "It's a very pretty name. Does it have a special meaning?"

"It means 'perfumed vine.' In Honolulu, I call myself Molly McIntosh." Seeing the surprise on Sarita's face, Maile laughed, revealing gleaming white teeth. "I'm here for the same reason you are, Miss Miller. I'm a lab assistant. It's difficult to find household help on Maui, so I also do domestic work for the Wycoffs because they paid for my education during my senior year at the University of Hawaii. I'm Scottish, Japanese, French and Polynesian. When I go to the mainland, which I will do to continue my studies at UCLA, I'll be Molly McIntosh there too."

Sarita couldn't suppress a smile at the earnestness of this last statement. She stood up and shook hands with her colleague. Well, perhaps colleague-to-be. "Please call me Sarita. And Maile sounds beautiful the way you say it."

Maile shrugged. "Molly will do just as well. I have to get used to it." She winked. "See you later. Have a nice day." The extraordinary mane of black hair disappeared through a doorway.

Sarita finished her Kona coffee, the homemade sweet rolls and the last of the fruit.

"Good morning."

Sarita hadn't heard footsteps, but Alex Firman stood directly beside her. His approach from the rear had been soundless. He glanced at Sarita's plate, empty except for a papaya rind. "Morgan's waiting for you in the office. I'll take you there if you've finished your breakfast. Did you sleep well last night? No disturbances?"

Sarita rose. "What could have disturbed me? Everything was fine."

"Good." Alex's pale eyes examined Sarita, her costume, her breasts, her bare legs. Sarita's lips tightened in annoyance. To her further discomfiture, the man began to hum a few bars from the melody Sarita had danced to by herself the night before. His eyes crinkled, but they were without humor. "Come along."

Sarita made herself walk at a leisurely pace behind Alex Firman. She wasn't going to hurry to keep up with him. Corridors led from one large room into another. Recalling Morgan's remark that he didn't keep guard dogs around the place, Sarita compared Alex's appearance to that of a Doberman pinscher. There was the same haughty, sharp profile. Except that Alex's meanness could actually make Dobermans seem lovable.

At the door to Morgan's office, Alex offered, "Take you swimming at the beach later."

"I may be busy packing to return home, but thanks just the same." Sarita was astounded at Alex's offhand invitation and assumed there was something obnoxious underlying it. She knew he was staring at her as she knocked on Morgan's door, so she kept her eyes firmly fixed on the finely grained wood. Why allow Alex Firman to think that any decision had been made one way or the other as to whether she'd stay on Maui or go back to Chicago?

Hearing no stir of movement around her, Sarita glanced over her shoulder. To her surprise, Alex had already started down the corridor. She remembered his silent approach behind her at the breakfast table, and a chill rippled across her shoulder blades. Then she reminded herself that anyone who walked with such a singularly quiet tread would never be guilty of carelessly trampling dry leaves underfoot in the night. Unless, of course, the noise had been intentional.

Morgan's deep voice called, "Come in," and Sarita forgot Alex Firman.

Wycoff rose from behind his desk and moved forward with the compelling ease that Sarita had visualized earlier. Again she felt an exquisite current running between them, but when she looked up into his face, she saw that his eyes were hooded as he politely indicated a chair. "If you'll sit down, Sarita, we'll have our talk. I have a couple of papers to go through first. You'll excuse me?"

Sarita nodded and sat down. She didn't feel slighted by Morgan's remote attitude. Instead, she felt gloriously entrapped, heady with the silken sensation of being in the same room with Morgan Wycoff. The sensible side of her understood that this feeling must be one of pure sexual arousal. Love at first sight was a myth that had been disproved.

She stole a glance at Morgan. His head was down while he studied pages in a folder in front of him. A thick sheaf of russet-brown hair fell across his forehead. A faded, tight T-shirt displayed the muscular width of his chest and shoulders. Hastily Sarita looked away, not wanting him to catch her staring at him.

As she glanced around the office, she noticed it was a well-used, no-nonsense working room. A large map hanging on one wall depicted the islands—Hawaii, Maui, Lanai, Molokai, Oahu and, in the far distance, Kauai. A world globe spun beside her. In the corner was a long drafting board covered with blueprints and architectural renderings. Metal files consumed another portion of the study, along with bookcases and a range of wall clocks that showed the time of day in Los Angeles, Houston, Chicago, New York and London. A late model electric typewriter and a word processor were also in evidence. A small computer system sat on a table.

Morgan stood up, put aside the folder and walked over to a casement window. He remained there looking out at the expanse of blue sky. Sarita knew it was time to be stern with herself, to stifle her emotion-charged feelings. Yet her heart still thudded at the sight of him, which was all right, because she was beautifully alive. She wondered—or was it a hope?—if Morgan was fighting sensations similar to her own.

But when he turned back to her, his gaze was steady and impersonal. His face wore the empty mask of commerce. It was as though all vigor and lusty life had been sucked out of him. This wasn't the same Morgan who had insisted last night that she stay here and not leave him, that it was important that she remain.

Why was it important when she didn't even know what the whole thing was all about? She started to rise from her chair in protest at her own ignorance. Morgan waved her back as though she were an irritating insect. He seated himself and steepled his fingers, bringing them to rest contemplatively against his lips and looking down their length, concentrating his thoughts. An annoyed Sarita had seen this ploy before. It was designed to make the interviewee uncomfortable.

If, for some obscure reason, he was trying to put her at a disadvantage, let him have his say and she would get out fast. She didn't know this man sitting across from her; she didn't want to know him. It was probably all finished—and she saw herself on the plane bound for home and familiar ice storms. She'd had enough of the seduction of the flowers in winter on this island. She told herself there was nothing wrong with the normal February weather of ten degrees below zero. Nor was there anything wrong with Chicago, Illinois.

Without looking at Sarita, Morgan began to speak, and she made herself listen. "Patrice would like you to stay here for a period of three months and work with her. It would be in the nature of a trial, I have to be frank about that. Personalities and how they bond are important too." There was a pause. "At the end of that time, if all goes well, we can negotiate a year's contract that would be advantageous for you. That is, assuming the market analysis of the product Patrice is interested in is up to expectations. I believe it will be. I still believe in my wife's talent." Morgan's smile curled briefly. Ruefully? Sarita wondered. "I meant to say my former wife. Domestic speech habits are hard to break sometimes."

Did this mean they went to bed together sometimes too? Sarita wondered. That was a domestic habit that might be equally hard to break. Patrice was an ageless siren, with all the lure of experience. Sarita felt helpless, hopeless—but then, she didn't intend to stay here with these people, so what did it matter?

Morgan's face was blank, and he wasn't looking at her. Sarita gazed coldly at him. She'd made up her mind. Peter Dome would be furious with her when she returned and told him she had made this decision without consulting him— and how could she explain it to Meg Kirby? By calling it Miller intuition? Meg would snarl at that and say, "You're supposed to use a computer *plus* your brain, Sarita—not some impromptu feeling that you label intuition."

Sarita might be letting down her colleagues in Chicago, but they'd told her the deal depended on her and what she found out and if she was comfortable with it. She wasn't. "And for what reason?" Peter would ask. She would have to answer that the Wycoffs were peculiarly evasive. Both Peter and Meg would pounce. Had she given the Wycoffs a chance?

The silence between herself and Morgan had lasted too long. As his dark eyes swung back to challenge hers, she said, "You haven't told me what this project of yours is all about. I think now it's better that you not bother to confide the details. I can give you the names of other consultants who might be interested. I'm sorry that your company has had the expense of flying me over here, but I'm beginning to think this isn't a venture that Dome Advertising should undertake."

Morgan spoke harshly. "You're making an emotional judgment."

"What did you say!" Sarita sprang to her feet. Her frustration with the situation boiled over into rage at his contemptuous comment, and she pounded her fist on his desk. "I came here a seasoned professional! My market procedures are tested, valid and original. In the promotion of tangible goods, I am probably the best you can get. My reputation in research analysis is excellent—and that's why I'm here!"

Sarita halted and took a deep breath. She was well aware of Meg Kirby's opinion of her. Sarita Miller, never a chip on the shoulder, a calm, controlled, reasonable woman. Right now she was none of these things. She was antagonistic and excited. Her eyes sparked electric green. Her fingers nervously ruffled her hair, turning it into a savage golden halo.

"I'd like to know exactly why I'm here," Sarita plowed on, her face pale and angry. "You haven't said. Your representative in Los Angeles didn't say. And your wife—forgive me, your former wife—hasn't given a hint of what's expected of me. It's not a normal situation. I've waited for this interview and for some explanation of the product you want me to handle. I'm not overreacting. It's all very *in*tangible, Mr. Wycoff. And you have the unmitigated nerve to say I'm making an emotional judgment because I refuse to take on some nebulous, pie-in-the-sky account! I—don't—like it!"

"You liked me." Morgan's look was one of total innocence.

She could have torn his head off.

"Under the circumstances, Morgan Wycoff, that's really a rotten thing for you to say." Sarita was at the office door, her hand choked on the doorknob. "I don't suppose there's anything as civilized as a taxi around here, so I'd appreciate it if you'd have your guard dog, Firman, drive me into Kahului Airport as soon as I'm packed."

"If you give up and go back, Peter Dome will fire you, and then where will you be? You know who will arrange it? Your old chum, Ross Bailey. Under the table, he's Dome Advertising's financial backer as well as its attorney. He's a heavyweight who knows your city and can pull strings. And he can also get rid of you."

How could Morgan Wycoff know so much of what Sarita herself had guessed, but hoped wasn't true?

"You're a terrible man."

"My character isn't the subject under discussion."

"Isn't it?"

Morgan stood up, granitelike, his look menacing.

"Don't come near me!"

All at once, as though her head were held in a vise and she were being forced to look at the jumbled pieces in a dangerous kaleidoscope, the pattern rearranged itself and came smoothly together. Sarita was released. Confusion disappeared. And he was Morgan again, her Morgan. The icy-eyed man vanished, to be replaced by a human being. Too human. The bronze eyes stared into hers with an intensity that shredded her pride. Their relationship was tentative, just beginning. He didn't want it to end this way. Both of them knew it.

"You don't want to leave," he said. "You be honest with me, and I'll be honest with you."

"Credibility twins?" Her smiled was jagged. She would not be so easily coaxed.

"I intend to tell you . . . everything. In my own way. In my own time. Let me choose the environment."

"Environment? This is business, Morgan. I'm a businesswoman. I'm not here on a happy holiday tour, you know."

"I know. And you're right. But I thought we'd work it this way. You come over to my place tonight, we'll have a drink there, then I'll take you to dinner at the Teahouse of the Maui Moon."

"The condo you spoke of on the other side of Napili Bay?" Morgan nodded. Sarita continued. "I'd like to see it, but I can't believe a name like Teahouse of the Maui Moon."

"It's a very good dining spot and not far from where I live. Stop holding up that door—the knob's going to come off in your hand."

"You are the most totally evasive man I've ever met. How did you get where you're supposed to be—major industrialist of his time, and all that?"

"By being evasive, of course. And I always get my own way. I don't negotiate."

"Whether you get your own way about this we'll have to see. Tonight is show and tell? That is, if I agree to go with you to the . . . the Maui Moon?"

"Yes."

"Shouldn't I talk with Patrice first? She might be induced to tell me a little more about our project than you have."

"I've told you nothing. And I notice you said 'our' project. Welcome aboard." He held out his hand.

"Oh, no." She stepped back and put her hand behind her. "I suppose one more night on Maui won't hurt. I'd like to hear your presentation, Morgan. It had better be a heart-pounder, because I'm tough. And I'm beginning to be curious," she concluded with irony.

"You've been curious all along."

Sarita shrugged. "Thinking back, admittedly I haven't been entirely the businesswoman I bragged about. Of course I'm curious. About Patrice. She's an exciting character, and with her background, whatever assignment you people have in mind should be out of the ordinary." Sarita paused, surprised. "I seem to be taking it for granted that if I agree, I'll be working with Patrice."

"You're intuitive. I like that."

"It's easy, Morgan. You have a chemistry major as a live-in domestic. That ties in somehow, doesn't it?"

"Maybe." Warily Morgan approached Sarita. "I won't bite you."

Sarita could have shouted with laughter. What if she said, "Please do. I'd adore it. Be my guest"? Damn, she hoped he couldn't read her mind. Sensing the swell of feeling building up once more between them, Sarita slipped away from his hand just as it would have captured her, and walked to the casement window.

The view below was that of an artfully shaped swimming pool, its water a turquoise contrast to the deep, vibrant green of the surrounding foliage. Feisty myna birds hopped around on the smooth lawn as though they owned the place.

Morgan came up behind her. Very close. She stared blindly out of the window, conscious only of the sound of his even breathing, of his broad chest an inch away. If she moved back a step, would his hands draw her close to him, slide up and over her shoulders and down to cup and tantalize her breasts? She knew she was quivering with the desire that this would happen, because then . . . she would revolve slowly in his arms, place a kiss on his heart and nibble at him, at that place on his chest where the neck of the old T-shirt dipped low to show the gloss of body hair. Her fingers would drift slowly up around his neck, and Morgan would incline his head, and, as had happened the night before, his tongue would explore her mouth with infinite tenderness. . . . Fantasy stopped there. She began to lean back gently. . . .

The voice behind her was brisk. "Now that we've come to an understanding, do you want to go for a swim in the pool? By yourself. I have work to do here."

Rigidly she straightened up. When she finally permitted herself to turn around and face him, her own tone was equally crisp. "I don't know that we do understand each other. For the first time, you may have to negotiate." Her smile was like cream as she concluded, "Alex asked me to go to the beach." She said it to test Morgan and saw his expression tighten.

"I'd rather you didn't go with him. In fact, I'm surprised he put himself out enough to offer to take you."

She tried to make her answer light. "I think he had drowning me in mind." She made a droll face to show that she was kidding. Morgan seemed amused then, and that was good.

He walked her to the door—at least her legs moved in that direction, but the rest of her was frantically trying to come up with reasons why she should stay here with him.

"I think Patrice will want to have a talk with you. She and I discussed the situation last night, and, as I've already told you, you're the one we want for this assignment." His eyes glinted mischievously. "After all, you do come highly recommended. You don't suppose your ex-fiancé would let you down, do you?"

When Meg Kirby had first discussed the possible linkup of Dome Advertising and the Morgan Wycoff interests, Sarita had suspected that the unnamed associate responsible for it might be Ross. Meg had dissembled, but Sarita's instincts had proved correct.

"You made it clear that if I decided not to take on this job, Dome and Ross would terminate me. Now you say Ross recommended me and would stand by me. Which is it?"

"Both. He's trapped you. Having met you, I can understand his feelings toward you. Of course, if you go back like a good girl and marry him, he won't mind Dome's losing this particular deal. What's a million or so, after all?"

"How do you know so much?" Having asked this, Sarita abruptly changed the subject. "I suppose I should be flattered that you and Patrice have made up your minds about me. But I'm not a puppet. I have some input in this matter. It will be my decision too." If she blew it, she blew it, she reflected.

They were in the corridor outside the office. "I'll see if Patrice is up." He walked over to one of the windows opening onto the circular terrace and shouted, "Maile!"

"Yes, Morgan?" Unexpectedly, Maile appeared on the lanai, holding a bamboo rake in one hand.

"Why aren't you with the test tubes?"

"I've been locked out."

Following this curious exchange, which seemed to faze neither Maile nor Wycoff, Maile went back to the garden. Nothing further was said about Sarita's having a talk with Patrice.

"Why don't you take your swim before lunch?" Morgan suggested. "I'll join you on the lanai at noon and we'll talk some more."

Sarita knew she couldn't put on that ribbon of a bikini and swim in the pool directly beneath Morgan's office window. Her private thoughts might be seductive, but she couldn't bear to play the role of sensual tease if he should look out and watch her.

"Is there a car I can borrow to drive into Lahaina?" She hoped Morgan wouldn't offer Alex Firman as chauffeur.

He didn't. Again he shouted, "Maile!"

What an arrogant bastard, Sarita thought with a sigh. Actually he was the type of man she detested. Last night she'd believed she'd seen the poet in him. But not today. Last night she'd forgotten his successful life and all that money and the fact that he could get whatever he asked for. Even so, right now she wished he would kiss her, and immediately. So what kind of person *was* she?

Maile appeared like a shot and seemed delighted to hear that she'd been tapped to drive Sarita into Lahaina. "Five minutes," she told Sarita, her brown eyes shining. "We will have fun."

Sarita's response was meek. "I want to buy a bathing suit. You think that's fun?"

"Anything in Lahaina is fun."

Sarita glanced around and realized that Morgan had returned to his office. "I'll run back to the guest house and get my purse."

"Five minutes," Maile repeated. "I'll have the car out in front. We'll go the quick way to the Napili road this time."

Sarita frowned. "How did you know Alex drove me the long way around? Were you here when we arrived?"

Maile's smile was prim. "I prepared the guest house for you. I left as your car stopped."

"I didn't see you. I'm sorry."

"You weren't supposed to see me. Don't you know when people live as the Wycoffs do that all service is invisible? Beds are made, tables are set, meals are prepared—but no one is supposed to see how these things happen. Isn't it that way in the best hotels?"

Sarita hesitated. "Maile, I don't know what to say to that."

Maile crooked an eyebrow above her doe-soft eyes and put a finger to her lips. "Then don't say, but I think, really, you know."

God, what am I supposed to know? Sarita stared for a moment at the lovely, childlike face that showed nothing of what Maile's experience of life and her four years at the university must have taught her. Maile wore a mask like the rest of them did on this Napili estate. Sometimes she was Molly McIntosh on her way to UCLA. Most of the time she was Maile, but not an unsophisticated daughter of the islands, as she had proved by her slightly caustic remark about the Wycoffs' way of life.

Sarita hurried down the path toward the guest house. Maile had seemed excited about going into Lahaina. Perhaps she had a male friend in town she was anxious to see. Sarita no longer felt as comfortable with Maile as she had this morning when they'd talked at breakfast. She wasn't sure she wanted to spend the afternoon in the young woman's company. On the other hand—and Sarita knew that she was being opportunistic—Maile might tell her everything she wanted to know.

Meg and Peter, back in Chicago, would be disgusted to learn that Sarita was still in the dark about this whole enterprise after an almost twenty-four-hour stay at the Wycoffs'. Sarita was disgusted with herself.

After reaching the porch, she took the key out of her pocket and inserted it into the lock. Then she realized to her amazement that the door had drifted open without any pressure from the key.

She pushed the door further ajar, wondering if she had forgotten to lock it this morning when she left. Of course not! She'd locked the door securely. She'd even held up the key afterward, looking at it, pleased because she'd obtained it from Morgan. As was her usual habit with her own apartment, she'd even tried the knob to make sure the door was locked.

Sarita quickly started toward the bedroom to check her tape recorder and camera, both of which were expensive items and would be difficult to replace on Maui if someone had walked off with them. She wasn't frightened. Something like this brought out the mettle in her. She'd warned Morgan she could be tough.

"Hello . . ." It was an unexpected, sibilant whisper.

Sarita froze. She hadn't sensed another presence in the sitting room. Slowly she turned around to locate the place from where that husky voice had come. It was the low chair near the bamboo screen by the door. Against the gold chair cushions sat a tiny figure, wearing gold silk pajamas.

"I didn't mean to surprise you."

Warily Sarita reversed her path away from the bedroom. She came forward, feeling tall and awkward and more than slightly betrayed. "Yes, you did mean to surprise me, Patrice. You certainly did."

Chapter Seven

PATRICE STARED AT THE ADVANCING SARITA. "You're angry with me."

Sarita halted. "This is an unexpected visit—but no, I'm not angry." She'd been trained to avoid anger in confrontations with clients. That was almost Rule Number One. "Just curious," she added diplomatically.

"I can answer that 'curious' of yours. Sit down, make yourself comfortable and we'll talk." It was distinctly the voice of a woman in charge.

Sarita knew that the guest house was no longer her personal haven. It belonged, and rightfully, to its owner, Patrice Wycoff. Sarita was the intruder.

Had she been asked to make herself comfortable? She glanced at the rattan couch on which she and Morgan had sat side by side the night before. The present situation was an ironic one. The low chair on which Patrice perched was close to the bamboo screen, and it was by that screen that Morgan had held Sarita, searching her mouth with his own while his touch had sent crescendos of desire swelling through her body.

The silence between the two women had lasted too long.

Patrice watched Sarita with probing eyes. "When you came in, why did you say that I meant to surprise you? I wasn't trying to put you at a disadvantage, if that was the implication. I want us to get along well together. I merely considered that today would be an opportunity to talk to you in private—to get to know you." Patrice put out that mesmerizing hand, her fingers moving rhythmically, like starflowers under water. "After all, Sarita, you *will* share my secrets."

Sarita thought, Here it comes. With suppressed amusement she recognized the melodrama behind Patrice's approach. Was the new, pouty sweetness in Patrice's voice intended to ingratiate? Or was Patrice conveying an apology for her unconventional appearance?

Sarita halted in her search for a neutral corner. "Maile is waiting to drive me into Lahaina. I'll have to let her know I'm not going."

"That's an intercom phone over there. Dial one-o-nine and tell whoever answers to see that Maile gets your message."

It was Nils who answered at the main house. He said he'd find Maile and give her the message. Sarita hung up the phone and turned back to Patrice.

The older woman swung her knees up in front of her, hooked her flat gold heels on the chair edge and clasped her fingers around her pajama-clad legs. She rested her chin on the silk curve of her knees, and peering at Sarita, plunged right into her talk.

"You haven't been here long enough to have had the experience of rain in the islands. Rain here is different from anything you've ever seen or felt before. It's a golden mist, like pale, wet sunlight. One simply walks through it. There's never an umbrella in use on Maui." Patrice raised one graceful hand, her fingers gesturing raindrops drifting down. "Most of the time Maui's rain feels like a fine, gentle spray. One can swim in the sea when it rains, dance in the rain, make love in the rain. Yellow ginger flowers are everywhere here, particularly potent during the fall season. I have a reason for stressing this, because their ginger fragrance tends to rise in the moisture that comes up from the wet earth. It's not overwhelming, you understand, but it is subtle and pervasive."

Sarita nodded, recalling yesterday's spectacular rainbow over the West Maui Mountains, a souvenir left by a rain flurry at higher altitudes. In Hilo a delicious odor of ginger had permeated the humid afternoon.

"If one is susceptible or inclined to hallucinate, that scented ginger mist can drive a person slightly mad . . . in a pleasurable sense, I mean. There's nothing at all remarkable in what I'm going to tell you next. To a person of my background and experience, it was obvious what could be done." Patrice paused.

Sarita's brows peaked thoughtfully. "You've captured a genie in a bottle?"

"Exactly. I've captured the rain scent, but not in a prosaic way. I'm not talking about a drugstore counter sale, Sarita. It's a seductive aphrodisiac—one for which I haven't yet found a name. The formula's almost perfected. Maile works with me. So does her father. He's a chemist in Honolulu. You must go over there and meet with him."

After the buildup she'd received, Sarita was a little disappointed, even deflated. Perfume? A nice idea, but why all the mystery?

A clever Patrice defined the expression on Sarita's face. "I'm not talking about a mere scent. Sarita, look at me. What is your impression?"

Sarita blinked, thinking rapidly before she spoke. "I see a successful woman with flair and imagination and creative talent. Your reputation—"

Patrice cut her off. "Don't bore me, dear, with compliments. We both know my reputation is nonexistent at the moment. I *was* a successful woman. But that's yesterday's rumor. It's what you have done today that counts. Take a man or a woman out of the cosmetic world for a few years, and who remembers—past reputation or not?"

"Gabrielle Chanel?"

"The exception. To go back—what do you think of me, *me?* Look at me! The exterior me. My face, my skin, my arms." The full sleeves of her costume flowed as Patrice extended smooth, tanned, graceful arms. Young arms. And that exquisite, youthful-appearing face . . . Sarita wondered what she was supposed to say if Patrice didn't want compliments.

"I've reached the half-century mark in my life," Patrice stated as she stood up and approached Sarita. Gliding forward, she maintained the posture of a demure goddess who expected offerings. "You're too young to be aware of this, but bizarre things can happen to a woman as the years go by. One day, alone in the bright sunshine, she catches a glimpse of the inner part of her upper arm. The skin is no longer taut, it isn't as she remembered it—instead, it's loose, it jiggles, it hangs there. In the inside curve of her elbow there's a microscopic withering—faint, but she can see it. She turns her wrist this way . . ." Patrice accompanied her words with a similar movement. "Those hideous little track marks won't go away. They're there to stay. It happens to most women of a certain age, except to those idiots who run laps and let themselves be pommeled either by torture machines or by a heavyweight masseuse."

Patrice began to smile. "You look startled, Sarita. Naturally I'm speaking about the women in my world, those creatures who lie swaddled in body wraps to rid themselves of massive dimpling flesh."

"I'm going to start taping," Sarita said quietly.

Patrice withdrew her smooth arms into her billowing sleeves. "You plan to stay." It was a statement. She smiled cannily without disturbing the egg-smooth planes of her face. "I know you'll stay, because there's more to all this than the superficialities I've spoken about."

"I guessed that."

"My background is European, and so I have a high regard for tradition. Today's new path is a return to old values."

Patrice's last sentence followed Sarita as she exited the

77

room, returning almost immediately with her recorder. She didn't want to miss a word.

Patrice reseated herself on the low chair. "At one time I used all those glossy pages of the big, important magazines to do my ridiculous advertising—most of it lies. I would okay huge centerfolds that shouted, 'Metallic is in! Bronze the lips, sequin the eyelids!' Next season we'd have to change everything. It would have to be cheeky earth tones instead. Kohl-rimmed eyes are out. Khaki-green mascara is in. Place a smudge of matte charcoal beneath the brow line. And, of course, we mustn't forget the year for 'Weird.' That fashionable face had a kind of museum armor effect. Medusa curls spritzed with silver gilt, the stainless steel approach. Sounds crazy? You're laughing? It *is* crazy. You can read all about it in that smart Seventh Avenue publication they put out . . ."

"But, Patrice, the average woman doesn't go for that stuff."

A singularly intense Patrice leaned forward and thrust out both palms. "Listen to me, now. What I am talking about has nothing to do with the vapidity of these seasonal cosmetic changes. I'm through with all that. I'm talking about a basic control agent from the laboratory. Science teaches us that our skin is an organ of the body—that age signs are programed genetically. Our parents' coloring, their bone structure, even their personality traits are all inside the tiny seed that starts us out."

"What can be done about that?"

"I am convinced this built-in aging timer can be reversed. My control agent is simple but extraordinarily effective. It's a spray-on cream that can prevent the damage of years, climate and sun. Those women who play golf and tennis have marvelous bodies underneath their panties and bras. And, of course, they have a great heartbeat. Blood pressure? The diastolic and the systolic are perfect. But their faces! Thickened skin, weathered and lined. My discovery will change all that."

Sarita sighed. Caught up for the moment by the delirium of Patrice's words and dedication, she'd wanted to believe. But the truth was that she'd heard it before—emollients of hydrolized protein, collagen, necessary fatty acids. And now what? Maui rain and ginger blossom scent?

"What are you thinking?" Patrice demanded.

Sarita's reply was prompt, if not strictly truthful. "I'm thinking that with your discovery, women's sun-ruined skins will be improved enough to complement the vigor of those healthy bodies you've described."

Patrice's one note of laughter resembled a short bark. "It's all right, Sarita. Keep your skepticism to yourself. In the past I've had business dealings with Ross Bailey. If he says you're good, you are. Your job is not to cater to me. Your job is to test the market for my product and tell me what's out there waiting."

Like a quick gold butterfly, Patrice fluttered to the door. "Tomorrow we'll meet in my lab. You'll need specifics, though I don't expect you to retain too much of those. You're not trained for it. In the meantime, talk over financial arrangements with Morgan. You'll find he's a man without a soul for anything but finance, but he's very adept at that."

Sarita would have to place that last startling sentence concerning Morgan on hold. There was more she needed to learn from Patrice. "I have to know your concept. Have you thought about formulating a strategy to counteract any stepping over the boundary that you might do regarding the medical associations around the country?"

"I pay a very good law firm to worry about that. Think with your heart now. Write me up some beautiful passages to tell the world what I have discovered."

"I don't do copy."

"Ah, that's right. You're all specialists now, aren't you? Anyway, we don't need fancy words, because I won't have any competition in the marketplace. Remember, Sarita, I have no competition . . . in anything."

It's true, Sarita thought. One has to be a complete egotist

to succeed completely. The saying fitted Patrice very well. Seemingly, Sarita had signed on with her. But was the woman too much of an eccentric?

The door closed behind Patrice. She reopened it to toss a piece of metal that landed next to the tray of shells on the glass table. "There's the extra key I let myself in with today. I promise you there's no other. No one will intrude on your privacy. I did, and I apologize."

The elfin face disappeared.

It was fortunate that the sentences of the brief interview were on tape. Sarita remembered very little of the strange conversation except for Patrice's derisive remark about Morgan's being a man without a soul for anything but finance.

Sarita tried to work, but she couldn't. Sitting cross-legged on the bed, she crayoned in the headings on her chart: Selective Buying Motive. Primary Buying Motive. Segmentation According to Demographics, Geographics, Attitudes, Values and Benefits.

To no avail. It was too early to do any preparatory forecasting with the meager information she had. Later it would all fall onto the graph, then into a computer, and the zig-zagging lines on her chart would have meaning for her.

She'd missed lunch. She didn't care. She would go down to the beach for a swim. If she didn't do that, she would spend the rest of the afternoon thinking about Morgan and the evening ahead and what it signified.

Sarita reflected that Morgan wasn't a man without a soul. He must only seem that way to Patrice because their life together had ended, though a business partnership apparently persisted between them. It was inevitable that a bitter residue could still be tasted after a broken marriage. On the surface the two were polite to each other. Yet Sarita recalled the sarcasm—and, strangely enough, the purring sensuality—in Patrice's dinner table remark preceding Morgan's appearance the night before: "Get set for the master."

* * *

David Mikimura, who had spent a decade in New York City's financial canyons after having been graduated from Columbia University, was speaking in the direction of Morgan Wycoff's back. "The shopping center mall has not become the rousing success we'd hoped for, but then, neither has it been a failure."

Morgan did not turn around. He continued to look out his office window toward the meadow in the distance. It was hardly a meadow in the classic sense, but more of an open space with matted grass and low, red ixora bushes.

Morgan sighed. "Not a success, not a failure? That's a little subtle for me, Mr. Mikimura."

"It's true there are no crowds and no foot traffic, as one would expect. But the few customers who do appear spend a great deal of money. The gallery that sells Niihau shells is charging ten thousand dollars for a fifteen-strand necklace, and a not-unusual day can see several sold. The paintings done by the young lady from Kiahuna Plantation account for fifteen percent of the sales volume. The people who do find their way to the shops in the mall demand quality, and they can pay for it. They're sophisticated in their purchases. Perhaps the original plans were too ambitious, but what we're achieving now appeals to the Princeville crowd."

"You mean those athletes over from the mainland on a six-week hiatus? Most of those professionals do have million-dollar contracts." It was said idly. Still, Morgan did not turn to face his desk and his colleague. A figure had appeared in the distance on the meadow path.

"I am talking about the people who are social and rich. They keep changing the decor of the condominiums they buy at Hanalei. These vacationers like luxurious appointments, sunken Japanese-style tubs, gourmet kitchen gadgets, beautiful furniture. All of this is available in the shops."

Morgan stirred. The figure was that of a woman with a brightly colored towel tied around her waist. The upper part

FLOWERS IN WINTER

of her body appeared to be bare, or else whatever she was
wearing there was flesh-colored. She was running swiftly,
with long strides. Her hair was fair, swept back by the wind.

David Mikimura was saying, ". . . with spectacular artifacts and artful decorations. I repeat, affluence has found
its particular niche here. Low volume in this case is better.
When will you fly over and take another look? You won't
be disappointed in your investment, I can assure you. But,
of course, before we do that, we must meet with my people
in Honolulu. The Tokyo group will be staying at the Kahala
Hilton. They arrive tomorrow. To talk with them is a priority."

"I didn't hear the question . . . sorry."

The woman was Sarita. She must be on her way to swim
at the uninhabited beach nearby. In a moment she would
disappear, following the path down the rock cliff.

Mikimura patiently explained that his private plane would
be at the Kaanapali airstrip. They could take off that afternoon for Honolulu. Otherwise he could be reached at the
splendid Kapalua Bay Hotel, which was owned by his international friends, and where he was entertaining vacationing bankers from Japan.

"Not this afternoon, Mr. Mikimura." Morgan turned
around and clasped both hands over those of his business
associate, whom he had never called David. They shook
hands heartily. David Mikimura beamed and bowed.

"I will telephone you at the Kapalua," Morgan promised.
"I have to go now. But tomorrow you and I will fly to
Honolulu. Please have Alex confirm the arrangements.
Goodbye, Mr. Mikimura."

Once again Morgan's gaze was drawn to the magnet of
the empty meadow. He must find Sarita.

The beach was totally isolated. Sarita shed her wrap-
around towel and walked into the lapping waves. A strong
swimmer in icy, freshwater Lake Michigan, she discovered
this ocean to be warm, salty and buoyant. She struck out

with a steady stroke. Freedom . . . the small top strip of her bikini barely contained her full breasts. The tiny band laced across her hips allowed her the illusion of complete nakedness. It was a marvelous feeling to swim this way in the limpid waters.

She turned over onto her back, floating, staring through tight lashes at a cobalt sky. A maverick comber, a big one, picked her up and rocked her gently into its back flow until it was ready to roll on and slide up the beach in a triangle of foam. Next, Sarita stroked face down, holding her breath, turning her head sideways for an occasional gasp of air. The stinging salty water didn't bother her. She could see clearly, far beneath her, the white sand bottom and the slice of her legs propelling her on through deep aqua-blue.

She righted herself, paddling, lifting both hands to smooth back the wet bang of hair from her forehead. A second swell caught her, this time with her mouth wide open. Salt water flowed into her throat. She gurgled, gagged, spit out, tucked her head down and began a strong crawl shoreward.

Her toes touched the upslope of sand. She found herself executing fanciful pirouettes as the waters dragged at her and swirled her around, rushing her forward, pulling her back. She abandoned herself to the spinning motion, watching the lovely scenery do carousel turns before her eyes with each dizzying sweep. On the final spin, the last surge of a wave sent her scooping along the wet sand on her belly. She lay there, panting, laughing. Then, on her knees, she reached for the next curl of water, letting it flow over her body to wash away every particle of sand.

The top of her bikini tugged at the soft flesh of her bosom. She stripped it off and raced back for a final plunge in the pulsing sea. Its waters covered her sensuously, its ripples exploring her inner thighs, its currents raising and cradling her full breasts, its cool breath tightening her nipples to a ruby-red tautness that was almost exquisitely painful. The sea was like a lover, fingering, probing, caressing. . . . Reluctant to leave its embrace, Sarita was astonished at her own sense of voluptuousness. The awareness of throbbing vitality within her body, the delicious extension of her breasts, the velvety rub and demand of her thighs as she walked up through the waves to the shore, were unique to Sarita, a revelation that surprised her with its primitive need. She wanted . . . something? She desired to take . . . or to be taken? A thrumming sensual rhythm now stirred deep within her.

She reached the sandy beach and bent to retrieve the two tiny triangles of material that were looped together and intended to cover her naked breasts. How ridiculous and extravagant and outrageous! Sarita thought. Languidly she fastened one of the loops, knowing the flesh-colored cloth did little to disguise the bounty of her breasts. The warmth of the afternoon sun was turning her rosy all over. She could feel the stinging burn of the sun's rays along with the salt drying on her skin.

At least she had not thought of Morgan for an hour. Or had she? Wasn't it really Morgan who was the creator of the sea's embrace? Wasn't Morgan the sea's force that had explored her body until she had writhed in its cool delight? Hadn't she plunged herself back into the wild current of the waves to become once more a part of the sea's sensuous rhythm . . . to become a part of Morgan?

She looked up toward the rise of ground where she'd left her towel and sandals. Puzzled, she closed her eyes. She must be concentrating too deeply, creating Morgan's physical image—the wide cheekbones, the tiger-bright gaze, the lips carved flat, like a Greek statue's. She was merely dizzy from the sun. That must be it. She was totally alone. No one was standing there observing her, as she had at first believed. The beautiful scenery was static. There was no movement, except for the vast, spatial sea, ghostly in the distance.

Sarita's eyes snapped open.

It was no apparition.

It was he . . . leaning, with his arms crossed, against the twisted trunk of a kiawe tree. A silent watcher, an onlooker, a voyeur!

She heard her own voice, hoarse and furious. "How long have you been there?"

"Long enough to make sure that you're safe. Never swim alone in unfamiliar waters." An insinuating smile touched his lips, his eyes. His expression seemed to mock her annoyance with him, but beneath the surface of his amusement, his own uneasiness matched Sarita's. He asked himself, What is my true feeling toward this woman? Am I caught by the lushness of her body, by the strongly physical attraction she holds for me?

He wished it were that simple. Infatuation would be much easier to deal with. If it were only that, then, crudely put, he would take her in his arms, set himself upon her and pump until lust vanished in weariness and his satiation with her flesh released him. Deliberately, cruelly, he fixed this image in his mind. But it could not reach his heart. And because of this, he suspected the truth. Sarita's appeal for him lay in some long-ago memory of beauty, in some place of serene enchantment where love could never disappoint, where honor was not frail, where there could be no rejection, where tenderness and understanding were imperishable.

Impossible? Utopian? Probably. Still, he knew his feeling ran deep. Sarita was someone he might have known—hell, *should* have known—far back in a less complicated time in his life. A time when his innocence could match her own—an innocence that knew nothing of deceits practiced, an innocence free from the moral and intellectual accommodations he had made, first to "get along" and later to "achieve."

He began to saunter toward her, his feet in their canvas sneakers crusting into the sand with each step he took. Sarita heard the squeak of the sand, the breath of the wind; the sun was in her eyes, and he kept coming. What had he seen of her? How long had he watched? She glanced down at her nearly naked body, wishing she were wearing a less revealing bathing suit. Then she saw that he was carrying the towel she'd left by the rocks, its pattern bright with red and yellow hibiscuses.

As he came close—too close—she reached for the towel to shield herself. Morgan hesitated only for a moment, his gaze lingering on her splendid body. Then his eyes rose to meet hers, which were now as ink-dark as the far stretch of sea at the horizon. Sarita's lungs filled with breath that seemed difficult to expel.

"I came to rescue you."

He tried to make it sound like a joke, easy words of social pretense to cover something that was awkward between them. He wasn't even clever about it, he thought. They both knew it. Why should he lie to her, to himself?

With a move so sudden it startled them both, he whipped the thick towel around Sarita's shoulders, bringing her in tight to the clothed length of his body. She was trapped against him, held hard by his strength, her arms pinioned together and her palms lying flat on his chest. Her touch accelerated and intensified the pounding of his heart. The response in her own body was like an uncontrollable shudder that flowed upward through toes, knees, thighs and belly.

She could feel him against her breasts and torso, against the warm place between her legs. She was no longer rigid. A longing so strong that it made her want to scream aloud at its insistence began to pearl moistly in every pore of her flesh. Was it enough to desire his mouth, his probing tongue searching hers? Was it his kiss she had to have, or something deeper, more vital and life-giving?

Her legs buckled beneath her as a wave of lassitude glided slowly, like drops of honey, throughout her body. Only his arms holding her kept Sarita from crumpling to the ground. When he lowered his head to hers, it was as though a great shadow had crossed the sun, providing relief from the glare of sexual heat that enveloped her. She knew his essence as their mouths thirstily matched and held. She was nervous and frightened, but this time her tongue darted to meet his, pointed, agile, keeping at bay the tormenting need but making her part of Morgan as she had been partner to the sea's embrace.

Finally, reluctantly, Morgan released her. Sarita stepped back shakily, staring at him. Then, as solemnly as a child, she knotted the bright towel around her just above her breasts; its length ended in a modest salute below her bikinied bottom. They walked up to the rock, and Sarita slipped her feet into the zori sandals she'd left there.

"Tonight we'll have dinner first, and then . . . my place," Morgan said.

Once more Sarita looked full into his eyes. "You've changed the order. Wasn't it to be drinks at your place, then dinner at the Maui Moon?"

Morgan did not reply. So, after a time, without speaking again, they smiled at each other, understanding. Tonight would be their night.

Chapter Eight

MAILE STEPPED ONTO THE PORCH OF THE GUEST house, knocked on the front door and walked through the sitting room and into the bedroom. Sarita stood there, swinging a garment in each hand, trying to decide which one she would wear tonight.

Maile looked around. "You've made your bed and tidied up. I'm supposed to do that."

Sarita put down the dress hangers. "Thanks, Maile, but I'll take care of things here. There's going to be a lot of paperwork around, and I won't want it disturbed."

Maile glanced curiously at the zigzagging lines on the graph sheets lying on the bed. "If you're sure you want it that way, I'll send one of the girls who works with the cook down here a couple of times a week to clean up. By the way, the extra key is missing from its peg."

Patrice had been telling the truth, then. Sarita did have the second key, and, as Patrice had promised, no one would surprise her again. "Patrice was here. She left the other key," Sarita told Maile.

The slightly slanting eyes in the girl's exotic face almost rounded in surprise. "She doesn't leave the house ever, except to go to the dolphin pool."

"What about her lab?"

"It's in the main house. A great setup, very professional. Why shouldn't it be? I understand she started as a lab assistant without too much basic training—just tremendous skill. I don't know about the cosmetic phase. That was before my time." Maile glanced around as though scenting Patrice's presence. "So she came down here?" She added abruptly, "Why?"

Sarita shrugged, trying to be patient. She was eager for Maile to leave so that she could be alone to think about Morgan, to make herself beautiful for Morgan, to decide on which costume to wear tonight for Morgan. "Patrice wanted us to get acquainted. Somehow the decision's been made. I'm staying."

"He made the decision."

"Who?" Of course Sarita knew.

"Morgan. Do you like him?"

"I don't know him really well enough to say whether I do or not," Sarita parried.

Maile stared at her. "I think you will."

"Naturally I will, in time. I'll be working here."

"Here, and in Honolulu, and over on Kauai. You'll meet my father, James McIntosh, in Honolulu. He has his laboratory there. And sometimes Morgan goes over to his big shopping development on Kauai."

"I'm not exactly a secretary-companion, Maile. After a few lab sessions and a lot more explanation of what's going on, I'll be able to do a workup on this project, and that'll be it. I can finish the consumer research on the mainland." Sarita picked up her chart. She'd forgotten the talk of a year's contract. Not even three months here would be necessary. As deeply as she was attracted to Morgan Wycoff, and even assuming what the night ahead would hold for them, she'd lived a lot longer with ambition.

Maile pointed to the chart. "What is that about?"

Sarita tried to hide her irritation. She really had to move Maile out of here as tactfully as possible so that she could start getting ready for the evening ahead. "I didn't get very far with this chart. I'll tell you about it later." Sarita paused hopefully, but Maile maintained a look of keen interest.

Nothing for it, Sarita supposed. She'd give Maile a quick interpretation. Actually what she did was something intangible, more a matter of feeling the pulse of future clients.

"Someone like me uses scientific methods to solve marketing problems. I have to gather, organize and analyze a lot of data. My responsibility in this case is to assemble the basics that will be useful in a marketing plan for Patrice's product. The Wycoffs are really interested in future potential, so that's my job—to evaluate consumer attitudes and opinions. Sometimes all the science and the computers and the data banks don't help. You have to use instinct, intuition and a background of historical behavioral tendencies." Maile shifted uneasily as Sarita went on. "We have to be subtle about this. First we find the problem areas. I'll make up an organized form that will be my guide. I'll tell you more about it when the guide starts working."

"Sarita, I'm not sure I want to hear more. I prefer chemical composition and testing with analytical balance in the lab."

"To each her own, Maile."

The two grinned at each other.

Maile started to leave. "You want to go into Lahaina anyway for an hour or so? It's not too late."

"I don't think so, thanks. I have work to do here." She flashed a quick smile. "You won't mind?"

Maile shook her head, the long black mane swaying. "I was supposed to have the afternoon off."

"I didn't know that. Did you miss out on it because of me?"

"Oh, no, because of Patrice. She's changed her plans for tonight."

"If that's the case, I don't feel too guilty about spoiling things for you. See you later." Sarita hoped she wasn't being too obvious as she edged Maile toward the door.

"We could have met Nils in Lahaina. It was planned. Too bad."

"Is he your fellow?"

Maile nodded proudly.

Sarita grinned. "This is a beautiful place, and I know it's a temptation to go out and play in the sandbox, but work comes first. Especially for you, since you're going to graduate school in California."

"Speaking of work coming first, that's another reason I came down here—to tell you we're working tonight."

"Who is?"

"Patrice wants to have a lab session with you and me before you go to Honolulu and meet my father and see his material."

Sarita sat down hard on the bed. "But I . . ." She stopped.

"If you don't want to do a quick tour of Lahaina, why don't we get started in the lab now? I'll show you what I'm doing so you'll be ready for Patrice and the heavy stuff. We'll probably have dinner on a tray and go on from there. Sometimes she works until midnight. You have a lot of catching up to do."

"Does . . . does Morgan know about this? I mean, that Patrice intends to work tonight with you and me?"

"She might have told him, but there's no reason to, really. They're not that close. It's business only with them. Probably always has been." Maile paused. "Why do you ask?"

Why indeed! Anything Sarita said would sound pretty limp. She turned away and carefully folded up the violet-colored blouse and pants and the white cotton dress with the halter top. "These just needed ironing," she explained. "I'll attend to them later."

Maile, distracted, told her where the ironing board was in the kitchen. She added, "Morgan's car went out a while ago. Alex said the boss was on his way to Kapalua. Mr. Mikimura's here."

"Yes, of course, Mr. Mikimura." Whoever Mr. Mikimura was. Maile didn't recognize the irony in Sarita's muffled comment. Sarita was feeling brightly stupid. And terrible. Even sick to her stomach.

"Those are pretty outfits." Maile glanced again at the smart garments that no longer swayed on their hangers but needed ironing, according to Sarita. "Listen, just wear any old thing tonight. You can get really spotted up in the lab."

Sarita replied softly, "Thanks for the tip. Maile, you don't need to wait for me. I'll make it up to the house on my own."

After Maile left, Sarita thought that if he had known about the change in plans, the very least Morgan Wycoff could have done would have been to call her on the intercom phone to say he was sorry they couldn't have dinner together. And as for afterward? She wouldn't think about that.

The lab was located in the lower section of the main house. Its walls were painted an antiseptic white and the floor was well-scrubbed tile. The long room was sterile and gleaming, with stainless steel sinks and rows of glass shelves holding a set of balance scales, test tube racks, and various sized jars and bottles containing powders and salves that ranged in color from the faintest shade of lavender to the deepest red. In one corner stood a blackboard on which a series of chemical equations was charted. Sarita guessed that these figures corresponded with Maile's correct proportion of color mix, and whatever else a chemistry major had to know in an operation of this kind. All that was missing was the elusive scent of ginger. Instead, the odors were chalky and medicinal.

An impassive Alex had guided Sarita to the door of the lab. Maile had opened it, her long hair bound back in a white scarf. She was wearing blue jeans and a smock that came to her knees. Patrice in a black, full-length dancer's leotard and slacks, her hair caught back and her smooth face looking elegant, was making notes on a smaller wall blackboard.

Patrice's greeting was a quick glance over her shoulder at Sarita. Her sharp command was, "Take notes." Sarita pushed the recorder's On switch. Immediately Patrice began lecturing.

As Maile had predicted, two hours later there was a break for a frugal meal on a tray. Sitting on a high stool, eating an apple and sipping hot tea, Patrice continued her monologue. This time it was directed solely at Sarita. She glanced at the recorder. "You probably don't comprehend half of what's in that thing. But the tapes will give you some background to feed into your computer, or whatever you use to get the results that Ross said you could come up with. They're very high on you at Dome Advertising. By the way, was your connection with Bailey an intimate one? He suggested as much."

Sarita's color deepened. "We were engaged, but then we broke it off."

"Ah, yes . . . engaged. A formal word to use these days, isn't it? But that sounds like Ross. He's a gentleman about such matters."

"It *was* a formal engagement." Sarita was furious. She wondered at her own patient insistence on setting Patrice straight. After all, her personal life was none of Patrice Wycoff's business.

"Sarita, I'm not prying, if that's what you're thinking. I couldn't care less what your status was with Bailey. I would assume that, being his fiancée, you would benefit greatly by association with him. He's even richer and more politically powerful than he was in the days when I first knew him."

Patrice slid off the high stool and began to stroll back and forth. "I must tell you this, Sarita. Maile's heard it before, and I'm sure she's profited by it. As an athlete does, one must keep the powers of one's body stringently aligned within oneself. Mentally *and* physically. A female can control her destiny only if she doesn't squander herself on emotional alliances with other people. At your age, Sarita,

I was already on my way to becoming a successful entity. Do you know what that word 'entity' means? It means an independent, separate, self-contained existence for a woman. Single-minded, single-hearted . . . that's the road to success. In order to achieve, one must abstain from all but the simplest foods, from stimulants of any kind, from alcohol, tobacco and sedative drugs. Now, if you've finished your dinner, you can watch and listen while Maile and I work for a while longer."

"I'd like to leave for a few minutes," Sarita said.

"Go ahead."

Sarita didn't dare exchange a glance with Maile. As she left the lab on her way to the bathroom, she thought that she could well understand Maile's preoccupation with Nils. Maile must make up for the dreariness of these lectures by romantic sessions with the attractive young man. More power to the two of them. Sarita knew that if she'd looked at Maile, they both would have burst out laughing. Still, there might be something to what Patrice was sponsoring. She was certainly youthful in appearance, but Sarita had supposed the woman's perfect complexion was a result of using her own cosmetic invention, even though it wasn't yet perfected for the public's consumption.

Sarita finally decided she'd stayed away long enough. It was time to return to the lab.

On her way back, she met Maile, who raised one slim black eyebrow and winked. "Now you know the secrets of success. I'm glad she didn't say to give up sex." This was said with such a beatific look of innocence that Sarita stifled her laughter and, straight-faced, entered Patrice's workshop. Earlier, she hadn't noticed the handrail along the rear wall. But now she saw that Patrice was using it as a bar at which to do ballet exercises, slowly, precisely and elegantly.

Near midnight, staggered with fatigue, ears numbed and eyes bleary, Sarita was handed a flashlight to make her solitary way back to the guest house. If she suspected that she heard the crackle of footsteps among the fallen palm fronds behind her, she was too tired to care. She unlocked her front door, remembered to relock it, walked into the bedroom, took three tapes out of her bag and stashed them and the recorder under her bed. It had been the machine that had absorbed all of Patrice's theories, quirks, abstractions and lectures. Sarita herself tried to blank out her mind, but without success.

Because so much had happened, it was hard to believe she had arrived here only yesterday afternoon. A little more than twenty-four hours ago, and all this . . .

Disregarding Patrice's recent lecture on sedatives, Sarita swallowed two aspirin tablets, drank half a glass of water and held her aching head in her hands. Perhaps she should give serious consideration to leaving Maui, and doing it right away. The career opportunity was here, and Morgan Wycoff was here, but could she take Patrice and her eccentricities? There was also the unpleasant Alex Firman, who had the cold eye of a security force. But that added up to only two negatives. Balanced against them was Morgan, and he was special. There was the island itself, and it was special. She had to admit her career was coming in third. Morgan was first. Morgan tipped the scales in favor of her staying. Morgan . . . Morgan . . . Sarita yawned mightily. She knew she was going to sleep the clock around.

That same night was a late one for Morgan at the Kapalua Bay Hotel. There was too much rich food, too many drinks and several difficult attempts to carry on a conversation over and under the orchestra's thumping rhythm. During the intermission the silence was filled by a young man at the piano who sang very loudly what he did for love. David Mikimura's friends, the bankers from the Orient on a holiday trip with their lovely and expensively clothed wives, found their surroundings entrancing. So much so that, with no important meetings to attend the next day, the visitors kept their hosts Mikimura and Morgan up until nearly three o'clock in the morning.

Another annoyance adding to Morgan's moodiness was Patrice's choice of this night to work in the lab with Maile and Sarita. Morgan considered it a deliberately contrary decision. He thought he might be wrong in suspecting that Patrice's ill timing had been intentional, but it had served to deprive him of his anticipated evening with Sarita. With his night hours subsequently free, he could not have avoided joining Mikimura and his vacationing countrymen.

At nine-thirty the next morning, by prearrangement, Alex Firman pulled up to Morgan's condo in the Wycoffs' station wagon. Morgan came out wearing white slacks and a muted shirt and carrying a light jacket over his arm, his tie in one hand and an attaché case in the other. He was sleepy-eyed and in a foul temper. He was bound for Mikimura's private, six-passenger plane that waited on Kaanapali's runway.

As Morgan approached the station wagon, he felt relieved that he hadn't had to pack a bag. All his gear was at the Illikai Hotel, where he kept a permanent apartment for his business trips to Honolulu. He also felt a nagging concern about what Sarita might be thinking. She'd probably decided he'd run out on her, even though he hadn't been the one responsible for aborting their plans for dinner. And for afterward. He himself wasn't sure about that "afterward."

He should have called Sarita, he supposed, but he hadn't. No doubt everything had turned out for the best. It might be destructive to get involved with a business colleague of Patrice. He certainly didn't need an additional complication in his life at the moment.

He opened the front door of the car and saw his "complication" sitting stiffly in the back seat, a briefcase on one side of her and a small piece of fancy-looking luggage on the other. Morgan glanced into the sharp eyes of Alex and growled, "What is this?" At the same time he uttered a strained "Good morning" over his shoulder to Sarita, who nodded and stared straight ahead.

Under the noise of the motor's coughing start, Alex

murmured in reply to Morgan's question, "Patrice wants her to talk to McIntosh in his lab. With Mikimura's plane flying to Oahu today, this is it."

Morgan turned halfway around, his arm resting along the top of the front seat. For the second time he said, "Good morning." Then, "How are you?" He added that amenity to make his greeting sound less grumpy and looked hard at Sarita.

She was dressed in the same skirt and blouse she'd worn over on the United flight. Her hair was no longer composed and tidy. It fluttered, wind-tossed, against her cheeks. Sarita's eyes were shadowed and she looked as wan as Morgan did, but her mouth was set stubbornly. Set against him, he supposed.

Ignoring Alex, he remarked, "This isn't my idea. I'm sorry if it's not convenient for you to fly over to Honolulu this morning."

Sarita's tone was crisp. "Why shouldn't it be convenient? I'm in the islands on business, and this is a very necessary part of the venture, according to Mrs. Wycoff."

"According to Patrice," Morgan corrected gently, using the name that in its commercial labeling set his ex-wife apart from both Sarita and himself. It was his intent to remind Sarita that there no longer was a Mrs. Wycoff.

She understood him, and understood that this was said in an attempt at an apology for his seeming desertion of her last night. It hadn't really been his fault that she'd had to work with Patrice, she knew. Sarita caught Alex's light eyes watching her in the car mirror with a curious blend of half triumph, half malice. She hardened her own expression. She didn't intend to let him guess that there was any degree of intimacy between herself and Morgan.

"Everything's fine, Mr. Wycoff. Patrice and I had a very interesting session. I understood about one-third of what she said, but that's all right. I know enough now so that I can go ahead and work out a short summary—"

Alex interrupted Sarita. "Here we are." They turned off

the highway toward the sea and in a few minutes were parking at the private airstrip. The day was blue and bright, with only a faint rumble of clouds in the distance, and the flight over the glittering waters was swift. Less than half an hour later, Morgan, Sarita and David Mikimura were landing at Honolulu's international airport.

Mikimura said to Sarita, "You must not be disappointed in Honolulu. It has become a big city. The climate and the vegetation are tropical, but there's a commercial and industrial boom going on. Apartments and hotels twenty stories high line the famous Waikiki Beach. You'll see multilane highways, heavy traffic, buses, tourists everywhere and, I regret to say, smog."

Sarita smiled. "I'm prepared. But no matter what you say, this is still pure magic to me." The plane door had opened, and they were walking down ladderlike iron steps. Sarita looked around. "It's busy, yes. You've warned me. But this is February! At home it's ten degrees above zero, and here it's eighty degrees. There are flowers blooming here . . . flowers in winter . . ."

Morgan caught up with them. Overhearing Sarita, he reminded her, "And flying over fabled Diamond Head back there was worth it all."

A long black limo met them and took David and Morgan to the Illikai hotel, which overlooked the yacht harbor, on Ala Moana Boulevard. As Morgan stepped out of the car, he looked back at Sarita. "I'll see you tonight."

David Mikimura smiled widely. "I will see you too. We will both be at the Royal Hawaiian for a meeting there in the main conference room. I'll look forward to another chat with you, Miss Miller."

As the limo drove away with its one passenger in the back seat, the young, uniformed driver wondered why the pretty blonde with the rosy sunburn and the look of a sunbather from Maui was laughing to herself. He flipped open the glass between the front and rear seats and asked, "You like it here?"

"Very much—but where is Waikiki Beach?"

"You'll see it. I'm taking you there. That's where the Queen sits."

"The Queen?"

"Sometimes it's called the Pink Palace. Anyway, that's where you're going."

Sarita was curious. "Do you live here in Honolulu?"

"Now I do. I'm originally from Kansas City. But after I got out of the service and had a little R and R here, I just stayed. I guess I smelled the ginger flowers." Seeing Sarita's eyes widen, he finished, "That means I fell in love."

"Tell me about everything."

"Not the love part, that's personal . . . but about Honolulu; well, it's more crowded than Hong Kong. Too many high-rises, condos and apartments." The driver gestured toward the city's background of volcanic mountains whose sharp peaks reared up into cloud masses. "If you hang around a while, all this gets to you, seeps inside and stays with you. Maybe you won't come back to Honolulu itself, but somewhere else you'll look for the surfers and the reefs and the purple sails of a catamaran, and wherever you are in the islands, you'll think about Waikiki. The tourist playground stuff will fade. Just the memory of this big half moon of sand anchored by old Diamond Head will stay with you."

Traffic grew heavier. The driver stopped talking. After several minutes had passed, he slid the glass closed between them. Sarita gazed dreamily out of the window as the car eased along through this compromised landscape of buildings and sea and commerce and palm trees.

Sarita's room at the Royal Hawaiian was on the ocean side, overlooking Waikiki. It was harmoniously furnished, big and clean and anonymous. The bed was queen-size and comfortable. Maile had made the reservation at Patrice's request. She'd also furnished Sarita with phone numbers, addresses and directions, as well as a very complete street map. Before starting out toward her objective, Sarita walked onto the balcony and leaned against the balustrade, gazing at the clear, turquoise-colored water. The surfers were coming in, standing upright on the big boards, though today there wasn't much sport. The surf was low, rolling shoreward in gentle ripples. The view was serene, the air balmy. Finally Sarita tore herself away from just looking and being. The remainder of the day would have to be spent in finding her way to the McIntosh Laboratories and interviewing Maile's father.

Sarita's tape recorder and camera went into the bag she slung over her arm. She hadn't had much to unpack, but when she returned, she'd buy a swimsuit in one of the lobby shops and go out into the inviting surf that splashed along one of the world's most famous beaches.

The phone rang. Surprised, Sarita stepped across the room to answer it. The caller was Morgan.

Sarita exclaimed, "You caught me just as I was leaving!"

"Is everything all right there? Is your room comfortable?"

"It's super, with a view like you've never seen."

There was a brief silence. Then he said, "Tonight maybe we can see that view together."

"I . . . have to go now. Thank you for calling." Thoughtfully Sarita replaced the receiver on its cradle. Did he mean the view from the terrace below, or this view, the one from her balcony? Whichever, her heart began its slow pounding. She took a deep breath, steadying its beat. Somehow she had to live through this day.

Chapter Nine

JAMES MCINTOSH SAT ACROSS FROM SARITA at his desk in the small office adjoining the crowded but immaculate laboratory on the third floor of the Kalakaua Avenue building. It was the end of a long afternoon, and Sarita had stashed away her notes and recorder in her carry-all bag. She felt relaxed in the company of the tall, sandy-haired man who was Maile's father.

"So they put you up in the old Royal Hawaiian?" McIntosh asked.

"Patrice warned me that the hotel couldn't be protected forever from being demolished to make room for a modern high-rise. She wanted me to stay there because it's a landmark, a part of Hawaii's history."

"Let's say Hawaii's history since nineteen twenty-seven, when the Royal Hawaiian was built. I wouldn't have expected a hardheaded businesswoman like Patrice to be so sensitive about historic preservation. But then, considering her background, one could call her an artist too, I suppose, working with the palettes of colors as she does. You know, the hotel stands on the site of King Kalanikapule's sea home of a century and a half ago. So, you see, everything changes. But changes come more swiftly nowadays."

McIntosh leaned forward unexpectedly and turned a

small, exquisitely framed picture toward Sarita. "This is Maile's mother. She and I would like you to come to our house for dinner. Tomorrow night, perhaps?"

"I'd like to very much, but I have to fly back tomorrow. Patrice expects me."

"Ah, yes, Patrice." McIntosh shook his head. "She still rules people's lives, doesn't she? Her cosmetics line was brilliant—that's why I say she's an artist—but that's all in the past. The therapy of being back in the laboratory again is good for her."

Listening to Maile's father, Sarita wondered why it had been necessary for the Wycoffs to subsidize Maile's final year at the university. The McIntosh Laboratory seemed prosperous enough. Then she remembered—last night Maile had told her there were eight sons and daughters in the McIntosh family. And what had Mr. McIntosh just said?

"Therapy . . . ?" Sarita murmured.

The sandy-haired man frowned, stood up, walked to the window and flipped the mini-blinds. "I meant in a general sense, not medical. Do you know the beginnings—or should I say the ending—of her active career?" Sarita shook her head. "Perhaps I've said too much, then," he continued. "Well, it's been a good afternoon. You've asked intelligent questions. I hope I've given you the right answers to assist you in your work, and I've enjoyed showing you around here. If you were staying longer . . ." He nodded toward the picture of his wife. "Aala would like to show you our island of Oahu. With all the growing-too-fast that we've done, we're still, as Mark Twain called us, 'the loveliest fleet of islands anchored in any sea.'"

Sarita recognized that McIntosh had carefully steered away from further discussion of Patrice. She'd seen the faint tinge of red on the man's freckled cheeks and assumed it was caused by his concern that he might have betrayed too much.

Sarita rose from her chair. "I've enjoyed the afternoon too. You've been very kind to give me so much time. The formula Patrice is working on sounds truly remarkable—if it works." She couldn't help adding that last.

McIntosh repeated, "If it works. We'll see. It might undo the face-lift industry, mightn't it? A creamy mist one can spray on to help retain one's youth . . ." He shook his head. "The principal ingredient is still secret. So far, all the chemical balance she's given me for testing has worked out. But one never knows. . . ." An uncertain silence. He appeared uncomfortable, and Sarita thought she knew why.

"Will there be a need for government clinical testing too?"

"I would say it's almost a requirement. Nevertheless, Patrice tells me she's impatient to get her market research under way. I felt it was premature, but that's what she wanted."

"Not having the tested product makes my work more difficult in a sense, but not really. I evaluate long-term future potential. I don't stand in a market and hand out samples."

McIntosh chuckled. Sarita put out her hand and McIntosh shook it.

"We two are commercial creatures bound to finance, I see," he said with a sigh.

"Yes," Sarita admitted. "Yet I think you and I understand each other, and we don't pretend."

The Scotsman informed her, "We do pretend. Our motives aren't pure. The beauty business is . . ." He hesitated.

Sarita gave him a straight look and bit off her words. "The beauty business is big bucks."

"Thank you for saying it for me." McIntosh walked Sarita to the door and watched until she was out of sight.

Sarita strolled slowly down Kalakaua Avenue on her way back to the hotel. She looked into each face she passed, reflecting on the tapestry of racial differences and cultures that was evident here. Yet all these people seemed to blend into a harmonious whole.

From the main avenue she walked through the street's arcade shops into the lush, tropical garden court of the pink stucco, Moorish-style Royal Hawaiian. A group of tourists was taking pictures of the monkeypod tree. Sarita unslung her camera and did the same, then went up the shallow steps and across the wide porch into the lobby with its black terrazzo floor. Coral-toned, hand-loomed rugs matched the pink of the high ceilings. Sarita smiled, recognizing the man who had "greeted" her on arrival earlier this morning. He was sixtyish and dapper, with a trim white mustache and wearing a very pink blazer over his pale pink trousers. He gave her a wink and hurried off to welcome a new stream of passengers descending from an enormous tourist bus.

In her room, Sarita checked her watch. The time difference between Honolulu and Chicago made it much too late to do what she should have done before—call Peter Dome in his office. Peter must be wondering what was going on out here in the Pacific. Tomorrow, she thought, I'll call him before eight in the morning. She ignored the fact that since she had Peter's home phone number, she could probably reach him there. But she didn't place the call. The languor of Polynesia had caught up with her.

Looking down from her balcony onto the tops of the shower trees and the coconut palms, with the scent of plumeria drifting through the air, she felt too relaxed and sleepy to get out to the beach to try some body surfing. She had worked late last night and risen early this morning. The large bed beckoned invitingly. She would take a nap for twenty minutes or so. . . .

She awakened to the sound of the phone ringing in a darkened room, and to the sight of the most enormous full moon riding up slowly from an iridescent sea. She fumbled for the phone, found it and croaked, "Hello . . . ?"

"It's not you?"

"It is me—I—Sarita!"

"How about the three of you getting down here fast? I'd like to buy you a drink before I have to meet with my associates. They're putting on a banquet with speeches, so I can't take you to dinner unless you want to eat at midnight."

"Morgan, it'll be at least half an hour before I can meet you in the lobby." That would be cutting it thin. Sarita switched on the bedside lamp and looked down at her wrinkled blouse and skirt. She would have to shower and do something to her hair and face before she put on the one fresh outfit she'd brought with her.

"I can't count on you to come down to the terrace right away? Have you seen the moon?"

"I've seen it." She waited. He didn't really sound as though her absence would matter one way or the other. Sarita was disappointed. Morgan's presence mattered to her. She could feel the excitement beginning to build in her, that crazy breathlessness that choked off speech.

"I'll try to get away when our friends begin to oil themselves up for their elocution. I've already heard what they have to say—'You do it to me, I'll do it to you. Just sign the contract.'"

Morgan's tone was that of a lighthearted, noncaring, disengaged man. He'd *try* to get away. It was as though he considered meeting Sarita a triviality that once was referred to as a late date. She supposed she'd built up in her mind something more concerning Morgan Wycoff than actually existed. Again she recalled how, back in Hilo, he'd let her go off on the interisland plane without him. This time there'd been no expression of concern from him, merely a bit of bantering talk. What was that delightful French word for an attitude like Morgan's? *Sangfroid*, that was it. Meaning literally coldblooded and actually imperturbable. She'd settled that one. Yet she couldn't help remembering yesterday afternoon on the beach at Napili, and his kiss. . . .

"Are you still there?" Morgan asked curiously.

Fortunately, she was again breathing in and out normally. "I'm here," she replied coolly. "If you can't break away tonight, I understand. Business and all that." She hoped he didn't think she sounded hurt and juvenile. Which, un-doubtedly, she did.

"Here comes Mikimura, looking for me. For once he's not smiling. He's probably about to tell me that if we make a vertical merger with our friends here, we'll have a court case on our hands due to the effect of so-called horizontal competition between firms that engage in the same produc-tion and distribution activity."

"You know something, Morgan? I don't give a damn!"

Sarita slammed down the phone on Morgan's quick laugh, which was deep and resonant. She knew she'd be-haved in a petulant fashion that showed she had a chip on both shoulders. It was unlike Sarita Miller to hunt up reasons to feel rejected. She'd always been poised and sensible, ready to roll with whatever punches life poked at her. But this—this— Oh! She felt like howling in her frustration. She did give a damn, she gave a million damns—she was quite insane about this no-good man with terrific charm, eyes that claimed her and a smile that melted her down. She was obsessed with Morgan. Admit it, admit everything! she berated herself. And she would have him!

Since she would be alone for dinner, Sarita decided to do something extra special. The evening was sultry, and the trade winds had died down. A thin veil appeared to be moving across the moon, which was farther up in the sky now, a smaller disc than it had been earlier, but still creating a phosphorescent path of light across the shimmering water.

As Sarita put on the white cotton dress with the halter top, she noticed that the rosy burn she'd acquired on the Napili beach was turning into a respectable tan. That was good. She was beginning to look as though she belonged here. What did the islanders call an old-timer, a *kamaaina?* She didn't qualify for that. Instead, she was a *malihini,* a newcomer from the mainland.

A half hour later she was wandering along the stone terrace that overlooked Waikiki Beach. She'd turned down a couple of offers to have a drink at the hotel bar with some distinguished-looking types. They were mature moths, however, and Sarita was not prepared to be their flame. Besides, there was something about their prosperous stance and impeccable manners that reminded her of Ross Bailey.

She hadn't expected to reach the far end of the terrace, where glass doors offered a view of what appeared to be a huge room, the kind that might be devoted to stockholders' meetings. This one was set up for dining, long tables covered with white tablecloths, silverware and flower arrangements. She could hear music from a trio in the corner. Waiters moved about, attending to side trays and serving drinks. Just as she decided this must be Morgan's banquet group, she saw him standing there, surrounded by a number of Japanese and Ameican businessmen.

Sarita couldn't help herself. She watched Morgan through the glass doors, unabashedly and avidly. He seemed taller, more electric, more vital, better-looking than the rest of the men gathered there. His light jacket sat on his wide shoulders with an ease that indicated a physique that was the envy of a tailor's art. His thick, mahogany-brown hair was well groomed, but he'd run a careless hand through it. Its slight disorder gave him a rakish air that tugged at Sarita's sensibilities. She wanted to reach out and smooth his hair for him. Which was asinine, she told herself in annoyance. Still, she shivered when she saw him turn his head away and chuckle at some remark made to him. She adored the back of his neck. It was deeply tanned above the white collar of his shirt and had a sturdy strength that made her want to trace it with her fingers.

When the first raindrops began to fall—no more than a dampish, fragrant spray blowing across her hair and shoulders—Sarita looked skyward in surprise. The moon was still shining, but its light came from behind the fine veil of haze she'd noticed earlier. So this was island rain? She turned her face up to it and let it mist her lips and eyelashes.

With one backward glance at Morgan, now almost lost in the increasing press of the crowd inside, she hurried along the terrace and into the foyer of the lobby.

The rain had stopped by the time Sarita had crossed the few hundred feet that separated the Royal Hawaiian from the Sheraton-Waikiki hotel. In its glass elevator, she rode thirty stories to the rooftop restaurant called the Hanohano Room and soon was seated at a small table providing a spectacular view of the glittering nighttime city far below.

After dinner, she again rode the glass elevator down to the lobby and browsed in all its shops. Then, feeling unutterably lonely, she walked back to her hotel. This time her friend in the pink jacket was again on duty. One look at Sarita's face, and he called over a young man with leis of pikake, ginger and tuberoses strung over his arm and insisted that she accept one. For good luck, she chose a ginger lei. He reminded her that the flowers that smelled the best died the fastest.

"That's life." Sarita smiled, thanked him, felt better and went off to her room, accompanied by the heady fragrance of the ginger lei, damp from the night rain.

Morgan listened and applauded when a colleague from his Houston office stood up to say that risk-taking paid off. Even though it hadn't been the best tourist year in the islands, the Wycoff Company was going ahead with the construction of a major athletic facility, including an adjoining hotel and restaurant complex. This meant using the human resources of the island, providing jobs. Another welling of applause.

David Mikimura leaned toward Morgan. "Why didn't you make the announcement?"

"I don't need a medal, he does."

Mr. Mikimura shook his head. "You've never been modest."

Morgan smiled too sweetly. "After last night with your friends at the Kapalua, I'm tired and I'm going to back out of here gracefully. I'll let my associate up there on the podium accept the congratulations."

Morgan made his move out of the banquet room in gradual stages. By the time he reached the double doors leading into the corridor, he was able to achieve a quick exit. Reaching the lobby, he loosened his tie, pulled it off and stuffed it into the pocket of his jacket. His fingers touched the envelope Alex had handed him just before he had stepped into the plane on the Kaanapali airstrip. Hell, he'd forgotten about it. He'd folded it into thirds and jammed it into his pocket. Of course it had to be a last-minute message from Patrice. In his mind's eye he could see those straggly lines she usually typed, full of estimates, bright ideas and sour comments accorded to rivals, and then always the firm directives: "Morgan, do this. . . . Morgan, you owe me one. . . ."

Sometimes the anxieties of dealing with Patrice interfered with his sleep. But not tonight. He was too tired. Nothing she could say on paper would reach him. Particularly, he couldn't be reached if he didn't open the envelope and read her message. Tomorrow would be soon enough.

He told the doorman he wanted a taxi. For a moment he thought about Sarita. If he were ten years younger, he'd go upstairs, knock on her door and say good night . . . for a long time. Instead, he was heading back to his Illikai Hotel apartment and bed.

Or was he?

"Wait a minute—cancel the cab. Thanks." He handed the doorman a folded bill and walked a few steps to the hotel bar, where he ordered a gin and tonic but didn't drink it. After moving the hurricane lamp on the bar closer to him, he opened the business-size envelope Alex had handed him and groaned. There were three pages of single-spaced material intended for Sarita Miller, not for him. He was supposed to read them first, approve the new ideas Patrice had thought up at four in the morning, then hand the pages over to Sarita so that she could discuss their contents with

James McIntosh. What the hell! Morgan supposed that Patrice had every right to assume he'd look over her communiqué on the flight to Honolulu this morning, but he'd simply forgotten all about it.

This was something Sarita should have, but she'd already seen McIntosh and was due to return to Maui tomorrow on Mikimura's plane. With this new material, she'd have to make another appointment with McIntosh first thing in the morning. If Morgan left the envelope at the desk for her, she would get it too late.

Morgan paid the bartender, started to the house phones and stalled. He'd better not call her room. It was almost midnight, Sarita was probably asleep, and, he remembered, she'd hung up on him earlier. However, he knew her room number. A quick trip in the elevator wouldn't take him that much out of his way. He would slip Patrice's envelope under Sarita's door, and she would see it early in the morning.

Reopening the envelope, he scribbled a brief recommendation across the top of the first page: *Sarita, go with this, but only if you agree. If you think P's ideas are out of line, don't talk further with McIntosh. See you in the morning. M.*

The elevator took him up to Sarita's floor, where he became a little lost in the maze of corridors. He retraced his steps twice, found the correct room number, knelt down and couldn't slide the envelope under the door. Everything was security tight. So he would knock, wake her up if he had to, hand the envelope to her and disappear.

Sarita, unable to sleep, was out on the balcony, which she was learning to call a lanai. The air was misty soft with moonlight and light beads of rain slanting in, intermingling, touching her with magic. The ginger fragrance from the lei she'd left on the dressing table scented the room behind her. Far beyond, shimmering and dazzling, the sea moved in gentle rhythm; closer to shore, the foamy white waves lapped up the dark surface of the sand, paused, then fell back again.

Someone was knocking repeatedly on her door. The sound finally penetrated her reverie, and Sarita left the lanai and crossed the room swiftly. Without opening the door, she asked, "Who is it? What do you want?"

What did he want? Standing out there in the hotel corridor, Morgan thought solemnly about what he really wanted.

Sarita faced the closed door. There was too much silence outside that door. She was curious, but not really afraid. She opened the door as far as the chain would allow and peered out.

Wordlessly Morgan handed her the envelope.

Sarita took it, turned it over and saw that it had been opened. She raised her eyes to his in surprise.

"I forgot this. It's for you from Patrice, but I was supposed to read it first."

"And did you?"

"I skimmed it." Uncomfortable at the half truth because he hadn't read it at all, he glanced over Sarita's shoulder. "How's the view from your lanai?"

Sarita hesitated, regarding him coolly. "It's like the view from every other lanai up and down the front of this hotel and its annex. I'm sure you've seen hundreds of views just like it."

Morgan wanted to smile. She was still mad. He kept a straight face. "Sarita, you're being very rude to a man who likes you very much, and who just got himself lost in a couple of corridors trying to find you."

"I thought you once explored Brazil or some such place. I read about it in a magazine. Have you lost your compass? And by the way, why don't you ever let photographers take your picture?"

"Seriously?"

"Seriously."

111

"Look, I can't stand out here much longer or the house detective will be along. Seriously, if I had my face plastered in every newspaper and magazine, I'd run the risk of being kidnapped and held for a huge ransom. Now *that's* serious."

"Oh, Morgan, truly?" Shocked, Sarita unhooked the door chain. "That is terrible."

"Let's not get excited. I'll tell you about it another time."

"You were exaggerating?"

"A little."

"I'm relieved."

"You should be. So am I."

Before she let him come all the way inside, she asked, "And how is Mr. Mikimura? Did you get the vertical and horizontal mergers all settled?" She couldn't resist this dig.

"I promise you, I won't talk business. I'll just look at your view." He grinned. She was still annoyed with him, but he knew her resistance was weakening.

Sarita's lips trembled into a smile, and she threw the door wide open.

Chapter Ten

THEY MOVED ACROSS THE WIDTH OF THE HOTEL
bedroom, Sarita leading the way. The night and the view
beckoned, but before they reached the threshold of the lanai,
Morgan no longer felt tired. From his plateau of thirty-seven
years, he'd dropped a decade. The notion struck him as
funny in some anti-inhibitory fashion. He was being handed
a release, freedom from a sharp trap that was partially of
his own making. Unrepressed, he could at last look,
touch . . . The spell that had held him seemed to be broken.

So he checked his stride. The focus of his gaze narrowed
on the lightly tanned feminine shoulders just ahead of him.
His hands were meant to encircle their firm surface. Within
his palms he could almost feel their tantalizing curve.

He saw that his hands were trembling. Fascinated by this
unexpected reaction, he quickly raised his eyes once more
to Sarita. If it were possible for a man to ravish a woman
visually, that was what he was doing. Sarita couldn't possibly know what she had provoked in him.

She was wearing some kind of halter thing around her
neck. The white material was cut into a low, fluttering dip
in the back. That was the only way he could describe it to
himself. He admired those lithe hips, with no spare flesh

113

on them, that undulated underneath the rippling cloth of her dress as she continued to move in front of him.

Sarita was unaware that he had halted in the dimly lit room, that he was staring after her, pursuing a vision of his own. This was a woman he'd held in his arms on a beach in the sunlight. He'd been intrigued by the thought that he could take her to his condo on Napili Bay and perhaps fulfill his desire. At the time, the "perhaps" had been just that. Under a bright sun, what could one really guess of the future? Tonight was the reality. He swore silently. He didn't merely want to plunge himself into her, he wanted to . . . love her.

"Sarita."

His voice strangled on her name, then grew mute. He was afraid that the thickened intonation would give him away. She was young, contemporary and open. He couldn't bear to be laughed at. He'd been laughed at by Patrice, an expert. The rawness and the hurt were still there. With this woman, he didn't want to be bedfellow to a stranger. With Sarita, it had to be something special.

Sarita reached the balcony railing and looked back over her shoulder. Morgan was standing in the middle of the room, watching her. He appeared strained, intent.

"Morgan, what is it?"

He approached her and responded almost roughly. "All right, where's your ocean and your view?"

His voice shocked her. It held the sound of dark pain, punctuated by uncertainty. Or was it hope? The two were contrary attitudes, but she couldn't distinguish between them. No experience she'd ever had could prepare her for the swift descent of Morgan's mask. Now she was looking at the indefinable face he could so easily assume to hide the other Morgan, the Morgan she . . . loved? Yes, loved.

Nervously, she tried to keep her response light so that he wouldn't know he had unsettled her. "Don't be a grouch. I invited you in. Now, you look out there," she commanded, indicating the lanai. "Isn't the view beautiful?" She paused. "Well . . . it was."

The curtain of rain was falling faster. Gentle and shimmering, it blotted out the moon. There was no scenic view of moonlight and Waikiki Beach, and the lanai was dripping wet. Sarita grimaced at this minor disaster and stepped back into the room. A silent Morgan slid the glass door closed.

"We can watch it from here . . . tropical rain," Sarita coaxed. "Mmmm, you can smell what the moisture does to the ginger flowers."

Morgan said nothing.

Sarita kept her smile bright. "Want to talk to me about what's in that envelope?" Why was she trying so hard? The business-size envelope Morgan had brought rested on top of the dressing table, near the necklace of ginger blossoms.

"No, not really."

One more attempt, Sarita thought. "The pink-jacketed greeter down in the lobby gave me the ginger blossom lei when I came back from dinner tonight." As though Morgan cared.

"Why?"

"I don't know. I suppose he thought I needed cheering up or something. I dined alone in that gorgeous Hanohano Room next door."

"You didn't mind being alone?"

Sarita shrugged. If one didn't have a dinner companion, either man or woman, one made the best of it. "I would have enjoyed my dinner and my glass of wine more if I'd had company, but, you know . . ."

"I don't know. I'd be interested in knowing. Tell me." He looked deadly serious.

Sarita had had enough of this drab conversation. She was sure she detected sarcasm in Morgan's remark. The spur-of-the-moment invitation to ask him into her room had been a mistake. She had dared, but it hadn't worked. Yet he was Morgan, the man she believed she loved.

115

Again she would dare.

Gently she touched his cheek with the palm of her hand. "Morgan . . . put your arms around me. Please," she whispered.

His face impassive, showing no surprise, he obeyed. So much could go wrong. Tentatively he drew her to him. The bold yesterday of their encounter on the Napili beach seemed to have vanished. There was a question in his eyes as his hands explored her shoulders and roamed the superb line of her back. She didn't flinch, so he let his hands caress her buttocks and move her in to him.

Sarita shuddered, then closed her eyes. He kissed her eyelids along their pale length, feeling her lashes flutter beneath his lips. Her fingers flattened hard against his chest, then moved up slowly along the thin cotton of his shirt until they met and clasped around his neck. Her body seemed to tighten convulsively against his. Because of her response, the charge of his own arousal began, like quicksilver racing toward his taut, private tension.

Was it only yesterday on the beach at Napili Bay that he had held Sarita's almost naked body in his arms? Why should I lie to her, to myself? he had thought then. Tonight he knew that Sarita had been honest with him. Delicately, without fully realizing the meaning of her action, she had offered herself. He would always remember the sweetly impudent curve of her full lips and her roguish grin as she'd thrown open the door to her hotel room, challenging him to come in and see the view from her lanai. The view was delicious, rain and all.

Sarita tipped her chin back from his chest, nudged her sandal tip against his ankle and muttered, "Why are you smiling? I'll kill you! You're making fun . . ."

"I'm making love. And so are you. I happened to remember . . . yesterday." His mouth came down over hers in a swift and passionate concentration of desire. It moved across her own, his tongue penetrating, taking secure possession. "Kill me, then, Sarita. How will you do it? This way?" His lips found her throat and bit gently, then traveled to her ear, where he nipped the lobe, his breath fanning out as warm and moist as the lick of a tongue.

"Or like this?" He spun her around, to face her away from him. With one arm he held her tightly, her back against his hard torso. She was forced to look in the mirror opposite and watch while he moved one hand across her breasts. It was as though he were tenderly crushing, fondling and smoothing a cluster of flowers. But the act was made erotically exciting because she was compelled to watch it.

The halter strap of her dress broke from the twisting tension on the cloth. Sarita's breasts with their tempting nipples thrust free. She had worn no underwear on this limpid night. A startled, panting Sarita stared into the dressing table mirror. Who was that female with the brilliant eyes, the full, red, parted lips, the tousled hair—held sensually against a man's body, his strong brown hand seeking the rosy points of her breasts? And now his hand moved down to do something outrageous to the rest of her.

"Morgan!"

Using all her strength, she forced herself around to look at him directly. He was not laughing now. His expression was riveted, his sun-flecked eyes half closed. Their bodies slowly revolved as they moved, mouth against mouth, fiery and ardent, in a pas de deux as relaxed as a great wave circling and breaking in slow motion. Leisurely turning, their two clasped bodies coiled sensuously onto the wide bed.

Somehow, in the course of their sinuous movement toward their objective, Sarita had lost her only garment, the white dress. Morgan's jacket lay on the floor, as did his slacks, shirt and shoes. He was wearing a pair of white briefs, his handsome torso smooth and burnished. Sarita was captivated. But at the sight of her own creamy nakedness, she gave a little whimper of surprise. Being unclothed felt right and good, yet how had it happened? She hid her face against the dark mat of hair on Morgan's chest.

In their turn, the white briefs were shucked off. Sarita kept her eyes from the periphery of the truly extraordinary part of him that she had desired, that she had known she wanted hazily, dreamily, in a fantasy. Was it to be here, now? So soon?

She couldn't cling and hide herself any longer. Morgan's lips sought hers as he slid her down between the pink sheets of the bed. Slowly, so slowly, he covered her body with the length of his. Her breath tightened, gasping in her throat. . . . Now! There it was, there it was . . . it happened, and while it was happening, Morgan seemed lost to her in a kind of arching world of his own. She wanted to cry out, "Take me with you!" Perspiration beaded her forehead and cheeks like tears.

When he returned to her from wherever his lone sexual journey had taken him, he looked down into her face with wonder.

"Morgan, I love you," she said. "I'm happy."

His face still darkened with sweat and passion, he nodded again and again. She was making funny little bleating sounds, as if she were a small lamb nestled against his chest for protection. He would protect her forever, love her forever.

Those were crazy ideas of his. The reality was that she was a beautiful, intelligent, luscious, grown woman, and she was his. He kissed the tips of her breasts and her belly. He soothed her thighs with caresses and let his kisses trail from her knees to her ankles to the soles of her feet.

Later, when he came back up to her, Sarita whispered against his lips, "Morgan, let's . . . again."

And, of course, he did exactly what she wanted him to do. This time the penetration was smoothly perfect, creamily lavished. It was good and exciting and full of love. And the rain outside was rushing down, tinkling like silver bells.

Morgan was telling her something funny about how he'd been tired from the night before at the Kapalua and that he hadn't been tired when he'd thought about her. Suddenly, in the middle of a sentence, he fell asleep in Sarita's arms. She didn't stir. She lay there beneath Morgan, listening to his even breathing and smelling the wet fragrance of the rain that kept falling through the night. From across the room there drifted the rising scent of ginger that had accompanied her precious night. And then the name for the Wycoff project came to her.

The Night of the Rain Ginger.

Chapter Eleven

SARITA HAD FALLEN ASLEEP TOWARD DAWN. When she awakened, she was lying within the circle of Morgan's arms. He was watching her, an amused smile on his face. As she opened her eyes wide, he bent and kissed her throat. Her own lips closed in a caress on his russet-dark head. She felt the warmth of his kiss stray from her throat to her heart to the point of her breast, first one breast and then the other. "I love seconds," he said. He sighed deeply, comfortably, laid his head against her bosom and closed his eyes.

She could look down and see his profile, reddish brows, strong nose, curve of eyelash, sensual span of lip, strong chin. Her free hand ran lazily down the sturdy column of his neck, her fingers tracing lightly into the furry tangle on his chest. In a leisurely fashion, her fingers slipped farther down, exploring with exquisite caution the hard-muscled torso. What a beautiful man, she thought. All of him.

Morgan murmured sleepily, "Keep doing that . . . just what you're doing . . . I love you."

To be loved, to love in return, to lie cozily together like this . . . close, closer. In her dreamy strokings she must have caressed a sensitive spot, some undiscovered area of masculine pleasure, for suddenly Morgan was alive under her hand. He gathered her in his arms, fully awake and ready to respond to her tender, unknowing stimulation.

This time for Sarita it was wonderful. This time Morgan took her with him on his journey into sexual climax. For Sarita, it was an ultimate pleasure, an excruciatingly joyous summit of their lovemaking. Caught up in the intensity of the rhythm churning inside her body, she cried out her delight. To Morgan this was as telling an admission of ecstasy as if she had articulated everything he had done to her, everything he had made her feel, all that he meant to her. He'd had more than enough words from Patrice at the beginning of their relationship. The untutored candor of Sarita's reaction bound him to her forever. And how long could forever be? he wondered.

The ringing of the telephone jerked them out of their comfortable exhaustion and into the business of today.

With an impatient exclamation, Morgan reached over and knocked the receiver out of its cradle. Sarita made a move to pick it up. He grasped her hands and shook his head. So they let the phone lie there, impotent, making curdling, distressing sounds until the hotel operator gave up.

"There's no answer in that room, madame," the operator told the caller from Maui. She wrote down the telephone number and the name of the party whom Sarita was to call: Patrice Wycoff, Napili Bay, Maui. The operator then turned on the switch that activated the red message light on the phone in Sarita's room.

But Morgan and Sarita were rolled up in the pink sheets, arms around each other, plotting their day ahead. "Don't go back to Maui," Morgan murmured. "I'll have Mikimura hold up his plane an extra day. I want you with me when I drive out to the Kahala Hilton. You can feed the penguins while I confer with the Tokyo group."

Sarita was gently amused. This must indeed be "the master" speaking. Nevertheless, she felt slightly unsure of herself, and perhaps of him. "What will Patrice say if I don't show up on Maui?" she asked nervously.

"What will Morgan say if you do?"

It was easy enough for him to make small jokes, to be whimsical. Last night had been fabulous, almost a fantasy. But this was today, and try as she might to be casual, Sarita was uneasy, even—and this was an odd admission—a trifle embarrassed. How was she going to unroll herself out of these pink sheets, release herself from Morgan's embrace and glide—gracefully, she hoped—out of this room and into the bathroom? She tried to think of a dignified way.

Her voice trembling a little because of the inanity of her thought, she managed to murmur, between kisses, "Who's first for the shower?"

"I am," Morgan declared.

When he came out of the bathroom, pulling on his rumpled white slacks, Sarita was wrapped in her dressing gown, looking out at the view, trying to appear unconcerned.

"Thinking?" Morgan inquired pleasantly, coming up behind her and kissing her neck.

Sarita turned. Who was this man? she asked herself. Morgan Wycoff, of course. Of course! She filled her eyes with the sight of him standing there, and some of her confidence returned.

She didn't think she sounded too rattled when she said, "I should read those pages Patrice gave you for me." Then she smiled guilelessly and dared to add, "I'm free to play with you today."

"Good! Let's start with room service. What'll you have for breakfast?"

After both had made their decisions, the order was called in and Morgan opened his arms. "Come here. It's been at least twenty minutes."

"Stay away from me." Warily Sarita circled him. "Do you know everything I have to do to get ready for today?"

He told her what she had to do.

She smiled widely, merrily. He was making it easy for her. "I'd like to do that too. But let's wait until after breakfast. I have to call Peter Dome. What time is it in Chicago? Never mind, I think I can catch him at the office."

"You can tell Peter that I made my pilgrimage to Pele, the fire goddess. She has granted my request. Peter may never see you again."

"Has Pele agreed, Morgan? Will I remain in the islands as long as my heart desires?" Sarita's eyes grew sober with the thought: Will you desire me always?

Morgan, in his turn, recalled his own fleeting reflection. How long would forever be? "Is that a question, Sarita?"

"It's nothing that I expect you to answer. We'll let Pele answer it for us." Why were they both suddenly so solemn? There'd been so much joy between them. Was it an uneasy future they faced—and did they both know it?

A knock sounded on the door, and a voice called, "Room service."

Morgan made a tactful departure into the bathroom before the breakfast cart was wheeled in. Though there was enough on the tray for two, the waiter's expression was blank as he watched Sarita sign the tab. He knew that he wasn't paid to conjecture.

"Do you want the cart on the lanai, miss?" he asked politely. "It's a beautiful day after the rain showers."

"It is indeed. But I think inside will be fine."

After breakfast Sarita quickly read Patrice's pages, then told Morgan, "There isn't anything here that will require my seeing McIntosh again. Everything's been covered. I've even thought of a name for the product. I'll tell you about it later."

They made their plans. Morgan would go off to the Illikai to shave and change his clothes. Sarita would pack her briefcase and her one piece of luggage and would spend the night with Morgan at his apartment. It would be more private

123

there than in her room at the Royal Hawaiian. Morgan would have Mikimura phone Alex Firman to say that his plane would not be returning to Maui today.

"I don't want either of us to talk on the phone to Patrice," Morgan said. "Don't return her call." He glanced at the winking red phone light. They both knew instinctively whose message was waiting for Sarita.

"Morgan, do you still have . . . Is it still something personal between you and her?"

Morgan stared at Sarita in surprise. "You mean you could believe that after last night? I suppose this is the time to tell you—at least part of the story. Experimenting again in her laboratory at Napili has worked well for Patrice. It's steadied her and cleared up some of the professional trouble she's had. I'd rather not go into that part of it now. I bought the place on Maui to give her a chance to regain confidence after her career had ended."

"You've helped her."

"I've been protective, that's all. Circumstances caused her to develop certain neuroses, but basically she's a strong woman. She's really helped herself."

"Morgan, tell me if I'm asking you something that is none of my business, but why, after the divorce, did you feel it was important to do as much for Patrice as you've done? You've sort of explained, but . . ." Sarita hesitated, wondering if she sounded tactless and as though she were prying.

Morgan stood up, paced away from Sarita, then stared out through the glass door leading out the lanai. "I'd like to look good in your eyes, Sarita. But in my relationship with Patrice, the only area in which I could possibly come out blameless is the ending of her spectacular success. I had nothing to do with that. She was going to be involved in a messy lawsuit with a chemist she'd worked with in Belgium. We bought her out of that by settling the man's claims . . . I don't want to go into what he might have been able to prove. It had something to do with formulas she'd brought with her when she came to the United States. But it did mean she had to close up shop and get out of New York for a while."

Sarita came up to Morgan and put her hands on his shoulders. She studied his face. "I believe Patrice will make a comeback. She has the energy for it. If it's not with this youth concept of hers, it will be something else, I'm sure."

"I hope you're right. You see, Patrice and I were equally important to each other's careers in the beginning. We saw in the other an image of what we wanted to achieve for ourselves. She went to people she knew who could provide part of the financing I needed on my first big construction job. Soon enough, I was paying her back by my own success, which grew bigger than hers. And so did my access to influential people, to funding, to all the network channels one needs.

"I backed off from actual site work—I have a great corps of people working for me. Never could understand why they're called 'bodies.' Loyalty is so much more important than that." Morgan stirred uneasily. "Patrice and I had a kind of crazy loyalty to each other, I suppose. We knew almost as soon as we were married that we didn't have any love between us. But what we did have was a great working partnership, along with our accountants and our lawyers and the IRS. When you marry for the wrong reasons, you always pay for it eventually." Morgan grew thoughtful. "And I've stayed for all those reasons. I've tried to be supportive of Patrice during her . . . troubled times." What he didn't say was that he'd been faithful to Patrice, who had worked him over and made him into the business partner she wanted. Not a bed partner. Patrice had never had time for that. Nor had he, if he wanted to be totally honest about it.

He looked at Sarita. "Anything else?"

Sarita stepped back from Morgan and leaned against the dressing table. She linked her fingers, looked down at them, then glanced up quickly. Her gaze held Morgan's. "Something confuses me. I have my own ambitions, so I should be able to understand about careers and the pressures to attain the highest point in whatever line of work one chooses. But that article in *Time* called you a financial magnate, or some such term. . . . Anyway, it was a very impressive description. How do you feel about that, Morgan? Do you truly enjoy the sense of power that comes with being part of a high echelon? I guess it's America's aristocracy, isn't it . . . the aristocracy of financial achievement."

By turns Morgan looked startled, baffled and finally amused. "Is that what they say about me?"

"You know very well what they say about you!"

Morgan erupted into a howl of laughter. "I hope you're not impressed by that stuff! I'm a small businessman who became a big businessman. How's that? I'm a hard-assed professional on construction sites and in board rooms. I've had adversaries and I've licked them. Some of them have booted me. But all that power stuff . . ." He shook his head and grinned. "Very few of us rich guys actually care about that, regardless of what is written. We keep on working because we like to work, and we have to support our companies and our employees and pay taxes. It all comes down to—we love to work! And we succeed at it. Simple." He looked at Sarita closely. "And I am far from a perfect man. Satisfied?"

Sarita kissed him fervently. "You're perfect. Love you, Morgan," she said.

Morgan gave her a bear hug. "Then I can't hate myself, can I?" He walked to the door, saying, "I'll be back in an hour to pick you up." He turned around and winked. "Get dressed, beautiful woman. I'll be back for you."

The limousine took them on a fifteen-minute drive along Diamond Head Road through the elite residential area of Kahala to the Kahala Hilton. As their driver parked, a large black Cadillac disgorged several small-statured men wearing dark business suits and carrying expensive attaché cases.

Among these visitors from Tokyo was one woman, chic in a black designer pant suit and a smart fedora hat. She carried a briefcase also. A glimpse of her face showed its Oriental perfection.

"That woman makes me feel shabby," Sarita told Morgan. She glanced down at her blouse and skirt, long tanned legs and sandals.

"I shall buy you diamonds instantly—but you don't need them."

"See how easily you get out of doing your duty?" Oh, Lord! Sarita gasped. What an awful remark to make! Talk about my big mouth. I hope he doesn't think I mean an encrusted wedding band! She reddened but then realized she needn't have been so sensitive. Morgan had already stepped out of their hired limo and was waiting for her. Next he was greeting the others under the portico, introducing them to Sarita, and suddenly Mr. Mikimura was in their midst.

Morgan seemed to have meant it literally that Sarita was to play around with the penguins. There were also giant sea turtles in a large, rock-filled pond as well as graceful dolphins leaping and frolicking in the hotel's private lagoon. Sarita assured Morgan that she'd be fine on her own, so he went off to his business conference in the Waialae Room, after they had decided to meet later for lunch on the seaside terrace.

Sarita wandered through the immense lobby. Overhead were multicolored driftglass chandeliers, a copy of the driftglass found on Hawaiian beaches. Underfoot was teakwood parquet flooring from Thailand, partially covered by circular, Polynesian-inspired rugs. The walls were lined with paintings of island landscapes and a frothing sea. Sarita peered down a winding staircase, its lava rock walls awash with orchid plants. The gallery shops were magnificent, filled with coral, scrimshaw objects carved from whale ivory, silken hangings from China, opals, jade bangles, pearls and Oriental antique pieces.

Outside, there were acres of gardens, bamboo groves,

waterfalls and exotic plantings. Sarita enjoyed her excursions through the grounds, and at one o'clock in the afternoon she reached the seaside terrace where she was to meet Morgan. She found a table for two and glanced around at the secluded shore with its white sand beach shaded by graceful palm trees, their trunks leaning into the wind that blew steadily. Sitting at nearby poolside tables were a number of the hotel's guests, stunning people who were casually and expensively dressed. There was also a sprinkling of celebrities, their faces instantly recognizable to Sarita. She knew this was not a place to be alone—it was too beautiful and romantic. One should share it with a beloved.

A pretty female attendant in a lavender silk kimono asked if Sarita would like a fresh pineapple. Sarita said that a friend was joining her and they'd be ordering lunch later. In surroundings like these, it was only natural that she'd be waiting for the man she loved.

Sarita opened her handbag, took out her writing pad and made notes to herself on all the points Peter Dome had brought up in their phone conversation from her room this morning. When he'd asked if he could call her back at the hotel with the information she considered pertinent, she'd hesitated and said it could wait, but that tomorrow she would be at Napili Bay and he could call her there. Peter had sounded curious when she'd told him she was checking out of the Royal Hawaiian. She was glad she hadn't had to speak to Meg Kirby. When Meg learned that Sarita would still be in Honolulu but couldn't be reached tonight, Meg would demand to know what was going on. Sarita grinned to herself. A long, complicated thought process, all that, but the way it was at Dome Advertising required one's knowing who was doing what to whom and why.

Footsteps approached Sarita's table on the terrace, and she felt a hand on her shoulder. She looked up, smiling against the sun. But before she could utter Morgan's name, her smile had become merely a shaky tremor across her lips.

Pale eyes fringed with bleached lashes regarded her with

an almost satanic amusement. "Fancy," Alex Firman drawled, "finding you here." Without being asked, he seated himself opposite Sarita. "But then, I'm not really surprised, seeing that Morgan's at a meeting in the Waialae Room and that you and he have been working so closely together. By the way, he's having lunch with his business associates. I've been detailed by him to rescue you. If you're hungry, here's the menu." Alex reached for the printed card propped against a centerpiece of loose hibiscus blossoms. "I've had your luggage removed from Morgan's hired limo. It's in a taxi out front, and the taxi is waiting for you and me. Nice?"

What did one say when the earth fell out from under one, when the stars chilled, when the magic shifted and vanished? Sarita felt her face stiffen, her body grow taut. Her mind raced as the adrenaline flowed. She looked across the table at Alex Firman and spoke softly. "I shall leave when I'm damn good and ready. And not with you, Dick Tracy."

"He was the good guy detective, wasn't he?"

"You admit you're not?" She didn't mean to snap the stem of the hibiscus flower she was holding. Quickly she put her hands in her lap to hide their telltale quiver, and then her handbag turned over. Its contents spewed across the table and onto the stone floor of the terrace. She bent and retrieved pencil and notebook.

Alex handed her a lipstick that had rolled in his direction. "To answer your question, I admit I'm not your everyday, straight-up-and-down fellow. How about lunch?"

"I have no appetite for lunch with you."

"Well, thanks."

"And don't forget, your taxi's waiting."

"Our taxi."

Sarita ignored that last. "I don't know why we're talking this way," she hissed. "I'm not leaving here with you. I'll return to Napili Bay tomorrow. Got that?"

"Listen, Miss Tough, you're avoiding the issue, which

is that you work for Patrice, and that Morgan Wycoff is in the middle of a big, big deal and doesn't want to be distracted. He's not going to run out here and chase you down and make excuses for himself. I'm the detail that takes care of that."

She remembered what Morgan had told her that first night in the guest house. He'd said he kept Alex Firman instead of guard dogs. He'd also said Alex was useful in a number of ways. This must be one of them.

Sarita's eyes narrowed. Alex's vagrant thought was that they were the exact shade of litmus blue. "How did you get here?" she asked. "How did you know where I was?"

"I flew. How else do you cross a channel if you don't have a boat?"

"I suppose little birds tell you everything?"

"I have eyes and ears. They're for hire."

"Is the guest house your stakeout?"

"You might say so. Does that explain what you want to know?"

"It tells a lot." Had it been Alex Firman's furtive footsteps she'd heard in the tropical night?

People at the next table glanced in Sarita's direction. She was not panicked—yet. But she was close to it. She had to get away from Alex and find Morgan. She stood up. Alex stood with her. She walked away from the table and knew that Alex was right behind her.

Sarita would never have left the Kahala Hilton with Alex Firman had it not been for Mr. Mikimura. He was in the lobby as she strode through, intent on finding the Waialae Room even if she had to interrupt the biggest deal to be consummated this side of the Pacific.

David Mikimura beamed his widest and rushed toward her. "I was on my way to the terrace to find you, Miss Sarita. Morgan gave me a message for you."

At Sarita's heels, Alex Firman hummed, "You got the message, didn't you, Sarita?"

It was an unpleasant admission for her to have to make,

130

but Morgan seemed to have a fondness for messengers. This morning he'd been reluctant to speak directly to Patrice on the phone about the change in his and Sarita's plans, and obviously he'd used a surrogate—Mikimura.

Now she heard Alex confiding to Morgan's business associate, "Good thing I was wearing my beeper when you reached me on Maui. That's how I was able to get to the nearest phone. I was on my way up-country in the jeep and had to change my plans. Sarita and I will fly back on the three-thirty plane. I have her luggage with me."

"Good, good. Morgan will be pleased. I'll tell him it's all taken care of." Mikimura leaned close to Sarita and whispered, "These Tokyo financiers are acting for a giant oil company, part of a Wycoff conglomerate. A cash infusion is needed, and this will be a significant new investment. I'll tell Morgan you understand the situation."

"I don't understand it, Mr. Mikimura. But if the rest of you do, that's just dandy." Sarita frowned. "I thought Morgan asked you to hold your plane's flight to Maui until tomorrow." And for a very special reason, to be shared only by Sarita and Morgan. What had happened to those plans? Perhaps Sarita had misunderstood them as well.

"Yes, he did." David Mikimura twinkled exuberantly. "But since this acquisition is going so well, it's twice as important that we not fly back to Maui until tomorrow. We'll be with these people the rest of today and tonight—can't let them get out of the net, you know!"

Good for Morgan, Sarita thought angrily. It didn't make sense, except that, in finance versus love, finance seemed to be the winner. Always. "Tell Mr. Wycoff that I send him my congratulations on the successful outcome of his oil venture. And tell him thanks for everything. It's been most illuminating."

"That's a lot to remember to relay to Morgan."

"It certainly is. Especially when a man's involved in a billion-dollar deal."

"Ah, you *do* understand!"

Sarita only shook her head.

She moved ahead of Alex on her way out of the Kahala Hilton. She didn't want to look at the man's face. His triumph might be hidden under a hollow expression of concern, but she knew it was there. He had just successfully stomped on a woman's pride. Or rather, he'd been a participant in the stomping act.

Chapter Twelve

THE TAXI TRIP TO THE AIRPORT WAS SWIFT AND silent. Along with the driver, Alex Firman appeared to be concentrating on the heavy traffic. Sarita stared unseeingly out of the cab window while struggling with depressing questions that seemed to have no answers.

Her body was still exquisitely sensitive from her and Morgan's intense and uninhibited lovemaking. They had shut out the world, and Sarita had gloried in her response to a sexual experience that was beyond her wildest fantasies. The reality was so exciting, her senses were so intoxicated, it didn't seem possible that a mundane business meeting could have caused her love partner to exclude her so abruptly from his life.

Just before reaching the airport, she turned to Alex. "You told Mikimura you were on your way somewhere when your beeper signaled you to call the house for a message, is that right?"

"Yeah." Alex was noncommittal, his pale eyes studying Sarita without expression.

"Why did you have to fly over here to Oahu?"

"Morgan wanted it that way."

"To see that I got back to Napili?"

"That's about it. Aren't you pleased he's looking out for your . . . comfort?"

"I could have made it on my own." Sarita knew she sounded snappish, but she was even angrier than she had been before. She and Morgan had been as intimate as lovers could be, but he was still an enigma to her. Why couldn't he have come to the seaside terrace and explained what had happened? Then she could have understood the impasse concerning their plans for tonight. But no, like some medieval merchant prince, he'd sent his couriers to deliver a message. One of them had been told to escort her back to the Napili estate. Were all unreadable rich men this way? she wondered.

The three-thirty Maui-bound plane was the regularly scheduled passenger flight from Honolulu, so Sarita and Alex Firman's late arrival put them in separate seats, for which Sarita was grateful. A few minutes before they reached Kahului Airport, she forced her mind away from its obsession with what had occurred in her room at the Royal Hawaiian and with the later episode on the Kahala Hilton terrace. Whatever, she thought caustically, she'd sent Morgan into an important financial meeting physically relaxed and mentally cued to achieve. Yet such bitterness wasn't like her.

As she walked down the ramp and into the baggage area of the small, busy airport on Maui, she grew disgusted with herself. What had happened to loyalty? Her random judgment regarding Morgan was pretty horrifying. How could she have doubted the man who had been her lover? Who *was* her lover! The magic was real. She would hold on to it. To doubt Morgan's integrity was to doubt her own.

She had almost forgotten Alex Firman until he came looking for her, toting her briefcase and her overnight bag.

"The jeep's in the parking lot. I'll get it and meet you in front."

Sarita spoke sharply. "I'm not driving back to Napili with you."

Alex stared at her, perplexed. "Look, none of whatever happened back there in Honolulu is my fault. Are you disappointed that Wycoff didn't meet you for lunch? Sarita, the man has major concerns in his life. Obviously you're not one of them. Not all the time, that is." He stopped just short of saying that Sarita had her place and she ought to recognize it and stay there. Other women did, so why not Sarita Miller? Was she someone special? Alex didn't think so.

Sarita's reply was cool. Without blinking at the fib, she said, "I don't know what you're talking about. I merely thought you'd want to continue on to wherever you were going earlier today. I can hire a car. I'd like to have a rental to drive while I'm here." She forced herself to smile at Alex. Be controlled, polite and distant, she told herself. She even added, "Thanks for making it easier for me to get back to Napili without having to bother about a plane reservation and luggage. Takes a local to arrange these things, doesn't it?" Thanks a lot! she repeated to herself.

Alex Firman appeared baffled. Before he could tighten his grip on Sarita's briefcase and overnight bag, she had whisked them out of his hands and was walking rapidly away from him. She'd already located the Hertz counter, so she acted purposefully—though she wasn't sure what she would do if Alex followed her and gave her an argument.

Alex didn't. He watched her until she was lost in the crowd of tourists carrying their string bags, tubes of suntan gel and souvenirs. He shrugged. This was a woman who could take care of herself. At least *she* thought she could. It would have suited Alex better if she'd fallen flat on her face. He went out to find the jeep, wondering what exactly had happened in Honolulu between Morgan and Sarita Miller. The way the woman was behaving now, he guessed he'd been mistaken in thinking there'd been some degree of hanky-panky—nothing serious, of course. Maybe a flirtation over a glass of wine and dinner. Alex was too sure that Patrice had Wycoff lassoed and roped tight. At least she'd told him as much last night. Alex had little use for women, but he kept his hand in with Patrice.

And speaking of lassos, he might as well get up to the ranch on the slopes of Haleakala Crater. The foreman had sent word that he was needed there. A nasty weather forecast had come in from the experimental station in Makawao. Something for Alex to handle, since Morgan wasn't here.

Still he sat in the jeep, watching until he spotted the Toyota rental with Sarita Miller at the wheel. He followed three cars behind and saw her make the left turnoff toward the coast. She wouldn't get lost now—not that he particularly cared. He set his sharp face toward Mount Haleakala and its vast expanse of cattle rangeland, five thousand acres of which belonged to the Wycoff interests.

Maile was waiting for Sarita when she zipped up in the white Toyota.

"What's that for?" A barefoot Maile came down the porch steps. She peered curiously at the car.

Sarita got out with a welcoming smile. "Hi, Maile. How did you guess when I'd get back? I'll bet you want to know how your father and I got along. Oh, about the Toyota." She turned and reached in for her briefcase. "I thought I'd do my own touring on the island."

"You could have used the station wagon or any of the other cars in the compound."

"That's just it. I'm not part of the compound."

"Mmm . . . independent." Maile took the suitcase Sarita handed her.

"Mmm . . . yes." Sarita grinned.

"Nils told me Alex flew over to Oahu to get you. I know the plane schedule and figured how long it'd be before you showed up here. How did you like Pa?"

Sarita unlocked the front door. "I like your father very much. We had a good session." She set down her briefcase by the bedroom door and looked inquiringly at Maile. "Tell me honestly, Maile, what do you and your dad think about the work Patrice is doing?"

Maile shrugged. "If she's successful—*vroom!*" Both of Maile's hands flew into the air like skyrockets. "Why do you ask? Is it something my father said?"

"Not exactly. He was most discreet."

"That's a strange way of putting it. Discreet!"

"I think you understand what I mean. You're a trained chemist—"

"Lab assistant," Maile interrupted. "Only an assistant."

"Is that the way Patrice wants it?"

"What Patrice wants, Patrice gets." Maile's eyes slanted at Sarita. "For instance, Patrice wanted you back here. Quick, like . . . *wikiwiki*. Not tomorrow, as Mikimura told her."

Sarita was glad her back was turned to Maile while she parked her suitcase on the luggage rack by the bed. "You mean that when Mr. Mikimura phoned to say I was staying over in Honolulu, it was Patrice who ordered those plans changed?"

"You work for Patrice, don't you?"

Sarita turned around and regarded Maile with surprise. "Someone else said exactly those same words to me today."

Maile was too quick with her response. "If it was Alex Firman, I suppose he had to say that—especially if you weren't keen on returning." Her voice lifted faintly on those last words, as though in question. Then, abruptly, she padded toward the doorway.

"Wait, Maile, I want to talk to you." Sarita realized Maile had sidestepped the question about what she and her father thought about Patrice's project.

Maile only said, "Glad you're back. We can talk about Pa later. I have to get up to the house now. I'll tell Patrice you're here, you and your Toyota."

"Stay and talk, Maile."

Maile halted. "Take it easy, Sarita. Let's not play questions and answers. You do your work. I do mine. Patrice has told you enough for you to know the potential of . . ." Maile hesitated. "Let's just call it Project Number One."

"How about 'The Night of the Rain Ginger'?"

Maile's brown eyes widened. "You thought that up? I don't know whether Patrice will like it, but I do. It sounds very . . . romantic." She repeated the words softly. "I can see the picture. A moist young face, sort of upturned to soft rain . . . pale ginger blossoms . . . the night . . . fragrance. Love. *Youth*. Isn't youth what it's all about?"

"Hey!" Sarita was laughing. "That's my job—to research the label!"

Maile stared straight into Sarita's blue eyes. "Speaking of research, show a little care how and with whom you do it."

"What do you mean?"

"Anything that once belonged to Patrice still belongs to her. She doesn't let go. Of money, power, men—anything."

Sarita recoiled. Please don't let Maile mean that Patrice still wants Morgan, Sarita hoped to herself. Of course that was what Maile's warning was all about. Only it was too late.

Maile gave Sarita a funny, bitter smile. Then she was down the steps and starting up the path. She halted abruptly and spun around. "I just remembered that Patrice isn't at the house. She's at the dolphin pool. Why don't you go tell her you're here?"

"Because once she said very distinctly that no one visited her pool."

"She didn't mean it. If I were you, I'd go down there. Just cross the meadow and follow the rock path."

"I remember where it is. The day I arrived, Alex stopped the station wagon on the cliff edge. I thought he was going to drop us over into the water. I didn't know then that the pool was down below."

"It's a pretty place. I'm sure she'd like to know you're

back." With that, Maile vanished, gliding along the path through the shadows and the greenery, the delicate ferns closing behind her. She left only a strange rippling motion among the leaves. Sarita stared after her in surprise. Maile was behaving differently today.

Sarita unpacked her overnight bag. In the arcade shops just off Kalakaua Avenue in Honolulu, she had bought T-shirts, shorts and a tank-neckline, cotton knit camisole to wear over a more modest white string bikini. She put away her purchases, then went into the small kitchen, still thinking about Maile. It was unlike the young island woman to urge Sarita to intrude on Patrice's privacy at the pool. Anyway, it was now after five o'clock and she was starved. She hadn't had lunch, and she couldn't wait for dinner at the big house.

In the fridge there was cheese and fruit. Sarita found a box of fresh crackers, a can of soup and a tin of Twinings' Darjeeling tea. She heated the soup, made tea, put everything together on a tray and took it out on the porch. There she watched the sun set behind the silhouette of graceful palm trees. Offshore, in the distance, lay the island of Molokai, dark against an orange blaze as the sun dipped into the sea and left molten pink and gold trails behind it.

Sarita was too tired to go up to the house to see Patrice and explain why she hadn't returned her call. After carrying the tray into the kitchen, she went into her bedroom, removed her skirt and blouse and collapsed onto the lavishly-colored bedspread. It was just as well that she hadn't opened the shutters, because the trade winds, which had been blowing at a steady pace, began to pick up strength stealthily, as though the salty spaces of the sea were communicating their force from some wild and unexplored deep.

Sarita thought about Morgan. If only there were a magic carpet to fly her through the sunset-colored air and over the darkening waters to his side. Forget about all the tycoons in the world that were so important to him, and all the fat bank accounts that beckoned—he would be glad to see her. He would fold his strong brown hands over hers, hold her wrists tightly, draw her in to him and let her know, by the hard male response of his body, that she was his love.

Restlessly she turned to listen to the ceaseless urgency of the wind as it banged against the closed shutters, pounded on the flimsy shake roof, roared around the corners of the guest house and vibrated along the length of the wooden-railed porch. She shivered at the eerie sounds, and pulled the edges of the spread around her shoulders and across her legs. Then, as though magnetized, her thoughts flowed once more toward Morgan.

Morgan had said, "I love you." Hadn't his body made an honest admission of that with its acts of sensual tenderness? Surely a man didn't do those things unless he cared. Sarita tried to articulate the names of special caresses but found there were really no words for certain of their lovely carnal encounters. What was the matter with her? Did she expect to chart their coming together? Statistically, and how many times? What about an up-and-down graph on the rhythmical pace of their movements? Sarita, just let it be, she told herself. She yawned and suddenly entered the dark archway of sleep.

The private plane would land at dawn on the Kaanapali airstrip. In Honolulu, Mikimura's pilot had been advised not to take off, but since he had grown up wind surfing from Maui to Lanai before he had entered the Air Force Academy, he was as much a part of the air as he was of the sea. Expertly he handled the buffeting that the plane received, while David Mikimura shrugged and told the other passenger, "It is not our time to go. I've had it from the Authority up there." He indicated the skies.

"You mean the control tower?" Morgan grinned. Hell, he didn't mind the danger. But there were two reasons he had to get back early this morning and not wait for the threatening weather to clear up. One was word from the ranch on Mount Haleakala. The other was . . . well, he hoped she was sound asleep through all this. He could almost see her—rosy skin, warm, curving flesh, sensitive profile, golden hair.

"I got word from a little higher up than Oahu's control tower," Mikimura replied. But Morgan had forgotten what his friend was talking about.

Patrice awakened very early. Actually, she'd merely cat-napped through the racket of the stormy night. In yesterday's late afternoon, while swimming in her pool carved out of black lava rock, she had been aware of the wind ruffling the channel waters and of the coco palms bending in more than their usual leisurely fashion. On this dry side of Maui, where the temperature usually hovered at a mild seventy-seven degrees, where the sea was warm at seventy-two degrees, she had not expected real "weather."

Patrice's companion, kneeling on the rocky edge of the pool, had brought Patrice's hand up from the water and kissed its salty palm. *"Pilikia* . . . trouble." Gray-green eyes had then raised to scan the sea and the horizon, looking south toward Haleakala.

Patrice's tanned shoulders had shrugged indifferently. "So?" She'd placed both hands flat on the pool side and, with surprising strength, had lifted her body, nude and glo-riously brown all over, from the water to stand upright. Then, enticingly, she had lain down and spread her legs to the sun.

Her companion's breath had shattered in his lungs. His dark head had bent, and his lips had offered several minutes of reverential courtesy to such beauty. "How can I leave you?" he had murmured.

"That's what I'm wondering." Patrice's look had ca-ressed his body from the expanse of broad shoulders to the trim, tight hips and truly splendid appendage. He had been embarrassed at its performance under her admiring gaze. She had laughed. "Must you go?"

"They'll miss me at the house."

"Who will? Maile?"

The young man had not answered.

"You can't go back to the house in that condition, you know." Patrice had indicated the interesting reason why he couldn't.

"I know," he had said. Sliding down beside her once more, he had covered her lips with his, sucking her breath and her sweetness. His hands had found their familiar place beneath her body, then had lifted her hips to meet his urgency. . . .

Thinking about Nils and what had happened the afternoon before, Patrice sat up and looked at her bedside clock. Six A.M. The wind had slashed at the house all night. She expected to see a ruined garden strewn with palm fronds. A storm like this rarely occurred, and when it did, the damage could be devastating. Nils would have the cleanup crew of gardeners set to work immediately. Patrice had heard crashes during the night. Many of the beautiful coco palms must have been uprooted. She could not bear to see the shambles the heavy wind had left in its wake. Ironically enough, this morning the trades barely sighed, which meant it would be *kono* weather—hot.

She lay back thoughtfully against the pillows. They had been foolish to take a chance yesterday. But Alex's absences were so infrequent that she and Nils had taken advantage of his trip to Haleakala. In that final orgasmic moment in Nil's arms, glancing up at the purpling sky, her mouth stretched wide to gasp out her writhing ecstasy, Patrice had been almost certain she'd observed a flash of white on the cliff above and the swing of a long black mane of hair disappearing into the red ixora bushes.

Patrice sighed. As it had done yesterday while she was held close in Nils's embrace, her mind was operating on several levels at one time. Now she was considering who was more important to her well-being—Nils or Maile. Could Nils's exciting sexuality be obtained elsewhere more easily than could an efficient and talented lab assistant, especially an assistant who owed the Wycoffs favors? It was an intriguing decision that would have to be made. How unfortunate that Nils had proved as seductive to Maile as he had to her—

She heard the sudden sound of car wheels spinning in the gravel outside. In one motion Patrice threw back the sheet that covered her and moved from her bed to the window. Hands on the sill, she leaned forward in anticipation. It was Morgan.

She ran to her dressing table, then paused. There were footsteps, but they were not coming up on the lanai. Their sound diminished in the direction of the path that led to the guest house. Goddammit, she thought—God damn his arrogance! But, of course, she had ways of stopping any nonsense that might be starting between Morgan and that blonde from Chicago. Yet here again, there was a contradiction in her needs.

Patrice removed her address book from the drawer of her bedside table and thumbed through it for Peter Dome's phone number. Then, slowly, she put down the little leather book. That market researcher Miller was smart. She could contribute to Patrice's project. Besides, she'd already been thoroughly indoctrinated in Patrice's lab and over at McIntosh's in Honolulu. Patrice knew she mustn't act hastily. In the background there was always Ross Bailey, to whom she could appeal.

Appeal?

Patrice laughed softly to herself, the sound resembling a low, enticing growl. She didn't need to appeal. She could crack a certain whip and Ross Bailey would be glad to jump . . . any which way at all.

Chapter Thirteen

AT THIS EARLY HOUR OF THE MORNING, Morgan expected to find Sarita still asleep. He took the porch steps of the guest house in two strides and, without thinking, pushed at the front door. To his astonishment, it swung open. She hadn't locked herself in, which was careless of her, but this way he wouldn't awaken her. He would just peek into her room to be sure she was all right. From the weather reports received on Oahu, and from the appearance of the landscape surrounding the main house, he knew they'd had a giant blow over here.

Morgan halted abruptly in the living room to muse on all the reasons why Sarita would be tired and need to sleep late. For one, there was the night before last in her room at the Royal Hawaiian. Thinking back on what had occurred there, he shook his head almost in disbelief. What a wonderful grown-up woman she was. Straightforward and candid, she'd enjoyed his body as much as he'd reveled in hers. No one more refreshing than Sarita had ever charged into the central being of his life. He recalled her words: "Morgan, I love you. I'm happy." He hoped she meant that.

For nearly ten years he had lived with Patrice's lies and clever, manipulative deceits. My own fault, he told himself grimly. You get stepped on, mashed down, emasculated even, it's all because you asked for it. Yet at one time Patrice had helped him as much as he'd helped her. He was grateful, but the partnership between them had been grinding, and he wasn't proud of it.

At no time had he thought that the bond holding them together was anything but tinsel. They'd stacked up the money. For Patrice, they'd maintained a celebrity status. For himself? He'd learned to wear the indispensable mask and hide all its variations while piling up currency in New York, cutting down forests in Brazil and building shopping centers in Florida and California during the days when these ventures were still profitable. It was a forgettable period in his life. He wondered how he could possibly be the man whom the woman in the next room could love—but oh, how he wanted to be that man!

He stepped softly, swiftly into the bedroom to look in on her while she slept.

And there she was—sitting cross-legged in the middle of the bed, dressed in jeans and a red T-shirt, staring at him with the brightest, bluest, most surprised set of eyes he'd ever seen.

"Morgan, it's you! Where did you come from?"

"You're awake?"

Their joint exclamations sounded so ridiculous that they both burst out laughing.

He said, "You should've locked the front door."

She said, "I forgot. I walked in here late yesterday afternoon with Maile and my bags, and we got to talking about . . . things. She left, and I scrounged up something to eat, took my tray onto the porch to watch the sunset, carried it back and . . . forgot to lock up." She wondered why she was rattling on so. "Why am I giving you a blow-by-blow account?" she asked.

"Tell me more. I'm interested in everything you do." He came around to the opposite side of the bed and stared down at the paperwork surrounding her. "Why are you at this stuff so early?"

"Why are *you* here so early?"

"Impolite to answer a question with a question."

"You mean you want to hear the rest of it? All right. I went to sleep about six o'clock last night. I woke up before daybreak. I've been working ever since, going over the main points in Patrice's notes. After all, I wasn't able to concentrate too well on them with you there in my hotel room."

Morgan gave Sarita a jaunty, understanding smile and bent over toward her. With the tip of his finger supporting her chin, he raised her face to his. "May I?"

"Go right ahead."

She closed her eyes and let his luscious good-morning kiss awaken her to this truly glorious day. Then, on her knees, she scrambled across the bed, over the charts and papers, and snuggled close inside Morgan's arms.

"I thought I was mad at you for standing me up at lunchtime yesterday. I seem to be very forgiving for some reason."

"Some reason!" he agreed. He kissed her again. "How do you think I felt about that? When I got back to my apartment at the Illikai, I stayed awake thinking about how you were supposed to be there beside me in bed—and you weren't."

"Didn't you have to see your rich friends in Honolulu today?"

"We knocked the deal together last night. I'll go back for the paper signing, but we're through for now. I'm on my way up to the ranch. Come with me." It was said spontaneously. He hadn't planned it. But there she was, his fresh-faced beauty with her blond hair growing out to the length he liked. No longer worn tidily and barely touching the lower tips of her ears, it fell instead in—how should he say it?—golden disarray. My God, he was poetical. What an effect she had on him!

"I'd love to go with you, Morgan, but I can't. I'm expecting a phone call from Peter Dome. He has some information I need. And I have to report to Patrice on my talk with McIntosh at his lab. As various people seem to keep reminding me, I work for Patrice."

"You're right about that, of course. I'm not going to try to convince you." He paused.

"You could . . . easily."

"How? Like this?" His dark head bent down to hers. The inner curve of her mouth tingled sensationally at the touch of his tongue. When their faces drew apart, he said, "There'll be another time for you to see the ranch. The fire goddess has promised you'll stay in the islands as long as your heart desires."

"You're very sure of your goddess friend Pele, aren't you? What if my heart desires it . . . forever?" She laughed nervously at her boldness. "No answer required."

Was he ready for forever? Was she? Once again they were both solemn-faced. But Sarita lightened the mood as she surveyed him now with amusement. "That's the tan drill outfit and those cowboy boots you wore on the flight from L.A."

"I dress somewhat like the other fellows. On our up-country ranches we call 'em *paniolos*—Hawaiian cowboys."

"Exactly where *is* up-country?"

"On the sides of Haleakala. It's higher and cooler there, with completely different vegetation—pines and eucalyptus trees. It's another world, unlike anything you see around here."

"Morgan, I want to go with you."

"I know you do. And you're dressed for it. Just grab a jacket and put on some shoes."

"I can't," she mourned. "I have a job to do here. Anyway, Alex Firman went up to your ranch. What would he think if he saw us there together?"

"That I have very good taste. Do you care what he thinks?"

"Don't you pay him to think?"

"That's no answer." Morgan released her from his arms.

"Of course you're right, Sarita. You do have a job to do. And do you have integrity! It's like a wave that rushes right at one and can't be deflected. That's what you remind me of."

"What kind of talk is that?"

"It's 'I love you' talk." Morgan's brown eyes were mischievous. "I'll see you when I get back. We'll have that dinner together at the Maui Moon." He grinned. "You haven't seen my condo yet, have you? In the meantime, do whatever Patrice wants you to do, but do it in a hurry."

"It seems to me I recall a conversation in your office in which you mentioned a trial period of three months, and then a year's contract if Patrice's product was up to everyone's expectations. That doesn't sound like hurry-up and get-through." Sarita slid off the bed and stood up. "Seriously, Morgan, you know I can do a lot of the work that has to be done for Patrice right on the mainland. In my Chicago office we have a super computer that'll give me answers faster than I could ferret them out for myself here."

"The computer does all your work?"

"No. I rely on it only for stats. The rest is up to my own judgment."

"Which I hear is very good."

"Oh? Whom did you hear that from?"

"You mean besides Peter Dome?"

Sarita shook her head. "Never mind."

She didn't want Morgan to say Ross Bailey's name again. Right now she only wanted to remember the echoes of Morgan's voice on her first night here, when he'd come to her and said he didn't want her to leave him.

She wondered what had happened to her plan for an independent Sarita Miller, creative and marketing strategist, complete with a logo design depicting her entrepreneurial efforts as organizer, owner, manager and assumer of risks in her own business.

Studying her, Morgan asked curiously, "What are you thinking about?"

"That I must get back to work. So must you. You haven't told me why you need to go to your ranch."

"Have you been outside to see what happened here last night? It's worse at Haleakala. That's why I have to get up there. The trades went crazy—close to hurricane force."

"I slept through it all."

He kissed her again. "Because you were tired . . . from making love?" He wanted to hear her say it. He wanted to know that their night had meant as much to her as it had to him. He had fallen asleep midway through, but hadn't he made up for it the next morning?

Understanding very well what Morgan wanted— needed?—to hear her say, Sarita responded, "I was beautifully tired, Morgan. Because of love, because of you."

He closed her lips with his own, murmuring, "Sarita, I want you now."

She turned her head away from him and looked over her shoulder at the bed with its coverlet of sensual colors. Again the thought came to her that it was a bed meant for ardor, for lovemaking.

Morgan's hands moved lingeringly around her waist. She felt his strong fingers gliding slowly underneath her T-shirt and up her bare torso, discovering the naked peaks of her breasts as they tautened, rigid with her desire.

In that instant there was a loud knocking on the front door. Maile called out, her voice sulky and strange, "Hurry up, Sarita. Breakfast! Patrice is waiting."

Patrice had listened alertly, translating into a warning signal the sound of Morgan's footsteps crunching along the path in the direction of the guest house. Even with the divorce behind them, it hadn't occurred to her that Morgan could be seriously interested in another woman. And blatantly so, it seemed, since he'd parked boldly in front of the house and rushed off to Sarita Miller.

Patrice dressed quickly in a thin white caftan and ordered breakfast to be served on the lanai. After telling Maile on the house phone that she should fetch Sarita immediately, Patrice wondered if she hadn't detected a cool tremor in Maile's usually warm tones. But it couldn't be. By this time Patrice had convinced herself that her imagination had again played its tricks. Maile hadn't spied on her and Nils from the clifftop. What she had seen was probably the flirt of a sea bird's black and white wing spread.

Patrice descended the long stairway to the large room below. The ceiling fan was revolving, stirring up the humid air, making it even stickier. She supposed they would have to close up the house and turn on the air conditioning, which she disliked and thought unhealthy. But without the trade winds blowing, the atmosphere was stifling. For a moment she felt light-headed, aware of the years passing—something she never allowed herself to think about.

On the lanai, she had to wait five minutes for Sarita, who finally came up the steps wearing blue jeans and a T-shirt. Patrice noticed that the younger woman's face was flushed. Probably the heat, she thought. Where was Morgan? She very nearly asked this question, then bit her lips together and said, "Good morning. Sorry to get you out so early."

"I was working. It's all right." Sarita's gaze, now ice blue, flashed like a laser beam. "Didn't you intend for Morgan to join us for breakfast?"

Patrice was so startled by the audacity of this remark that she spilled her papaya juice and swore aloud as she watched it ooze through the caftan's crinkly material and spread its cool stain across her belly button. She mopped at herself with a linen napkin, her action giving her time to think.

"I did hear his car," Patrice managed to drawl. "Was he with you?" She achieved a look of marvelous innocence, which didn't seem to fool Sarita Miller at all, a girl, Patrice thought, who must know that the best defense was a quick attack.

All Sarita said was, "I'm sorry about the juice. I hope it doesn't spot. Try cold water."

At that moment Morgan walked up the terrace steps. In his hand he held the envelope containing Patrice's notes. "Hello, Patrice," he said, and tossed the envelope on the table between the two women.

To Sarita he said, "You'll probably need this. I picked it up just now from the rest of your papers."

Patrice interpreted this remark as an indication that he and Sarita had been working together. Once more she was happy to delude herself. No doubt about it—the envelope must be the reason why he'd gone down to the guest house. She relaxed. "I expected the winds would turn into a typhoon last night. Look at the garden, Morgan—it's a terrible mess. How was it on Oahu?"

"Rough, but not as bad as here."

"Are you having breakfast with me?" Deliberately she excluded Sarita to give the phrase its proper intimacy.

"I've eaten." He barely glanced at Sarita. "I'm off to Haleakala."

"Cheers." Patrice raised her coffee cup and regarded him over the edge with inquisitive eyes. "See you tonight?"

"I don't think so. Goodbye, Sarita."

Sarita said nothing. The two women turned their heads and watched his broad shoulders disappear through the archway. Then Sarita quickly touched the envelope with her fingertips. "I was interested in your ideas about surgically reversing the mark of years on a human face. That's a widely accepted restorative, no question. But I'm concerned that your discovery might be considered similar to a chemical peel, even though you don't use phenol."

Patrice shuddered. "Don't even mention carbolic acid. There's nothing like that in my formula."

"You showed me the equation of hereditary factors plus environmental ones that can cause skin damage. But the market is up to here with moisturizers and sun-screening agents. You understand, Patrice, I'm trying to work out an approach that will guide your product around the years of laboratory testing that the government might insist on."

Patrice looked sullen. "That's up to McIntosh and my lawyers. They have the connections to avoid trouble of that sort. My product is pure, harmless . . . I guarantee that."

"Unfortunately, the government's testing lab won't take your word alone for it."

"I've been in the business for years. I'm not stupid, and I'm well aware that it may present a difficulty, or, rather, a hurdle. Why do you bother me with this sort of thing? Your job is to search out potential clients' attitudes. At least, that was my understanding."

"I have to start with the basic questioning of procedures. In this case, the minuses are as important as the pluses."

Patrice's face darkened. "If you don't want to go forward with this—"

"But I do." Sarita paused, her glance alert. "Even though advertising *isn't* my part of the job, how do you like the sound of 'The Night of the Rain Ginger'? Could it be a label for you?"

Patrice closed her eyes. After nearly four minutes had passed, she spoke. "I see a waterfall and ferns and a marvelous face. I also see a commercial splash in all the big magazines. Yes, it's very good . . . for that slogan trade. It produces an image in the brain that's alluring . . . even the words themselves are. But I had intended to use something a great deal more professional—some equation that's part of the formula. Perhaps we could go with both." She opened her eyes. "Temporarily, we can call it the Rain Ginger line. I did describe the island rain to you, didn't I? And the scented ginger mist when the moisture rises from the wet earth? It's not surprising that you came up with that little phrase. I practically gave it to you."

Sarita stood up. "Is there anything else?"

Patrice's eyes narrowed. Was Sarita deliberately asking for it? She leaned forward, her shoulders elfin, her small hands clasped in front of her. At the moment, her fingers were not elongated and graceful. They were tightly linked and looked inordinately strong. "Since you ask me, there *is* something else, Sarita. You should know that Morgan and I will probably remarry. I mention this only to explain why he is so much a part of my current operation. You must have guessed it from the way we worked together, with his office being here as well as my lab." Patrice realized it would have been more effective if she hadn't said "probably." Why make it conditional? She was about to correct her own error when she became aware that Sarita had left the table and was racing down the steps.

Patrice rose from her chair and called after her, "Peter Dome phoned from Chicago and wants you to call him back. I took the liberty of speaking to Peter myself. He's a friend of an old friend of mine."

Sarita halted on the pathway but did not turn around. When she replied over her shoulder, her voice was hoarse. "I'll return the call later. I have to finish my charts."

"Well, my dear, you've forgotten to take along all my suggestions. They're still here in this envelope." Her voice carrying like the notes of a steel flute, Patrice continued. "The old friend I mentioned is Ross Bailey. I thought you'd be interested. I've invited him out here to get away from that dreadful Chicago weather."

The invitation was a lie, but the moment that she said it, Patrice convinced herself it was the truth, and if not the truth, at least a brilliant idea. One that she would have to put to work immediately.

Sarita turned slowly to face in Patrice's direction. From this distance she hoped that Patrice Wycoff could not read her expression. A jumble of fierce emotions boiled inside her. She was sure she must resemble a wild woman, shocked and disconsolate. She'd been all right, sparring with Patrice right up until the end. But the end was what had done her in. There was just the faintest ring of truth in the notion that the marital as well as the business partnerships between the illustrious Patrice, once the darling of the fashion mags, and Morgan Wycoff, financial industrialist without a soul, might very well be indissoluble.

Then there was the business about Ross Bailey. Even though her feelings for Ross were a thing of the past, Sarita shivered at the thought of Patrice's throwing him and Morgan together, with herself as a not-so-innocent bystander. She felt sickened, horrified and defeated.

Something made Sarita raise her eyes to the sky. The heat in this Eden was almost unbearable. With no breath of air stirring, it was as though she were gazing into the inside part of a giant white porcelain cup. Little flickers of bitter green were in the air, a myriad of insects flapping their bronzed wings. Sarita's lips were dry, her body was drained and her skin felt feverish. She turned and stumbled down the path. She didn't care what Patrice might think of her clumsy movements.

But Patrice was no longer on the lanai. The heat and the flying insects had driven her inside the house. She saw Nils and ordered him to close all the windows and doors and to turn on the air conditioning. When he glanced around surreptitiously and would have advanced on her in an amorous way, she screamed at him to disappear and fled up the stairs to her room.

Alex was at the ranch, but she wanted him here and she wanted him now. He could make her the reviving drink that would cool her, soothe her, quiet her. She didn't need any more physical pounding from Nils to relax her. If anyone touched her hot flesh, she would be instantly sick. God, she felt a million years old! She stripped off the caftan and stepped into the shower. She couldn't even think about Sarita Miller, so young, so very young. She hated Sarita. She hated Maile.

But she had herself and her beautiful body and her extraordinary brain, and she would concentrate on that. Patrice Wycoff and the big comeback she was going to make. She would show them all.

Better than that, she'd get busy right now. She stepped out of the shower, found her address book and dialed a number halfway across the rest of the United States. When

154

the secretary answered, Patrice asked to speak to Peter Dome. As soon as he came on the line, she told him she wanted Ross Bailey's private number, which she hadn't needed for a long time. "Thanks, Pete," she said when he had given it to her, and hung up on him, leaving Peter Dome wondering what the hell was going on.

Chapter Fourteen

WORK HAD TO BE THE ONLY ANSWER!

Sarita made herself a cup of instant coffee, so hot that it scalded her mouth. No matter. She picked up her notebook and pushed the recorder's playback button to start her tapes. What she heard were the husky accents of Patrice's voice lecturing in the lab. Sarita snapped off the machine and stared straight ahead. Acknowledge your anger, she told herself—and try again.

She went into the bedroom, sat on the bed and spread out the big chart. Slowly, carefully, she printed the heading "The Night of the Rain Ginger" in block letters. But the words shimmered together, summoning a soft night . . . a passionate encounter . . . the remembered fragrance of ginger petals drifting on the air of an impersonal room made personal by the embrace of lovers . . . the rain pattering on a lanai that overlooked a moon-touched sea veiled in pale mist. Sarita rocked back and forth on the bed, her arms cradling her upper torso. To lie within the warm encirclement of Morgan's embrace, to know the power of his body, to feel the fierce tenderness of his lips on hers and his hands stroking, caressing, loving—these were the real embodiment of the night of the rain ginger.

Sarita's bones ached, her throat felt choked. She mustn't think of Morgan. What a funny, funny joke *that* was! Not to think of Morgan would be the same as not breathing, as her heart not beating.

There was another image, one she couldn't think about at all: Morgan and Patrice together. She might be grateful for tears at this point, but they wouldn't relieve her pain.

The humidity in the guest house was becoming more unbearable. There was no sign of an air-conditioning unit anywhere. Sarita walked to the porch. Not a stir of air there either. She was more than ready for the return of the trade winds, even for their rough urgency when they blew at a steady pace from the island's north bluff.

While she watched gardening crews clearing away last night's debris, Sarita thought about Patrice's saying that she'd invited Ross to Maui. What Patrice hadn't added to this bit of shocking news was whether he had accepted the invitation. Sarita was sure her ex-fiancé wouldn't leave Chicago. There were too many hot irons in his fire that no one but him could attend to.

She'd have to return Peter Dome's phone call. With that out of the way, she might go to the beach and swim, though today even the ocean looked sultry.

But there was a cool place.

Up-country Maui.

Morgan had asked her to go there with him. Why shouldn't she? Patrice's attitude at the breakfast table had canceled Sarita's incentive to work. In a clutch like this, she really wasn't ready to deliver. And she could not forget the burning desolation of hearing Patrice say: "Morgan and I will probably remarry."

A lie . . . it had to be a lie. . . .

Morgan had told Sarita that all she needed was a jacket and a pair of shoes. She was still wearing the blue jeans and red T-shirt. She got out her one pair of sturdy shoes and a denim jacket. She had the Toyota and knew the general direction to take. Someone could tell her how to find the Wycoff ranch.

Sarita drove past fields of pineapples and sugar cane, past Pukalani, then up a narrow hill road to the old cowboy town of Makawao, its weathered buildings huddled along a short main street. There was no one about. Sarita parked next to the bakery, went inside, bought some homemade sugar buns and asked the Japanese woman behind the counter for directions to the Wycoff ranch.

The Olinda road snaked steeply upward past rolling meadows and through stands of fragrant eucalyptus trees. The coco palms, sandy beaches and surf had long since disappeared. It was cooler here, and incredibly green and lush. At one curve of the road, rain spattered the windshield. At the next rise, misty sunlight streamed through the trees. In the pastures there were flocks of white sheep and roaming Arabian horses with cream-colored manes and tails. Silhouetted against the pale noon sky were jacaranda trees, starting their purple bloom for an early spring in February.

Sarita stayed on the two-lane country road and abandoned herself to the sights and smells of this different world. The road twisted upward through a landscape of fertile soil and tall pines. Hereford cattle grazed in dark green meadows. From the signposts she had been given, she knew she must be coming close to the ranch. She rounded the last hill at a two-thousand-foot elevation, and there in the far distance was the sea, a blaze of blue spread out in metallic splendor.

It was only then that she thought about Alex Firman. She had seen the remains of the onslaught of the winds up here— fallen trees, a giant boulder that had tumbled onto the road from the heights above, a crushed siding of weathered fence. Alex had been sent for, and she supposed he was still attending to the damage in order to make his report to Morgan. If there were to be a confrontation with Alex right now, she didn't care. She was feeling fiercely competitive, sure of

herself. The hired car had leaped to her bidding, shoved
into second gear by Sarita's knowing hand as she'd urged
it forward. Morgan was her objective, and so was the truth
he would tell her—that Patrice had been lying.

Sarita heard sharp rumbles in the distance and stopped
the Toyota to put on her jacket. It was more than cool, it
was chilly. She looked over her shoulder in the direction
of the weird canyons and peaks that hid the Iao Valley.
Morgan had told her its legendary history. There Kame-
hameha the Great had fought the decisive battle for the
island of Maui against the followers of Maui's hereditary
chief. As though the dark stains of ancient warfare still
remained, heavy thunderclouds boiled up from the jumbled
masses of distant rock. Sarita had been warned about these
island squalls, but so far she'd experienced only the fine,
misting rains that disappeared quickly into sunshine. This
was going to be something else, she knew.

The black-bellied clouds raced so swiftly that in minutes
the green valley below her was hidden beneath thin slants
of gray rain. Sarita revved the car's engine and jounced
forward once more. The bakery woman had told her that
after her first sight of the ocean from the higher elevation,
she would see the side road leading to the ranch house. She
couldn't miss it. But she almost did.

She turned left on the unpaved road. At the half-mile
mark stood a gate with an iron scroll bearing the Wycoff
name and the insignia of the ranch's cattle brand. It was a
closed barrier to her passage.

Approaching her from the other side of the gate was the
first vehicle she'd seen on her drive up Haleakala's slopes.
The jeep didn't have to travel any closer for her to recognize
Alex Firman in it. She sat behind the wheel of her car until
the jeep came to a precipitous stop a few feet from the gate.

"Halloo . . ." Alex spoke as though seeing Sarita Miller
in a little white Toyota across the fence from him were a
natural sight, part of the expected landscape.

Sarita extended her hand out the window and gave him

159

a casual wave. Alex jumped out of his vehicle, sidled over to the gate and licked his lips. He could tell her that Morgan wasn't here. That news would send this twit of a girl back down the road. He glanced skyward. If he did that, she would meet up with the damnedest deluge she'd ever experienced. If he let her stay here, however, he could observe her terror himself, firsthand. He'd like that. Alex opened the gate.

Sarita drove through and stopped beside the jeep. If it was required, she'd give Alex an explanation of sorts for her presence. "I had to get away from the heat down below."

"You've gotten yourself into something worse. Severe weather, maybe even a hurricane." Alex watched Sarita closely.

"I doubt it. They're relatively rare here." She wanted to ask about Morgan. She didn't. She asked instead, "Where's the house? It's here somewhere, isn't it?"

Firman was on his way to the agricultural experimental station to pick up some data. He didn't want Sarita to go to the house without him. Morgan was there. Signed for and delivered, Morgan belonged to Patrice—he always would. Which made Alex's position in the Wycoff compound more secure. If the two Wycoffs stayed together, Alex Firman was needed, because one of them had to be kept in line.

"Listen, Sarita, you'd better get back down the mountain fast. You can still make it while the road's dry and safe. Over at Napili Bay it may be humid without the trades blowing, but the sun is shining and the climate's great. Besides, Patrice is waiting for you. She's bound to be. She employs you, and she has the right to expect you to be there. It's her time, not yours."

"How do you know she's waiting?" Something in Alex's manner brought out the perversity in Sarita. She looked away, toward a thick stand of pine trees, and thought she caught a glimpse of a white house in the background.

"Thanks, Alex, for opening the gate." She gave him a false smile of courtesy and drove on.

Alex stood beside the jeep, hatred spewing from his narrowed pale eyes. The woman was a fox. He was torn between the necessity of getting down to the agricultural station and his wish to head Sarita Miller away from the ranch house.

How did he know whether Morgan wanted to see this intruder? How did he know that Morgan didn't? Was something going on between them?

Alex moved quickly into his vehicle. He would go down the mountain and call Patrice from the station below. Then he would hightail it back here.

When Nils answered the phone, Alex snarled at him to get Patrice on the line. A few moments later he heard Patrice's soft, panting voice say, "Alex, come back here at once. I need you."

"I can't. That woman from Chicago is here."

"Sarita Miller went up there? Why?"

"You tell me."

There was silence on the other end. Then Patrice groaned. "Get rid of her, Alex. Get her back here any way you can. Morgan . . . I think that Morgan . . ."

"No, Patrice, don't worry. You'll never lose him. But do you really want me there?"

"I didn't say I want you, I said I *need* you." She hung up abruptly. Alex stared at the phone in his hand. He knew what she needed.

The road ahead of Sarita curved through the pines. When the house came into sight at last, she saw that it was long and white and green-shuttered. It looked sleepy and serene, a part of this rural, old-time Hawaii. There was nothing here to remind one of the burgeoning condominium communities on the coast below, nor of the tourist industry and the stereotyped view of Hawaii with its surfboards and sandy beaches.

An old-fashioned garden full of snapdragons and carnations bloomed in front of the house. Vegetables were thriving in a nearby patch. Sarita could smell the pungent odor of Maui sweet onions as she sat at the wheel of the Toyota and looked around her. The scene was remote and tranquil, except for the paling sky overhead, the uneasiness in the air and the faint grumbling sound emanating from the high peaks surrounding Iao Valley in the distance.

Morgan's station wagon was parked in an area close to the house. On seeing it, Sarita smiled greedily and got out of her car. She guessed Morgan could be considered as her quarry, and she had run him down.

But there was no one in the house. Sarita knocked at the front door, then went around to the side and the back. She remembered this was a working ranch and headed in the direction of the barn and corrals. A slim young man with shoulder-length black hair, wearing Levi's, boots and a tight denim jacket, came around a corner leading a spirited horse. Man and horse halted in surprise. The man stared at Sarita from beneath a curled-brimmed straw hat, its band decorated with feathers and shells. He was probably one of the *paniolos*, the Hawaiian cowboys Morgan had told her about.

"You want somebody?"

"Is Morgan Wycoff here?"

"He's over at the twenty, bringing in some steers. Had a bad blow last night."

"I know." When had the industrialist learned the cowboy trade? Then she recalled that he owned a ranching and lumber operation in Brazil.

"You new here?" The young man asked her the classic question.

"Not really. I'm staying at Napili."

The *paniolo* shrugged almost disdainfully, then led the gelding into the barn, with Sarita following. He went into a tack room and took a saddle and a blanket off a peg.

162

"Got to dress up this dude." He grinned as he adjusted the saddle pad and threw the saddle on the horse's back, then reached for the cinch strap. "You ride?" The man glanced sideways at Sarita.

"Some." Sarita smiled, recalling her grandparents' southern Illinois farm.

"Work cattle?"

"Some." She'd helped drive her folks' beef cattle into summer pasture at the end of the winter.

"Get on. I'll shorten these stirrups for you. You go along the fence there to the eucalyptus grove, you'll meet Morgan."

"What?" Had the *paniolo* actually been saddling this horse for *her* to ride?

The young man continued. "This fellow looks frisky, but he's gentle. I wouldn't let you on him otherwise. Think I want to get fired?"

Sarita shrugged. "Maybe you do. Maybe you're tired of working."

"I like my work, but if somebody like you hangs around, I won't be able to do any of it." His black eyes looked straight into Sarita's sapphire gaze. "You want Morgan, you go find Morgan."

"You mean it?"

The man nodded.

Sarita shook her head wonderingly, gathered the reins in one hand, put her other hand on the pommel and let her new friend give her a boost upward. What would Morgan think when he saw her come riding after him on one of his own horses? She swallowed nervously a few times. "You sure this is okay?" she asked, looking down at the young man's tanned face.

"Why not?"

Indeed, why not? Sarita nodded gravely, gave a flick of one sturdy leather heel into the horse's side and started off. Just before her mount went into a quick trot, she called back, "What's his name?"

"Brownie."

Brownie tossed his head, tugged at the bit, shook his mane and danced around. Sarita gentled him while the cowboy shouted, "He's a pacer. Put him into his gait."

Sarita coaxed Brownie into the comfortable lateral gait that was like riding a rocking chair, and off they went. She hadn't been on a horse for two years, but immediately her knees responded in a tight grip, and she held the reins with an easy pressure. Gusts of wind charged across her face, carrying a breath of meadow grass.

The agricultural station had forecast hail if the clouds became heavier over Iao and moved in this direction. Astride his own horse, Morgan shouted and hazed the steers, working them into the lower pasture. Assisting him were two *paniolos* who'd grown up on the place. Since they'd been here longer than he, Morgan didn't mind deferring to their greater knowledge of the terrain. When they told him a large part of this herd would be safe on the less exposed side of the slope, he agreed to leave the cattle there.

He cantered by the eucalyptus trees and along the fence, holding the reins in one gloved hand and patting the sweaty neck of his big red horse. The animal whinnied and jerked its head up and down. Morgan stared ahead of him. Brownie was coming up the line, and it looked as if a light-haired woman were astride the bay. Morgan halted his mount and stared some more. A wide grin cracked his solemn, deeply tanned face. It couldn't be Sarita, but it was.

She rode up to him, her face flushed and her eyes sparkling like blue pools that he could fall into. Morgan knew Brownie's temperament. He could put his arm around Sarita while she was still in the saddle and draw her close to him, and the horse wouldn't spook.

He did just that and held her in a one-armed embrace. "A surprise for me?" he asked.

Sarita couldn't answer. She was breathing hard, her heart pumping. She was probably happier than she'd ever been in her life. "Morgan, you aren't angry with me, are you? I had to ask you something."

He released her. "You did? You came all the way up here for that? Tell me, who put you on Brownie?"

"One of your *paniolos*."

"He didn't tell you his name?" Sarita shook her head. "Then I won't have to fire him, will I? Who told you that you could ride?"

"I *can* ride," she answered with spirit.

At that moment Brownie nipped the neck of Morgan's horse, then kicked out with his hind legs. The two animals shot forward in unison, jolting their riders. Sarita stuck like a burr as Brownie won the race to the barn. When they reached it, Morgan jumped down and caught Sarita as she slid out of the saddle.

Again Morgan stared down at Sarita, studying the full lips, the delicate cheekbones. He brushed his hand across the ends of her light hair. "As soon as I get these fellows into the barn, come inside and tell me what's going on. You wouldn't drive up to the ranch with me, but you came on your own. Why?"

"I had to find out the truth about something. But not this minute, Morgan. I'll wait for you."

"You're all right?"

"Of course." Why shouldn't she be? But she loved his solicitude.

When he returned after unsaddling the horses, he moved Sarita into the shadow of the tack room. She leaned against the wall, facing him, as he supported his weight by stretching out his muscular arms on either side of her shoulders, the palms of his hands flat against the wall.

When she didn't speak, Morgan prompted her gently. "Sarita, aren't you going to tell me what's bothering you?"

Earlier, it had seemed so simple to relay Patrice's words and ask Morgan if it were true that he and Patrice would reestablish their life together someday. Now such a question seemed offensive and awkward. She couldn't look into those amber-flecked eyes that observed her curiously. Morgan's body had wooed hers in the most intimate manner possible. Right now, this minute, she could feel sexual responses rising within her. He was standing so close to her that she felt invaded by the almost physical contact of his broad chest, by the taut strength of his legs, by the masculine odor of him, compounded of skin and sweat and male power. Tension boiled inside her. Her heart plunged like a wild thing. An electric current of breathlessness seemed to capture her throat and breasts, making it impossible for her to breathe. At that moment she knew she was totally his. She could ask no questions of him; she could only accept.

The silence was velvet. It was as though he were reading her mind and heart, seeing the thoughts behind her eyes, as he slowly leaned forward to move his lips against hers. And through that warm, impassioned kiss that seemed to part her soul, she could hear him murmur, "It is I who need you, Sarita. Don't ever think it's the other way around. You are my strength more than I am yours."

And then Morgan's lips coaxed and caressed hers. His tongue glided searchingly, sensuously, inside her mouth. Involuntarily she pushed herself back against the wall, but his hands caught and held her face motionless for his lips to savor. He took away and he gave, and Sarita, her eyes closed, felt herself sway against him . . . the victim and the victor.

Chapter Fifteen

MORGAN LED SARITA TOWARD THE RANCH house and smiled down at her quizzically. "Step into my parlor," he said, opening the screen door.

Sarita could see that the large and comfortable-looking room they entered was used for both relaxing and dining. An overstuffed green couch and several sturdy chairs were flanked by windows curtained in a plaid of green and red homespun. An oval-shaped rug woven in warm tones of deep rose lay on the plank floor. At the far end of the room were a stove, a refrigerator, a sink and a wooden chopping block. In an adjacent alcove there was a round table covered with a red cloth on which was placed a wicker cornucopia basket containing fresh garden vegetables—squash, an ear of corn, winter pea pods and elongated green beans. An old-style oak sideboard stood in one corner, its shelves filled with hand-painted stoneware plates in a design of pink rosettes and green leaves. Antique pieces were also displayed inside: a ceramic bean pot, a fine old soup tureen and ladle, a blue stipple pitcher, a pair of column candlesticks.

"The original owner was a retired whaling captain who came here in the eighteen-fifties," Morgan explained. "The house stayed in the family. We bought it from a great-great-granddaughter."

167

Always that "we." To Sarita it indicated the continuing alliance that must exist between Morgan and his ex-wife. Was their relationship a permanently retired one or not? To find out, either she'd have to wait until Morgan himself mentioned Patrice—as he had that night in their hotel room at the Royal Hawaiian—or she'd have to come right out and ask. She saw how easy it was to fall into the trap of the possessive! This time it was "their" hotel room—hers and Morgan's.

"Morgan . . ." She swallowed nervously.

"If we're in for a storm, we might be without electricity. I'll fix something for lunch. You hungry?" While he spoke he was opening the refrigerator and the cupboards, bringing out a skillet, eggs, ham, bread. "Fill this pot for me, will you?" He reached for the coffee can.

Sarita turned on the faucet, filled the pot, then put it down. "Morgan . . ."

This time he heard her. "Yeah?"

"Morgan . . . could you and Patrice ever get back together again?" Said like that, it really didn't sound so bad. Or did it?

He just looked at her easily, his eyes half closed, so that all she could see was their glitter. The rest of his face was expressionless. What could he be thinking? Sarita was panicked. Was he thinking that Patrice would never come out with such a faux pas, that Patrice was tactful and smooth and wouldn't ask a graceless question like that? Well, what was really wrong? And how long was he going to look at her in that remote manner as though she were someone far away?

She wasn't far away. She was right here. And she was mad. "Morgan, are you going to answer me?"

"No." At least he spoke.

"Why not? Because you don't choose to?"

"Because you shouldn't have asked me that. You should know better. How could you even think of such a thing?

168

Oh, Sarita . . ." He shook his head, remembering how well he knew Patrice and her ways. "It was something Patrice said, wasn't it?"

Relief soared through Sarita. "Yes, but please, let's forget it, Morgan."

"I want to straighten this out. What *did* she say to you?"

"That you and she might remarry."

"And you believed that?"

"Not really, but yes . . . maybe."

"You're becoming as cryptic as Mikimura can be sometimes. What is this 'not really, but yes, maybe'?"

Sarita's face crimsoned. "Can we change the subject?"

"I think we'd better. How about this? They're forecasting rain and hail. Doesn't happen up here more than once or twice a year, usually between October and April. On the crater rim eight thousand feet higher up, there can be a snowfall."

Sarita couldn't help laughing at his good-old-weather ploy. Then she said, "Snow? In these tropical islands?"

Morgan also chuckled. "They tell me Paradise has different levels for the tourists. Sometimes they ski on the slopes of Mauna Kea in the winter. Of course, it's no Aspen." Morgan picked up the flatware and began to set the table for the two of them. He winked at her. "Watch me. I'm handy to have around the house."

Sarita agreed. "You certainly are. But we were talking about hailstones."

"These aren't the monster kind you have in the Midwest. Here they're a quarter inch or less in diameter. Nothing much."

He had done a great job of changing the subject. Sarita leaned back against the sink. She was smiling dreamily at Morgan's chatter, but she was no longer paying very much attention to his words. She was wishing it could be this way always, Sarita and Morgan together in a plain, comfortable setting like the ranch house. She wished he wasn't rich. She

169

wished she didn't have that little niggling ambition to start a small research company of her own. She wished . . .

Morgan crossed to the stove. He turned it off, came up behind Sarita and put his arms around her, touching her breasts, pulling her against him, breathing ardently into her ear. "Do you want to eat lunch? Or make love?"

Sarita started to tell him what she wanted to do in the words he wanted to hear. Then she gasped and swung herself around in Morgan's arms. "What about Alex Firman?"

"What about him? He'll hit the experimental station, pick up the material they have for him and then hike off for Napili."

"How do you know that?"

"I know." Morgan nibbled at her throat. "Because the fellow in charge down there told me on the phone, right after Alex left, that he was going to ask Alex to drive to the county seat at Wailuku."

"Morgan, you were riding herd up on your property when Alex left!"

"I was, wasn't I? Well, maybe I called the guy myself and told him what to do with Alex. Maybe I got tired of seeing Alex around. So if he gets to Wailuku, I know him—he won't want to come all the way up the slope again. He'll go back to Napili. Wouldn't you?"

"No." She gave Morgan a meaningful kiss. "But Alex knows I'm here because he let me through the gate. You'll see—he'll outsmart you and come back."

"To chaperone us?" Morgan laughed. "That's not his function. He has a special mission in life, and that's to make *my* life easier."

"Let's hope he remembers that." Then Sarita asked, "Do you always stay here alone like this?"

"We have a cook. Right now she's putting a meal together at the bunkhouse for the *paniolos* who work on the ranch— the ones who don't have families here."

It was sentimental of her, she knew, but she wanted to say, "You don't have a family, Morgan. Let me be your family." Fortunately, she was tongue-tied on that subject. She only murmured, "I'm not hungry for lunch."

It was midafternoon when they woke up in Morgan's bedroom. Sarita opened her eyes, looked at the clothing on the floor and remembered how delicious their time together had been. In fact, it had been better than ever.

She gently dug her chin into the tanned shoulder beneath hers. Morgan's head turned on the pillow, his eyes a crescent gleam of amusement and tenderness. He raised a hand and ruffled her shining hair. "You are the most beautiful woman in the world," he told her in sleepy contentment. "And the nicest . . . and the sweetest . . . and the smartest . . ." He simulated a gentle snore.

"Morgan, no!" She poked him awake in all the hospitable places of his body—his hard-muscled stomach, his lean thigh, his broad chest with its curly mat of dark hair. She kissed those places and mischievously placed her body over his.

"Oh, Sarita, yes!" he groaned in answer to the delicate tracing of her lips along his chest, nipples and inner thighs. In response to the intensity of each other's desire, once again they joined their bodies.

This time it was Sarita who was the bold one. Inventive in a way that amazed her, she sought and found the rhythm, and its special sensitive object, to give Morgan his greatest sensual pleasure. Nature and the overpowering love she felt for him guided the instinctive, caressive movements of her hands and mouth to bring him to a climax that consumed them both.

Intensely stimulated, this refinement of their lovemaking finally led them to a kind of nirvana. The peace they both felt was more than an erotic trance. They lay together, breast to breast, their breaths mingled, their loins clinging, his strong legs gripping hers. Sarita's eyes were closed. Her arms were clasped beneath his, then tightened around his torso. The palms of her hands stroked the long muscles of his back. Rich with contentment, they told each other by touch and reassuring tenderness what their needs were and how skillfully those needs had been eased.

Outside, there were no bolts of lightning, no thundering of clouds. The predicted storm had passed, to lose itself in the trade winds that had resumed their journey across the island.

They were so hungry that during their late meal of scrambled eggs and ham, toast, coffee and sliced fresh pineapple, they didn't talk at all. Later they sat back, and as though they were continuing a dialogue, Morgan asked, "Are you on the executive ladder, Sarita?"

She almost laughed aloud. It would have been better if he'd said, "I love you and I want you to stay here with me forever," but perhaps this was his way and he might be leading up to something important.

Sarita waited a thoughtful few moments, then replied, not exactly brilliantly, "I don't know. I actually don't know."

"How old are you—twenty-five? Isn't it a little late not to know?"

She spoke hesitantly. "Sometimes things happen to change one's plans." Immediately she was annoyed with herself. He'd think she was waffling. Or worse, he might think she was angling for a commitment from him. She put down her coffee cup. "I'm not yet in an economically viable position, but when I am, I intend to start my own research company. In a small way at first. Just myself and a good secretary-assistant." She grinned wryly and pointed a finger at him. "Bang-bang. That ends that. Let's change the subject. I don't want to talk about me."

"I do. I'm interested in your future."

She wanted to tell him that he was her future. She didn't. She merely flipped another piece of bread into the toaster on the table and said, "I'll go for the ace when the time comes. I just don't want to talk about it."

He grinned suddenly, understanding. "You mean you don't want to talk about business *now*."

She buttered the popped-up piece of toast without looking at him. "Perhaps."

He reached across the table, took the butter knife away from her and stayed her hand. "All my life—and that's far too long—I've only been accustomed to upper-tier investor's talk when I sit across the table from a lady. Now I don't know how to—" He stopped.

Sarita's blue gaze was steady, and amused. "You mean you've confined your table conversation to something like 'What media-buying giant do we have waiting for us this morning on the CVR?'"

Morgan nodded. "Something like that."

"Over breakfast, lunch and dinner it's been business talk—even with the lady you've just been to bed with?"

There. It was out. The words sounded brazen. Morgan must realize she was referring to his life with Patrice. Sarita stood up from the table and moved toward the sink, dishes in her hands, her face flushed a deep pink.

Morgan caught up with her. He tumbled the crockery aside. "Leave that stuff. We have to talk."

What Morgan's next words would have been were unknown, for he was silenced by the sound of Alex Firman's jeep humping to a stop near the back door of the house. Startled, Morgan and Sarita looked out the kitchen window. Then Morgan moved swiftly to the door.

Just as quickly, Alex jumped over the vehicle's side and hustled up the back steps. He was still irritated that the agricultural station had asked him to do its errand at the county courthouse. Once in Wailuku, he'd been torn between Patrice's need of his presence in Napili and his own intuitive guess that he'd better get back up to the ranch to see what was going on. He'd reassured himself that whichever choice of action he made, he would be doing Patrice's bidding.

It was obvious Morgan wasn't too happy to see him.

Alex's sharp eye took in the situation. It was a little late to be having lunch, but maybe Morgan had just gotten back from the upper twenty acres—and of course Sarita Miller had had to wait for him. Alex looked around for the cook. "Where's Agnes?"

Morgan leaned against the kitchen table and crossed his arms. "You want Agnes, she's at the bunkhouse."

Recalling his manners, Alex belatedly changed his expression to one of concern. "Good thing the storm passed us by. I see you got here okay." The smile he turned in Sarita's direction resembled a piece of splintered glass.

A blank-faced Sarita refused to bleed. "My short stay has been an interesting experience." She didn't dare glance at Morgan as she said this. Instead, she made herself savor the puzzled look on Alex Firman's face.

Concealing his amusement, Morgan said, "I'll see you to your car, Sarita."

Sarita gathered up her jacket and handbag, hoping she hadn't left anything in the bedroom but the rumpled bed, which she was counting on Morgan to remake. Before she followed Morgan out, she addressed Firman. "Goodbye, Alex. Any message for Patrice?"

"Tell her I'll get there as soon as I can."

"Will do." Sarita nodded gravely.

Morgan held open the door of the Toyota. Sarita slid inside and turned the ignition switch. His lips barely moving, Morgan murmured, "I love you. Stop at the Lahaina Broiler. It's that restaurant on Front Street. I'll meet you there."

The car keys jangled nervously against the back of Sarita's hand while she released the brake. "What did you say?"

Morgan said it all again, including the "I love you" part.

In that moment Sarita wondered how she could possibly be any happier than she was. Lately, life seemed to be a succession of happy moments. Now, if they could all blend together into one permanent bliss . . . Through the rear

view mirror Sarita watched Morgan's lean, broad-shoul-
dered figure as he in turn, watched her leave. What a beautiful man, inside and out, naked or clothed. This exciting
thought made Sarita turn the wheel too sharply, and she
almost skidded the Toyota into the slippery pine needles at
the side of the road. Quickly Sarita fixed her gaze ahead.
She had to find the Lahaina Broiler on Front Street.

Sarita turned left off the highway toward the sea and the
old whaling village of Lahaina. She stopped near a huge
banyan tree to ask directions of a young woman who was
about to step off the curb. Sarita was told that the Lahaina
Broiler was straight ahead at the north end of Front Street.
The young woman, stylish in beige poplin pants and stiletto
heels, fished in her handbag and handed Sarita a card imprinted with the address of a tropical fashions boutique.
"My place," she said, smiling. "Come there and shop."

Sarita drove along the narrow street fronting the sea wall
beyond which small boats bobbed in the harbor. She found
the restaurant hidden away in a brown wooden building.
Hanging vines almost obscured the entrance.

Once inside, she was greeted by a Japanese woman, who
asked, "Have you come to watch the sun set?"

Sarita nodded. "A friend is joining me."

Since it was early, she was led to her choice of tables
on a porch overlooking the ocean. In the blue distance the
island of Lanai could be seen, outlined against the deepening
flame color of the sky. Water lapped peacefully six feet
beneath the wooden flooring. Tiny brown birds flew out of
the branches of a nearby tree, pecking for table crumbs and
sailing to a jaunty landing on the railing next to Sarita. The
air was silken against her bare arms.

The waitress brought a shallow dish of macadamia nuts.
Sarita ordered an iced drink, then sat back to let the tran-
quility of the view take charge. She wished that she were
wearing her new violet silk pants and blouse and her emerald
earrings. She wanted to be beautiful for Morgan, yet here

she was, in her red T-shirt, blue jeans and sensible shoes. She should be working on a cost-analysis survey. Instead, she had forgotten the marketplace and was remembering Morgan's caresses.

It was nearly dark when she saw his tall form loom in the entrance near the crowded bar. The hostess gestured in Sarita's direction, and Sarita sat up expectantly. Morgan had said, "I love you." Everything was going to be marvelous. He was the first real love of her life and would be forever.

He was wearing tan trousers and his familiar cowboy boots, but he'd changed into a white pullover. He looked immaculate and handsome. As he strode toward her table, Sarita noted that he was gazing at her with an expression that seemed to say he'd overtaken and passed all those bleak yesterdays in his life and that this day and tomorrow belonged to the two of them. Please, she begged silently, let me have read him right.

He sat down opposite her, his amber eyes warm and deep as they flicked across her lips and searched her own shining eyes for what he wanted to see there.

What he said was, "Did you find this place easily enough?" Sarita nodded. "It's been here a long time—my favorite spot. Do you want a drink?" Sarita shook her head. Morgan picked up a menu, looked at it, then murmured, "You do talk, don't you? Or are you just beautiful and bright and as silent as the Mona Lisa?"

"I can't say the words."

"I know." His eyes gleamed, but his face remained serious. "Let's just hold hands and look at the sea."

The interlude was serene, peaceful and full of a love that didn't need to be talked about. Then they ate the fish called _ono_ and an Oriental rice dish.

When they had finished, Morgan said, "I have something for you." From his pocket he took out a rare gold coral bracelet, sculptured perfectly to fit Sarita's wrist.

"It's exquisite!" she gasped. "Where did you find it?"

He raised her wrist, and smiling, kissed its tender underside. "I know a gallery and an artist. I stopped there on my way here. Another time we'll visit it together and have her create a design especially for you." His smile broadened. "By the way, do you still sleep in one earring and nothing else?"

Sarita leaned forward to answer. As she did so, her gaze was caught by an insistent stare from the shadowy bar. The face was male and very good-looking, with eyes that she instinctively knew were smoke-green. Hastily she looked away.

"Morgan, Nils is at the bar."

"It can't be. Lahaina's too raunchy for Nils. Kaanapali's his territory."

"It's he."

Morgan didn't turn around. "It doesn't matter." He signaled for the check. "I'll walk you to your car, Sarita— follow you back to Napili."

"I'll be fine driving up the coast. I know the way."

Neither of them wanted the spell of their being alone together to be broken, so they didn't look in Nils's direction as they walked past the bar and out into the tropical night.

At her parked car, Sarita turned to Morgan. "Nils is a good friend of Maile's. Does it matter that he saw us together?"

"Of course not."

But their privacy had been ripped and scattered, and they both knew it.

Chapter Sixteen

A FEW DAYS LATER NILS ARRIVED WITH THE IBM Selectric that Sarita had asked to be rented for her. She plugged in the cord, touched a button, and the machine hummed into life. She turned it off. "Everything works. Thanks, Nils. See you later."

But Nils gave no indication that he was about to leave. His striking-looking face had perfect immobility about it, except for the expression in the sultry gray-green eyes. They were narrowed, curious, observing Sarita carefully. He placed his shoulder against the side of the open door, his body at an angle, with legs extended and ankles crossed. He folded his arms across his chest.

"I saw you at the Lahaina Broiler the other night. With Morgan."

"You did?" Well, she knew it was coming, didn't she? Her reply was offhand. "Lahaina's a nice place." She wondered if Nils had seen Morgan put the beautiful sculptured bracelet on her wrist. It upset her to think that her special time with Morgan could be intruded upon. She didn't want them to be watched by speculative eyes.

"Could you ask Maile to come down here?" she asked Nils.

"She's busy in the lab."

Sarita frowned. "Have you and Maile had a falling out? She seems unhappy these last few days."

"I hadn't noticed."

"Maybe that's the trouble." Sarita ventured a pleasant smile. Anything to divert Nils's curiosity about the night at the Lahaina Broiler—and anyway, why shouldn't she and Morgan go out together? "Come on, Nils, you know Maile likes you. Why don't you two go off and have some fun? I've seen you board sailing. Somebody told me you've been clocked on a twelve-foot board with only sixty square feet of sail at twenty-eight miles per hour. I hear that's faster than any sailboat has ever moved." It was blatant flattery, but every word was true.

Nils was young and proud. She could see the bravado of self-confidence replace the questions in his eyes.

"You want me to teach you? I'm off this afternoon. When do you finish up here?"

"I can meet you on the beach at three."

Nils straightened himself and flipped a hand toward his temple in a casual salute. "See you then. I'll have a beginner's board waiting for you." He swaggered off the porch.

Smiling, Sarita looked after him. She might as well have a little fun and exercise. Morgan had returned to Honolulu to do some contract signing, and she'd had no word from him. Fortunately, she herself had been busy. It was her purpose to see the Wycoff project through as soon as possible. She'd assured Peter Dome of this during their last phone conversation. It was also true that Maile had been sullen and distant. As for Patrice, she was spending time in the lab and no longer took her meals with Sarita.

Sarita stood up and moved restlessly about. She suspected her reference to Maile's unhappiness might have touched a source of guilt in Nils. She thought she'd glimpsed a flicker of anxiety behind his eyes. If she were right about that, it made for an interesting premise. What had Nils done to Maile? Had he dropped her for another woman? Had there been another woman all the time, and had Maile just found out about it? With a man of Nils's looks and inclinations, that wouldn't be surprising.

Sarita had gotten herself into a session of sailboard lessons. Better Nils as a teacher than Alex Firman. Once she'd told Morgan that Alex would probably try to drown her if he got her on the beach. A joking exaggeration. There were other methods of drowning people. She was sure Alex knew them all.

In the lab, Patrice was feeling alert and capable. She sensed that her juices were at full tide. Alex always knew how to minister to her. The drink he had created needed his special attention. They had titled it Nature's Tonic, which meant Patrice was still an abstainer from liquor.

"This is going to be a great success, Maile!" The fact that Maile didn't answer went unnoticed while Patrice carefully analyzed and mixed the new liquefying mass and then weighed it on the scale. She continued intently. "A woman's skin needs clinical treatment, not camouflage."

Finally Maile murmured, "And your age-retardant factor—"

"Is worth millions!" Patrice cried jubilantly. "I know that, and so does your father. He's canny, that Scot. He hasn't shared his part of the formula even with you, has he?"

Maile shook her head, momentary anger wavering in her eyes like a flame. "Do you need reassurance about that?"

Patrice stopped what she was doing and looked sharply at her assistant. Might it have been Maile, after all, who had watched from the clifftop while she and Nils had contorted savagely in a passionate embrace? The memory of their naked limbs on that last afternoon together fired a stirring in Patrice's blood. "I'm thirsty," she said. "Pour us some orange juice." She looked away from Maile's brooding eyes.

Not Maile, she told herself. The girl was too open to be

able to work silently side by side in the laboratory with Patrice if she had seen Nils with her benefactress. Patrice liked the proud sound of that last word. She accepted the glass of juice. "You know, Maile, we're planning to take care of your expenses at the university in the fall."

"I've made the necessary arrangements already. Your help isn't needed." Maile hesitated. "Though I appreciate your offer."

"You've earned it."

Maile merely shrugged, an eloquent bit of body language whose meaning Patrice privately frowned over. Usually she understood this young island woman very well. But, it seemed, no more.

Also, Maile had been slightly cavalier in her rejection of Patrice's offer of financial help, which had always been taken for granted. Feeling sulky herself, Patrice muttered, "I've had enough today. I'm going for a swim." She peeked at Maile's face. There was no change of expression at the mention of the dolphin pool. Patrice added, "Nils has the afternoon off." Even with this teaser, Maile's face still told her nothing. It was as blank as an empty sheet of paper.

The younger woman stolidly replied, "I'll finish up here."

Patrice began to feel relieved. Her suspicion must be unfounded. "Good girl," she said briskly.

But outside the closed door of the lab, she paused. She was clever at reading people's hostilities. And for all that passivity in Maile's face, Patrice knew the girl's eyes had been diamond bright. Was their gleam one of malice or of unshed tears? Patrice shuddered. Enough of complications. Her body was truly ready now to receive Nils.

Three hours at the typewriter, and Sarita's muscles had cramped. She stood up, placed the plastic top on the machine, stretched and then touched the floor with her fingertips a half-dozen times. She glanced at her watch, which told her that if she was going to meet Nils, she'd better move. He'd seemed friendly at the end of their brief conversation, and perhaps a little indulgence of him would make him overlook Morgan and Sarita's presence at the Lahaina Broiler. She supposed Morgan would say it didn't matter what Nils thought or suspected of their relationship. But Morgan wasn't here, so she couldn't ask his opinion.

Sarita got into her swimsuit, went out to the Toyota and headed for the beach. This time she didn't walk across the meadow to reach her destination. It was midafternoon, and she didn't want to be late. She drove along a narrow lane to the brow of the cliff, parked the car, grabbed a beach towel and started down the path to the sandy stretch below.

Halfway there, she paused, shaded her eyes and stared in bemusement at the lithe brown figure far out on the water. She knew Nils was on a specially engineered surfboard with an underwater stabilizer, its sail and mast assembly fixed to the board by a seagoing universal joint. She was familiar with sailboard terminology and knowledgeable enough about how it worked. One had to get the hang of standing upright, balancing on the board and steering by shifting body weight while the wind in the sail took one over the water.

In the distance Nils was sailing with the wind on a straight course, but the other afternoon she'd seen him do stunt sailing—riding up a rolling swell and jumping off the top of a fifteen-foot wave. She had to admit this man whose blood was both Hawaiian and Nordic was beautiful to watch—part of the sea and the sky combined with an animal purity of form.

Nils had left the beginner's board for her on the sand. Sarita advanced toward it curiously. She threw aside her towel and made a try at picking up the board. Staggering a little, she guessed it weighed about sixty-five pounds with its gear rigged and ready to go.

She should wait for Nils, as he had expected her to, but she didn't. She wanted to see what she could do herself. She struggled with the board and got it into the water, where the salty buoyancy took over. Before she was ready for it, she and the board were out beyond the surf. One hand on its surface, she guided it through the backwash of the swells.

Her confidence returned. She would try to get on top of the board anyway. She did this and lay flat, nothing to it, really. She would surprise Nils by standing upright. Shakily, first down on her knees, then slowly straightening her legs, she stood, balancing. For a few seconds she was able to maintain that balance.

In the distance Sarita could see that Nils was shouting, waving an arm. He was signaling her to stop, telling her not to take chances. Sarita knew this, even though it was impossible to hear his warning, which the wind picked up and tossed aside.

She'd maneuvered small sailboats on Lake Michigan, so, balanced on the center of the board, she carefully pulled on the sail's boom. So far, so good. She was pretty sure she could manage this. She squinted skyward. She knew the idea was to accelerate, steer and stop by changing the sail's position. But this time there was a brisk ocean wind to contend with.

It looked easy the way Nils did it. It wasn't.

The skillful Nils was approaching fast on his own sailboard. Seeing him coming this rapidly toward her was unnerving. He seemed to be bouncing along on the top of the blue water as though readying for a collision course. Sarita panicked and turned directly into the wind. She knew instantly that to have done that was a gross mistake. The sail billowed, fluttered like a wounded wing, flared wildly once and then dipped. Attempting to swing her board about, Sarita made an awkward lunge for the line. With her footing unsteady, everything went out of control at the same time.

She skidded on one heel, tried to maintain balance, slipped, lost the line and plummeted on her back into the sea. The water cushioned her fall but closed over her head as she hurtled downward. Here goes Sarita, she thought; it's all over for me. A stupid, bloody accident, and everything to live for! But she wasn't knocked out, she was conscious, and almost immediately she bobbed up to the surface.

The capsized sail was on its side, heaving around in the water. The board itself was buoyant and floating. Nils was there, straddling his board and reaching out to give Sarita a hand. "Climb on," he ordered. In seconds she was back on her own board, panting and disconcerted, but not as unnerved as she'd expected to be.

"What next?" She looked at the lightweight mast in the water.

"Can you stand?" he asked. Sarita nodded. "Then let's see you do it." Nils's face grew serious. "Sure you're not hurt?"

"I . . . am . . . okay."

She stood shakily on her board while Nils helped pull the sail back up.

"Nils, I just can't take off again. I'm sorry."

"What are you sorry about? Of course you can't. You should never have taken this thing out alone in the first place. Couldn't you wait for me? There are certain fundamentals you're supposed to learn. You can't come out here on the water like a crack wind surfer and solo-sail right away. Especially the way you were doing it—at full speed. Here, get down and lie flat. I'll tow you back."

When she was on the beach again, Sarita watched Nils while he hauled the boards from the waterline. Her left knee was bleeding a little, and she hoped he wouldn't notice it. "Does anyone go very far on these things?" she asked.

Nils was untangling lines and sails. "Once somebody went nonstop from here to Molokai in a twenty-five-knot wind." He looked up. "Six-foot seas."

"You?"

Nils was self-mocking. "Yeah, me. Not such a big deal."

"Oh, Nils!" Sarita sank down on the sand beside the boards. Her legs were unsteady. After a few moments she asked curiously, "What do you want to do with your life?"

"I have plans."

"You don't want to talk about them?"

"Nope."

"I didn't mean to pry."

"I know you didn't."

Sarita got to her feet. "I think I'll go on back. I've had enough for today."

"What's the matter with your knee?"

"A scratch. It's all right. I'll wash it off when I get up to the house."

Nils examined her knee. "You do that. The cut's not very deep. Well, another time . . ."

"Yes," she said, "another time." She picked up her towel and grinned.

Nils watched Sarita climb up the path toward her car. She was trying not to limp, Nils was pretty sure of that.

From around the rocky point beyond the sand beach, Patrice had watched the entire sailboard episode. Hardly an expression had chased across her smooth face, even when Sarita's sail had billowed backward and knocked her into the sea. Patrice had been confident there wouldn't be a disaster. Nils was strong and swift in his own watery element—and unless the blonde from Chicago had hit her head on the board, she would be fine. But a rescue from a near drowning by that brawny male with his handsome face might give the young woman ideas about him.

Patrice grew impatient with herself. Never before had there been a need to feel the jolt of suspicion or jealousy. She was Patrice—preeminent in the desirable-woman category. Yet recently she'd imagined a connection between Morgan and Sarita, and now one between Nils and Sarita. And, of course, there was always Nils and Maile.

An irritated Patrice turned back from her observation post on the lava rock and dived deep into her pool. She came up shaking sparkles of water from her face. She was alone, quite alone. The dolphins came to visit early in the morning or at the end of the day. As yet, there was no sign of them. So she wouldn't have aquatic company. As she swam, she watched the frothing waves lap up and over the black rocks that kept her water inlet secure.

Alone.

She thought about Morgan. She had the distinct impression she wasn't reaching him. These days he seemed satisfied with the stale plateau of riches he'd already accumulated. He would bestir himself to keep his contacts and to devote sufficient time to his investment partnerships—especially the one with Mikimura—but other than that, Morgan appeared to have withdrawn from the passionate ambition for acquisition that both he and Patrice had shared. Los Angeles, Houston, New York—those bases seemed to be running themselves, thanks to the installation of first-rate people. Such detachment on his part was dangerous, and no one knew that better than Patrice.

She turned, floating on her back, feeling the lowering sun warm her closed eyelids. She had cost Morgan a lot when her own world had collapsed following the enormous settlement they'd had to make to that small and virtually bankrupt Belgian pharmaceutical firm. There had been no proof that she'd lifted the chemist's formula and used it in one of her greatest successes, but she'd been blackmailed by the threat of adverse publicity, scandal, and loss of reputation. She'd lost anyway—first her own empire, then Morgan.

No matter that she was clever and talented. There had been that one false step, and here she was, in exile. Supposedly content and protected by the walls Morgan had built around her, but hating all of it just the same. She could spit at the blue sky and the everlasting balmy temperatures . . . balm. There was no balm anywhere for Patrice.

Angrily she pulled herself up onto the side of the pool. She'd worked hard in the lab on this estate that Morgan had provided for her. She knew he considered the lab as recovery therapy. It had turned out to be much, much more than that.

What he thought was her toy could breed another fortune. Her own this time. The preliminary report Sarita Miller had put together was good, as far as it went. But neither Morgan nor Sarita Miller knew that Patrice planned to take The Night of the Rain Ginger out of their hands.

Only Peter Dome in Chicago knew that she wouldn't be alone much longer. Solitude was fine, but she needed a partner. For some time now, Morgan had outlived his usefulness. She'd realized that on the day she'd heard his footsteps go down the path toward the guest house and Sarita Miller.

Ridding herself of the lower part of her wet bikini and pulling on white cotton slacks that clung to her damp legs, Patrice was aware that the cool, salty water had removed her urge for Nils's sexual servicing. Which was fortunate, because if desire had continued to torment her, she wouldn't have been able to gratify it with Alex stalking the compound.

"Hello! May I came down?"

Startled at the coincidence of the intrusion, Patrice glared fiercely up into the sunlight. "No!"

"I've got to talk to you away from the house." Alex Firman hung over the ledge of the cliff.

"Can't it wait?"

"I don't think so," he shouted.

"Stay there—I'll be up." Only the exotic Nils had ever shared the privacy of her pool area. She didn't want Alex here.

Patrice darted around the rocks and threw on her cotton shirt. Alex was just sleazy enough to have watched while she took off her bikini. When she started up the path, she deliberately slowed the pace of her climb to the clifftop. Alex Firman was another one she'd have to throw out. Her dependency on him and his tonic drinks had become tiresome and, in a real sense, dangerous.

On the slope of the cliff Patrice halted and faced Alex. "Well?"

Alex flinched. A bully himself, he could recognize

harsher intimidation than his own. Besides, Patrice was one
of the two people who signed the checks. His sharp face
blanched beneath its tan. A tremor in his vitals told him this
wouldn't be easy.

Patrice was impatient. "You shouldn't have come here."

"I thought you and I had an understanding."

"Only a minor understanding." Patrice looked away from
the man whose perspiring discomfort she could smell. The
blue distance seemed to hold her gaze. "Come on, Alex,
what's the matter?"

It was easier for Alex Firman to say what he had to say
without those mournful dark eyes staring at him. "Morgan's
playing cozy with your researcher. I wouldn't talk, but I'm
here to protect your interests."

"Playing cozy?!" Patrice bit out the syllables in disgust.
"You can speak plainer than that."

Alex did speak plainly. He used a coarse phrase to tell
Patrice exactly what it was that Morgan and Sarita had been
doing.

Patrice inhaled a deep breath, then expelled it. "That's
better. Now we comprehend just what's going on, don't
we?" Black eyes spun back toward Alex. "How do we
know—for sure, that is?"

"From the beginning I've checked around the guest house
when he's been there with her. Nothing. But at the
ranch . . ." Alex shifted his shoulders. There was a possibility he was rather enjoying this. "Plenty of evidence
. . . you know the kind."

"Do I? Go on."

"When I got back from Wailuku, she was still there. I
told you about her on the phone, and you said to get rid of
her. He walked her to the car, and while they were gone,
I hustled into the bedroom."

"How clever of you, Alex. You found it all untidy-like,
I suppose. Morgan never made a bed in his life. I don't
think he knows how. So that's what makes you think they've
been messing around." When she had merely guessed about

Morgan and Sarita, it hadn't been so bad. To know definitely was infuriating. She had always intended to hold Morgan until she was ready to let him go. "Why did you wait to tell me?"

Alex managed to get control of himself. "I have no answer for that. Maybe I wanted to be sure."

"You've been sure for days." With a nip of her long fingers, Patrice sliced off the head of a red flower from the ixora bush.

Alex moved closer. "So I have."

"Get away from me!" Patrice was tiny, but her exclamation was ferocious. It set Alex stumbling backward and made her realize she had to handle him the right way. She'd been blackmailed once and had lost everything. It couldn't happen again. With an effort which Alex was sly enough to see through, Patrice regained her composure. "I'm nervy, and I'm sorry. Listen, Alex—thanks for looking out for things on my account. You'll get yours."

I'll get mine? Alex reflected to himself. What the hell does that mean? "Patrice?"

But Patrice had started across the meadow toward the main house. The flame-red sun was fast sailing down into the claret-colored sea. She turned, and her face was flushed by the crimson light. "What?"

"We know a lot about each other."

"Is that a threat?"

"How could it be? You know what I think about you."

Patrice smiled suddenly. "I think I'd rather not know, Alex." Her smile twisted. "We'd both better be careful." Her back to Alex Firman, she continued to walk quickly through the rough grass. Her musing was silent, expressed only in the tight fury of her shoulders: And you, Alex, had better be the most careful one of all.

Chapter Seventeen

THE HAWAIIAN WOMAN WEARING A FLOWING red muumuu was in her middle years, her hair graying. She was very fat and yet, as she danced, incredibly graceful in a manner that no slim mainlander—even one who had seriously studied the art of the hula—could possibly imitate. Her abundant bulk didn't matter at all. She rolled her lush body, gestured with her lovely arms and hands, while her song told the audience that though she no longer had her young lover, she still had her beautiful hands, beautiful eyes and beautiful body.

Sarita sat forward, her eyes sparkling with delight and pleasure. At last she was in the Teahouse of the Maui Moon with Morgan at her side. They'd had a delicious dinner, and now this wonderful entertainment. Afterward Morgan was going to show her his condominium on the beach.

The Teahouse was situated at the opposite end of Napili Bay from the Wycoff estate. The darkness of night was gentle, outside lights shone on the white waves that broke languidly across the distant reef, then moved in a zigzag pattern up the pale sand that sloped to the restaurant level.

Morgan held Sarita's hand, but this time discreetly, beneath the cover of the white tablecloth. She was wearing the bracelet he'd given her in addition to a pair of perfect pearl ear studs which he'd brought her from a recent trip to Honolulu.

He looked at her, smiling. "The pearls are becoming to you." He enjoyed their glow next to her fine, lightly tanned skin.

"I love them." She raised a finger to touch the perfection of one of them. At the same time she tossed back her lengthening, sun-streaked hair. She seemed to be doing everything to please this man, even to the extent of not taking a scissor to hair which she thought was growing out of bounds. Everything she did now gave her a different image from that of the trim businesswoman who had stepped out of the elevator in Phoebe Adams's building in Century City. But then, Sarita had never really had this kind of relationship before—love, passion, gifts, flowers. She looked down at the loose gardenias next to her plate. "You're spoiling me," she told Morgan.

"I bought those pearls for me to enjoy too," he admitted. "Aren't you the one who sleeps in one earring and nothing else? I wanted that earring to be suitable to the occasion."

Sarita flushed. At first she was incredulous, and then she believed him. "Is that really what you thought about when you were buying them? Oh, Morgan!"

His attractive smile widened. "Can I help it if I have these romantic fantasies when I shop for you?" He released her fingers which he'd been holding against his thigh under the table, and he placed his arms on the table edge. Linking his hands together, he said, "Let's talk."

Sarita wrinkled her nose delightedly. As though taking part in a conspiracy, she whispered back, "Let's. What about . . . ?" As if she didn't know!

"You. Me. What we're going to do about us."

There it was. Her future looming. Sarita's throat tightened, her heart hammered. She reached for the stemmed water glass and sipped at its contents, hoping she wouldn't choke and embarrass them both. The woman who had danced the hula so divinely had departed, to be replaced by a trio that strummed softly on stringed instruments. The lights were dimmed, and the music became a soft backdrop to conversation.

"I have a proposition to make to you."

This was a strange way to begin a loving proposal, but he was a man iron-bound in the business mold, so what else could she expect? Her one other experience like this had been with Ross Bailey. While they had been dining one night, he had reached across the table, captured her hand, slid a diamond solitaire on the proper finger and announced, "We're engaged." Then he'd gone on to tell Sarita about the great racetrack deal he was setting up for the benefit of the city of Chicago. Later she'd found out that the racetrack deal had been for Ross Bailey's benefit alone.

Morgan's words began to penetrate her consciousness. She caught up with them. "Sarita Miller, I admire your efficiency, and original thinking, and I respect the discipline you've shown. Everything you've handed to Patrice has gone across my desk—every chart, graph and report. I've studied them carefully. The concept you've plotted for the introduction of Rain Ginger will get the project off and sailing without too much preliminary promotion. I like that label you hung on it—The Night of the Rain Ginger. Didn't you hint something like that to me in Honolulu?"

"Did I? Yes." In Honolulu—that magical night. Go on, Morgan, she said to herself. This isn't what I expected, but let's hear it.

"You've done a lot more than you were hired to do—which was to research Patrice's probable clients and determine how this youth-texture idea would go over with them." Sarita nodded numbly. "I haven't had time to talk to McIntosh, though. Does he have confidence too, do you think?"

Sarita had to start talking. She hoped her voice didn't sound as strange to Morgan as it did to her. "I haven't spent much time with McIntosh, just that one day when we were on Oahu. He showed me around his lab. We didn't get

192

down to specifics. After all, I'm on the outside. But he did give me some philosophical rhetoric concerning motives and Patrice's need to prove herself. He cut himself off rather abruptly when he thought I was about to ask questions."

"Why did he do that?"

"First off, he was right—the background of this project is none of my business. Secondly, he didn't want to say too much because he's uncertain right at the moment about how it will turn out. By that I mean, it takes years to get through the government testing labs if there's any question as to safety. The consumer is more sophisticated these days."

Morgan frowned. "Go on."

"On the other hand, McIntosh is aware that a break-through like Patrice's could result in huge sums of money being made. He wants to be in on it."

"You've talked to Peter Dome?"

"Peter understands the possibility of such a time lag before the product can be marketed."

"It hinges on the safety factor, then."

"Right."

"Patrice has done some preliminary testing on her own skin. Even Maile has volunteered. Neither had any reactions—at least none that I've been told about."

"Morgan, why are we talking this way?" For an instant Sarita covered her mouth with one hand. Then she removed it. Was the gesture a subconscious indication to herself to keep still? "Never mind."

Morgan looked at her in surprise. "I don't understand." When she didn't respond, he shrugged and continued. "I have to dispose of this commodity of Patrice's before I move on to another area. You want to know what I'm leading up to? Just this, Sarita. I'm headquartered in New York, though I've been spending too much time out here in the islands."

"Enchanted by Pele?" Sarita asked.

"Something like that. I'm out of touch with both the L.A. and the Houston offices. Phoebe Adams brought this up last time I was on the mainland. I need someone like you, someone I can trust and depend on, to step in and time everything that's happening on the West Coast. We need quality control there, and I've been hanging too loose. I know Patrice thinks so. As for Patrice—she's on her own now. I won't have to worry about her much longer. Wouldn't you say she's got a grip on things?"

Sarita wanted to scream, to release all her pent-up astonishment, rage and disillusion. She'd been the recipient of a proposal, all right—a very fine and flattering business proposal!

She stared down at her dessert fork for a moment, then lifted her gaze to meet his. "I appreciate the offer, Morgan, and the confidence you have in me." She stopped, swallowing the taste of bitter disappointment. "If I were going to take you up on this, we'd have to talk about the authority I'd have, about remuneration, executive title and length of contract. But since I have my own plans for my career, the rest of this conversation won't be necessary." She almost added, "And you will never see me wearing only one pearl earring when I go to bed at night!"

She stood up. "I'm going to the ladies' room. I'll be back."

Morgan half rose from his chair as she left the table. She could have kicked him in all manner of sensitive spots. What was she going to do? She walked rapidly through the aisle of tables and hoped she was headed in the right direction. This evening that she had so looked forward to was turning itself around in an unbelievable fashion. Maybe she should consider herself lucky to be offered a pivotal position in the Wycoff enterprises at the age of twenty-five. Maybe all those years in school and the long hours directed at research analysis in Peter Dome's agency were all paying off, and she wasn't bright enough to recognize an opportunity when it slapped her in the face.

She followed a sign and went through an outside corridor and into the coral-toned powder room. While she was washing her hands and staring into the mirror, she wasn't seeing the image of Sarita Miller at all. Some other woman might have been complimented by Morgan's offer to join his Los Angeles office as overseer, whether or not she knew anything about finances, banks, shopping centers and construction. Or about oil, gold and antique coins. Sarita was a quick study, of course. But was she going to be Morgan's surrogate, his agent, his spy? Whatever had happened to her identity as his lover? Even—and wasn't this what she'd expected—as his wife?

Sarita was mortified to think how mistaken she'd been about the degree of their association. Oh, fine, she told herself. Is that what I'm calling love—degree of association? And did Morgan plan to have sex with her whenever he flew out from New York? With their heads together on the pillow, was she supposed to whisper to him everything that was going right or wrong at his West Coast office?

She dashed cold water on her face, her wrists, her temples—whatever needed reviving in a crisis. She would have to go back to the table. She couldn't just walk out. This wasn't a big city in which she could lose herself. This was one small island surrounded by the Pacific Ocean. Island fever occurred when one could no longer bear to know that there was nothing out there at all but water. One was stranded on a pinpoint of tiny land with no escape. Sarita guessed she had the fever.

On her way back to the table she walked through the long archway that contained a dress boutique, gift shop and miniature art gallery. All were closed, but brightly lit from within. To give herself time before facing Morgan, she stopped to look at the pictures on display in the gallery window. A very large watercolor depicting a cluster of pink and silver shells stood on an easel near the window. Sarita had learned to recognize conch shells and cowries, and the manner in which they had been painted seemed oddly familiar to her.

The shells appeared to be resting on a saffron-colored tray, similar to the one on the table in the guest house. She

moved closer to the window and peered inside. There was
no doubt—this large watercolor was identical to the smaller,
unframed paintings on the guest house wall. This one was
signed; the others were not. She turned her head sideways
in an attempt to read the fine brush stroke of the artist's
name.

One word only—Nils. Startled, Sarita stepped back.
Could this really be the work of the Nils she knew?

In the Teahouse dining room once more, she sat down
at their table, still dazed by her discovery.

"Is something the matter, Sarita?"

"There's a large watercolor in the gallery, signed by Nils.
Is it our Nils?"

"Yes. He's very talented, they tell me. He's always had
a fascination for shells. He used to dive for them. There
aren't many around here any more, but they're brought up
from the Philippines and Tahiti. It's interesting . . .
archaeologists have found shells in tombs thousands of years
old. There was a period in Africa when a wife could be
bought for a quantity of shells. American Indians used shell
beads for currency. Now they're subject to limitations. As
is true with so many beautiful objects, they're becoming
rare. Many can't be collected at all. But let's get back to
you, Sarita. To you and me."

This time she couldn't be caught by that seductive phrase.
"You and me" didn't mean the same to Morgan as it did
to her.

She picked up her handbag. "I've said all I intend to say
on that subject, Morgan. I couldn't possibly take over the
assignment you outlined. Again, thank you very much for
the offer, but . . ." Her voice diminished in intensity, and
she was terrified that she might cry. She never wept, but
the words he had spoken to her were so different from those
she had hoped to hear. She had believed true what she
wanted to believe. She had blithely ignored the reality.

"Look, we're going over to my place as we planned. I
wanted you to see it, remember? We'll talk some more.

Perhaps I can convince you to accept my offer. You don't want me to feel rejected, do you?"

It seemed to Sarita that Morgan spoke in a light vein, almost with amused disinterest. Wordlessly she shook her head. His rejection? What about her own?

"Something is bothering you. Can you tell me?"

Why did he have to sound so gentle now, and not disinterested? Why did she have to remember the wonder of what they'd had together, which had brought her so much joy? Sarita's eyes welled with tears, and she turned away hastily to pick up a silk scarf she'd worn earlier and tied it slowly around her neck. What would he think if she asked to be taken directly back to the guest house? To hell with what he'd think!

She turned back to him, her eyes dry. "Morgan, I've had a lovely evening. It's been an interesting talk. You've given me a lot to consider, but nevertheless, I can tell you the answer to your proposition will have to be no. I'm returning to Chicago to Peter Dome's agency. Eventually I'll be in business for myself. Didn't you once say that at age twenty-five, I should be picking up my options?"

"It was a joke. Twenty-five's very young."

"It's not too young to know what I want."

"And that is . . . ?"

Their conversation was halted by the arrival of the check. Morgan paid it, and they left the restaurant in silence. The darkness outside was only partially lighted by flaring torches placed at intervals along the path to the parking area. They went through an archway and over a small footbridge that crossed a brook in whose shallows night fish darted with the green and red iridescence of jewels. Their senses were assaulted by the seductive fragrance of plumeria.

Morgan stopped next to the side of the Jaguar he was driving tonight and repeated his question. "Sarita, what do you want?"

Sarita looked at the man she desired. It's you I want, Morgan . . . for all time and forever, she said to herself.

Morgan, love me with your heart as I love you. You've taught us both to love with our bodies, and we've said the words, but let your heart love me too.

The tearing emotion of her interior cry was so powerful that she almost believed she'd spoken aloud. But Morgan was still looking at her questioningly. Why couldn't he understand what she wanted? What was the matter with him? What was the matter with *her?*

Since she wasn't brave enough at the moment to speak the truth—that she wanted only Morgan—she replied, "I know what I don't want. And that is to share a business relationship with you, Morgan." When he looked confounded, she pressed on. "I do not want to go to an office and work for someone else—even you. I don't want to go home every night and return every morning and spend all my physical and mental energies in building something that isn't mine and never will be. That's what I'm doing at Dome. Do I sound selfish? I don't think I am. I don't want to talk business with you across a dinner table every time I see you." Her voice sank. "Or discuss commerce in bed with you." She tried to conclude on a lighter note. "It seems to me you've had enough of that in your life." As she said this, she sensed that these words were tasteless and could easily refer to his shattered marriage with Patrice.

Without a word, Morgan opened the door. Sarita got in. He slammed the door and went around to the driver's side and slid in next to her. His hands curved tightly around the wheel, and he looked at her. "We'll go to my place for no other reason than that I need time to answer you . . . tonight."

"Morgan, take me back to Napili." She almost added that she had a headache, but bit her tongue on that stupid lie. She spoke firmly. "It's late. I really do want you to drive me home." Was the guest house home?

The silhouette of Morgan's profile was darker than the night itself. He didn't bother to reply as he glided the Jaguar out of the parking area and onto Honoapiilani Highway. In silence he drove for a mile or so until they came to a turnoff that was unfamiliar to Sarita. Next they were on a tree-lined lane, heading toward the sea in the direction of a low-rise building set among the coco palms.

The car braked to a stop. Before Sarita could protest, Morgan was out of the Jaguar, opening the door on her side, gripping her arm and forcibly moving her toward a back staircase that led to an upper level. "Do I carry you?" he said grimly.

Sarita glared. "This is childish."

Suddenly he swept his arm around her and propelled her up the stairs. "But we're not kids, Sarita—we're man and woman. Grown-up people, remember?"

There was a brass lamp set above the door to the condominium. As Morgan inserted his key into the lock, Sarita stood stiffly in front of him, still held within the circle of his arm. She muttered, "Ridiculous," and refused to look out into the night or at the gardens and the pool below.

Morgan ushered her inside. The wind had begun its uneasy prowl, rustling the palm fronds that extended to the long balcony upon which they'd been standing. The reflection of lights from other occupied condos gilded the white railing. Sarita knew she couldn't make a scene. It was an impossible situation.

Morgan closed the door behind him, lit the interior lamps bracketed high on the wall and slid open the screen that led to the lanai. Sarita remained standing in the center of the room. She looked around her. Everything here was open; she could hear the ocean rumbling outside. Morgan reached up and pulled down a bamboo shade. The cooling winds still penetrated, but now she and Morgan had privacy. It was a simple and comfortable room, the seating arrangement covered with a sturdy blue and white cotton whose primitive design was one of deeper blues and earth tones. The floor was teak, the lanai laid with ceramic tile. The walls were painted a pale blue that seemed to extend the space around them.

"Will you sit down?"

Sarita continued to stand, slow anger kindling inside her. She'd meant every word she'd said to Morgan Wycoff. She wondered if he thought her actions were intended to tease; or worse, if she might be fishing for a stronger commitment from him of either a business or a personal nature.

Morgan was exasperated. He started to pace restlessly, then restrained himself. He knew his own tensions would only increase hers. "I invited you to dinner, Sarita, and asked you here to see my temporary home. It was going to be a special evening, I thought. Then I blew it for some reason when I made you a business offer. I considered it to be a good deal. For me first, admittedly. But for you too. Where did I go off tack? Why?"

"I told you why."

Morgan came forward, placed his hands on Sarita's shoulders and, with insistent pressure, urged her into the nearest chair. She collapsed there, unhappy and still wrathful. She glanced down at the violet silk blouse and pants she was wearing and thought with irony, And I saved these for a special occasion!

Morgan seated himself on a settee across from her. She eyed him warily.

"I guess you did tell me why," he said. "And I told you I was going to answer you, but that I needed time. I'm beginning to see what happened. You believe I'm following the same pattern with you that I had with Patrice all those years that she and I worked together, became very successful, then clawed each other like two caged cats. We did that—I agree. But we weren't compatible mates in that cage. You see that, don't you? If took me ten years to figure it out, and I'm supposed to be smart. But no one wants to fail in a marriage, even though the circumstances are bad." He paused. "With you and me it's different. My God, Sarita, you should know that, after what's happened between us."

Unsure, she continued to watch him silently.

"How could I expect you to understand what we have

physically?" he muttered. "You're not that experienced. Sarita . . ." He leaned forward, his fingers catching her wrists and holding them tight. "Let's end this evening the way we planned it."

"You planned it." The slightest smile crept into the full curve of her lips. She couldn't admit even now what it was she wanted.

"All right. I planned it." He rubbed his free hand gently along her jaw line, then smoothed back the tousled blond hair that touched the silk scarf around her neck. "There . . . that's the way I like you, Rapunzel."

He released her wrists and drew her closer, and since the settee in which he sat was designed for two, Sarita found herself in his arms, resting against his chest, her legs curled across his knees.

He cupped her chin in his hand, not realizing his urgent grip was hurting her, but she didn't care. Looking deep into each other's eyes, they seemed to share a glittering image of their bodies, unclothed and free, sensuously entwined. A wave of languor eased through Sarita, then shuddered into excitement as Morgan bent his head to hers. A tantalizing surge of desire quickened within her as she opened her mouth to his kiss and lifted her tight-budded breasts to his touch. She felt the firm pressure of his hand on her belly, and experienced an explosive prod of passion as he guided that hand downward inside the waistband of her violet silk pants.

Alex Firman climbed out of the nondescript small car he'd borrowed from an acquaintance. Keeping to the tree shadows, he walked to the phone booth at the rear of the parking lot. He left the door open so that the overhead bulb wouldn't go on, found the change he needed, inserted a coin and dialed.

When his party responded, he said, "They've been in his place since they left the Teahouse a couple hours ago. Lights still on. Nothing unusual. I'm going to pack it in." He listened, then complained. "No, I can't go up there. All those condos are occupied. There are plenty of people around. I'm a stranger." He waited a few moments. "You don't have to say that, you know. I'm doing you a favor."

Alex hung up, pondering. He could do one of two things. He could go to Morgan Wycoff and tell him that the bitch was having him watched. Or he could keep still and continue to hold Patrice's hand. He'd already told her it was evident what was going on with Morgan and Sarita. The girl was smart and pretty. Morgan was a free man. Why not? Alex was aware that Patrice had her own diversions. He was also sharp enough to realize that, although he'd tried to keep his distance from Patrice, each was beginning to learn too much about the other. When that happened, it could only be bad.

If he jockeyed around a little longer doing Patrice's errands, his curiosity might be satisfied as to why she was so keen on knowing Morgan's moves, financial and otherwise. If Morgan found him out, Alex could always say that keeping tabs on Patrice was part of the deal. Either way he was covered.

He felt better about the situation now. He went back to his car and thought some more. Smiling to himself, he took a match folder out of his shirt pocket, and using his left hand to disguise his handwriting, wrote a few words on it. Then he reached in through the open window of Morgan's Jaguar and tucked the matchbook onto the steering wheel.

He'd sleep better tonight having done this, but he'd still manage to watch the guest house when Sarita Miller returned. *If* she returned tonight. As he backed his car out of the lot, he glanced once more at the stairway leading to Morgan's apartment. He hoped the couple were having a good time up there. It would be very nice to pay Patrice back for being a woman—and a successful and rich one at that. Alex winced. Sometimes he suspected that something was wrong with him and that he might not be as shrewd as the security-background check on his résumé had promised him he was. He'd think about that another time.

In Morgan's condo bedroom he and Sarita drifted in and out of sleep, in and out of each other's embrace. They made love, they whispered their passion. In this bedroom of his, which was beautifully decorated in jade green and deep blue, like a sheltering cavern beneath tropical waters, Sarita felt safe—safe in Morgan's arms, safe in his love. No one could touch the two of them, ever. His lips on hers, his arms holding her, meant that everything would be wonderful for the rest of their lives. So it seemed. Sleepily Sarita thought, It's winter in other parts of the world, and outside those distant seas rock and roar . . . but here it's always bright summer. . . . The Maui waters are smooth . . . and on the island's enchanting shores grow orchids, white flowers and ferns. . . . She wasn't sure whether she was dreaming or really awake, until Morgan kissed her and she woke up and told him her dream about a cavern under the sea.

"We're not water babies," he teased, laughing.

"The reality is close to the dream," she said. And, of course, it was.

Chapter Eighteen

THE WORDS THAT SPUTTERED BETWEEN PATRICE and Alex Firman were low-pitched so that no one in the big house could hear them. The cook and his two assistants were sleeping downstairs. Nils was in his own quarters, and Maile was in hers. The distant sea lay like a band of dark silver while pale light from the emerging dawn tinged the scallops of lava rock that etched the shore. Patrice paced nervously, stopping momentarily to peer through the wide windows in her bedroom at the calm serenity of the scene far below.

Alex Firman sat gingerly on a chaise longue. "The sun rises in the east, Patrice. It's a sure bet. You can't do anything about it. In the same sense, you can't do anything about Morgan's having an affair with the researcher you hired."

Even at this early hour—the end of a long night for him—Alex's slacks were immaculately creased. His white shirt fit without a wrinkle across his chest and shoulders. He shoved the neat bang of sun-whitened hair from his forehead and blinked through his pale lashes to stare at the small woman in front of him. Alex had the appearance of a man sucked dry of emotional juice. With Patrice it was just the opposite. Her face was flushed and drawn tight, as if to conceal a boiling turmoil within. Her mouth was dry, her eyes bleak.

"Have a drink . . . relax, Patrice."

By rote she repeated, "Alcohol is poison. Why should I drug my brain? What—" She broke off her words as Alex stood up.

A warning nod of his head indicated the sleeping household downstairs. He walked out of the suite and into a connecting study. The room was small, with paneled walls, pale furnishings, a desk and many books. Alex opened a mirrored cupboard door behind which was a wet bar. From his trouser pocket he took a gold key chain, selected a key and opened a boxed compartment. Reaching in, he removed an oddly shaped bottle. It was one of the last of its kind left in the United States, where the possession of its contents had been prohibited for many years. Known as absinthe, the liqueur had at one time produced the exhilarating dreams that had enabled writers, painters and dilettantes both to relax and to experiment with enchanting ideas on paper and canvas.

Alex, who had introduced its delightful but forbidden effects to Patrice, partially filled a squat crystal glass with distilled water, then added a careful tablespoon of the green liquid in the bottle. He sniffed at the bitter liqueur, flavored with wormwood, anise, fennel and other aromatic spirits. He wanted to make sure that it was sufficiently weakened to provide rest and creative fancies without the danger of hallucination. The mixture had to be just right.

As he turned around, Alex was surprised to see Patrice standing behind him in the doorway. He moved forward gracefully and extended the glass to her. "Your tonic." Their eyes met. Alex had often wondered if Patrice was truly the innocent she seemed regarding this special drink.

Patrice accepted the glass, the faintest smile rimming her lips. "You are a fool, Alex," she complained. He wondered what she meant by that, but he was afraid to ask. Let whatever knowledge each had of the other remain in the shadows, undisturbed.

Patrice raised the glass to her lips. Alex saw her face

smooth, her color restore and her eyes darken until iris and pupil seemed to blend together. With a quirky, half-ragged smile, Patrice finished off the drink. "Spinach juice, isn't it?" Then she scowled. "I never act on impulse," she said, a remark that seemed decidedly non sequitur.

Alex's eyebrows shot upward. "Asking me to be your sentry last night at Morgan's condo was plenty impulsive. And I didn't like what you said to me over the phone. I had no idea you had such a bizarre vocabulary."

"Firman, don't give me trouble."

"Someoné else is giving you trouble, not me, ma'am. I'm doing what you ask me to do."

"And doing it badly."

Without explaining that last, Patrice spun around. She still nursed the crystal glass against her bosom. She was wearing a pastel-striped robe, tightly belted, that emphasized her small, pointed breasts. Impatiently she kicked a stool out of her way and reentered her bedroom to resume her pacing as well as her constant glances out the window. "That woman hasn't come back here yet."

"She's still at Morgan's," Alex commented unnecessarily. He didn't bother to add that Sarita was undoubtedly sleeping in Morgan's arms.

Recognizing the innuendo in Alex's voice, Patrice regarded him frostily. "You and I don't have a partnership, so be careful what you say. And think!"

"Talking like that doesn't help!" Alex snapped back. Realizing he had fired at Patrice too quickly, he gave her an apologetic, deprecating smile. "It's late—or early. However you want to look at it. Let's knock it off, shall we? You haven't been to bed tonight, and neither have I. A few hours sleep, and it'll all straighten itself out."

"What an idiotic thing to say! 'Straighten itself out.' What kind of Pablum is that?" Patrice bared her white teeth.

Was she smiling? Alex wondered. Or was she about to chew him up into little pieces and spit him out? Since he was uncertain of his position with Patrice at the moment, he felt very uncomfortable. So he said what could be interpreted as a safe remark in a situation like this.

"You're a beautiful woman—a brilliant and talented woman. But you're only doing yourself an injury by letting this thing get to you. Will you go to bed? Let me put you to bed." Tentatively he approached her.

"Just leave me, Alex." Patrice turned her head aside so that he couldn't see her expression. She was thinking, as she had thought before; Leave me forever, Alex, and that will do us all nicely. Aloud, she muttered, "Good night. Good morning. Whichever it is."

Alex Firman edged quickly and gratefully out of the room. He hurried down the wide stairs into the ivory-walled living area, in which the wooden paddle fan still revolved lazily. His next steps took him on a silent passage along a corridor toward his own quarters. He heard the sound of a car, cocked his head to listen and wondered if Patrice was at her rear window—the one from which she could survey the driveway in the back. He wished he could conjure up a magic trick and observe her reaction when the Jaguar stopped and Morgan and Sarita Miller emerged into this cool new day.

A smile skimmed Alex's eyes. He also wondered what Morgan had thought about the note left pinched into his steering wheel.

Sarita looked up at Morgan, her eyes the same color as the blue of the sky overhead. She was embarrassed at their bold arrival in the early morning light, since she was beginning to think of the Wycoff estate as Patrice's territory.

Bothered by the same feeling, Morgan said, "Look, we've discussed this . . . situation. We've agreed it's awkward, your staying here. You've finished most of what you were sent to do. So call Dome in Chicago and tell him what you've decided. I'll speak to Patrice about your leaving. I can't let you face her on that."

Sarita nodded slowly and wished they could share one

last kiss. Impulsively she leaned forward and encircled his hard-muscled waist with both arms. She could see the darkly tanned skin revealed beneath his unbuttoned shirt. She wanted to press her lips to his chest once more, to hear the thudding sound of his heart quicken at the nearness of her flesh. Certainly, she didn't want to let him go. Then, mentally ridiculing herself—what did she suspect could go wrong?—she stepped back quickly, sturdily.

"Don't walk down the path with me," she told him firmly. "We'll see each other later, won't we?" She waited for his answer. He gave her none, but his glance said enough.

Aware that he was watching, she ran down the path toward the guest house. At the last minute before the ferns closed behind her, she turned to look at him and lifted her hand. He was standing where she'd left him, in the driveway next to the Jaguar. She could feel the dark intensity of his gaze, the almost tangible reach of his passion. It seemed to Sarita as if she could open her hand and touch Morgan, touch love.

She placed one finger to her lips and blew Morgan a kiss. Slowly, and after a long moment, he raised his own hand in response to hers, then turned away. Sarita was startled at his next movement. She had expected to see him get into the car and drive off to his condo. Instead, Morgan entered the main house.

He had seen the flicker of shutters sliding against an upstairs window. At this hour it could only be Patrice observing from her bedroom. He moved through the silent house, entered his office and shut the door behind him. After crossing to his desk, he glanced out toward the swimming pool and the overhanging shrubbery, then beyond that to the meadow and the sea. His hand came slowly up to his shirt pocket, and he took out a small object, turned it over and reread the crude lettering upon it.

The torn outside half of the match folder was an anonymous blue shade. Almost undecipherable words were scratched across the inside. Morgan had extracted the note from the steering wheel when he and Sarita had entered the Jaguar a half hour ago. He might have tossed it away as a useless scrap of paper that had blown into the car, except something about it had scorched at his fingertips.

Translated from the language of the street, the message was clear. Whoever owned the Jaguar was being told to watch his step. Anyone could have left such a message on the steering wheel—a wealth-hating transient who had seen an expensive car left unattended, or a drunken tourist who had thought it would be a wonderful joke to play on the owner of a Jaguar. Even one of the guests at the condominium who might have observed Morgan and Sarita entering his apartment there could have reverted to a playfully coarse vulgarity of his—or her?—youth. But none of these possibilities were likely.

Morgan struck a match and watched absorbedly as the blue cover crumbled into its own curled ash. He made sure the ashtray was cool before he dumped its burned contents into a shell wastebasket under the desk. Then he sat down and waited. He'd heard the footsteps descending the stairs.

From his seat behind his desk, he faced the door as it opened. Small and perfect, wearing the gauzy type of costume that she affected, the woman he had once believed he was fond of walked toward him. He rose out of habit, at the same time thinking he was not a contemporary man at all and that etiquette and politeness still persisted.

"You've been around somewhere all night," Patrice said. "Mikimura's due today."

He threw back his head and laughed, a long, rolling, immoderate gloat of amusement. First he laughed at her euphemism—"You've been around somewhere all night"—when she knew damn well what he'd been up to. And secondly he laughed at her businesslike efficiency. Not only was she correct—he did have a two o'clock appointment with Mikimura—but the purpose of the meeting was important. For a long time now, he had wanted to finalize his company's plans to lease some desirable land from a Hawaiian family near Kahana. They all could be staggering under mortal blows, but Patrice would not allow him to forget financial acumen.

"Thanks for pointing out my duties to me," he responded dryly.

"Now that you've had your laugh . . ." Patrice picked up her flowing skirt and settled herself into a small chair near Morgan's desk.

Morgan thought she looked firmly planted there. He sighed. There was no getting out of this one, he guessed. "You saw me just now from your window?"

"You and my employee. It's an indecently early hour in the morning to bring her home."

"Which would lead you to suspect I've been out with Sarita all night—right?"

"Not 'suspect'—know! I know, Morgan. And I'd say you haven't been out, but that you've been inside all night."

Morgan didn't answer her. He was wondering if Patrice was being deliberately crude, which was not like her. Perhaps she didn't realize how that phrase might sound.

Finally he said, "We were at my condo."

"It's none of my business, of course. You're free—have been for years."

"But I've never stepped out of line before, is that it?"

Patrice shrugged. "I don't know what you mean by that cliché."

"I think you do."

"Then it's serious between the two of you?"

"Very."

"Send her back to the mainland."

"One doesn't 'send' Sarita anywhere. She's an intelligent woman who's done an excellent job of analyzing your prospective clientele and working out the pattern of your marketing structure."

"The strategy is mine."

"It's all yours, Patrice. No one takes that away from

you." There was a long pause. "You don't need Morgan Wycoff any longer."

Patrice's smile glistened. "Don't forget that the rich, corporate sound of 'Morgan Wycoff' has been built, in great part, by the Patrice label."

"Credit—monetary and otherwise—was given to you in our divorce settlement."

"A reminder to me?"

"As you've said, we're both free to do as we want. You too, Patrice. Not that you haven't."

Patrice wanted to ask Morgan what he meant by that. Wisely, she decided not to. She said instead, "Let's drop this. I do agree Sarita Miller's fulfilled her duties. She needn't move out of the guest house until she's ready to fly back to the mainland. I can see we won't need her for a year, as I'd supposed. But a week or so more . . ."

Morgan frowned. "Since you know about our relationship, I don't want any clumsy tactics on your part, Patrice. I trust you to handle this with discretion . . . and kindness."

"My public relations policy has always been impeccable." Patrice rose and moved toward Morgan. "You stood by me when I needed you."

Morgan also rose. He didn't want to let Patrice get too near him. Sentimentality was not her style, but, as she had pointed out, she was very good at public relations—and private ones as well. As one small hand with its undulating fingers reached out to touch his arm, he forestalled her intent by grasping that hand and shaking it firmly. "Man to man," he said, forgetting in the moment's unease that he mustn't be a male supremacist.

"Woman to man." Patrice's smile was alluring.

"I stand corrected."

"How original of you." Patrice's smile turned wry.

"Well . . . I'm tired." His look was a reminder of exactly why he was tired.

"Oh, yes." The way she said it, with a sibilant, hissing

sound, made Morgan wonder if it was wise to let Sarita stay at the guest house. But that was a ridiculous notion; they were all civilized people.

"Go on back to your place and get some sleep so you'll be able to bargain this afternoon. By the way, does Miki-mura have to go with you? Won't his Oriental presence ruffle the insular feelings of the Alunnua family?"

"Maybe you're right. Always thinking of my best interests, aren't you?" He gave her an enigmatic smile.

"Always." Her smile was equally cryptic.

Morgan eased past Patrice and held open the office door. Patrice gave him an arch look, which was somewhat out of character. "I'll catch a nap," she said, "and then I'll be in the lab." She seemed absolutely cheerful as she wandered out into the corridor in her gauzy dress, the sunlight from the lanai backlighting her perfect figure.

Morgan thought she might be up to something, but because the discussion concerning Sarita seemed to have gone smoothly, he was grateful enough to let matters ride. Now was not the time to rattle Patrice. He wanted some peace, and he wanted to get back to his place, shower, shave and grab some sleep before the two o'clock appointment.

He picked up the attaché case next to his desk, checked to be sure he had the appropriate papers for the Kahana lease arrangements, yawned hugely, then looked around his office with the thought that he would then be packing up soon and moving out. It had been nice here. The island was beautiful, with the myna birds, the sliding sea, the coco palms, the cloudless sky. Pele, the fire goddess, still held him in thrall, but he had other matters to enchant him now.

Sarita slept for four hours. When she opened her eyes, she felt more vividly awake then she had at any other time in her life. She was rested, hungry and aware of an acute aliveness. Vitality flowed through her, its alert energy seeming to burnish the room around her till the walls shone and the ceiling glowed. Her skin could still sense the soothing pressure of Morgan's arms. It was as though the palms of his hands, his embrace and his passion still claimed her. Her full breasts tingled at the memory of him and of his ardent lips . . . here and here. She raised her arms above her head, shivering agreeably as she recalled the sensual pleasures they had shared.

She kicked aside the covering sheet and flexed her legs straight up in the air. She admired her toes. So they were pearly delights, were they? She grinned, thinking of the audacities Morgan and she had perpetrated on each other's bodies. Their sexual expression hadn't been a swooning kind of thing—it had been fun! In fact, she wanted more of the same. Slightly embarrassed, she discovered her body was lushly ready for Morgan. Ah, Morgan . . . we have to be separate sometimes, she told herself.

She couldn't possibly work today. She'd have to evade both Patrice and Maile. Anyway, there was only one more report to finish. The conflict between herself and Patrice had never directly surfaced, but she knew she must tell Patrice that their association was at an end. The Night of the Rain Ginger, she thought dreamily. A fantasy title for what had turned out to be a very temporary project. She hoped Patrice's product would become successful, but her own part in it was concluded. She knew she had done what had been required of her, but now it was time to leave.

Today she would take the Toyota and do some sightseeing. She wanted to drive to Pineapple Hill and also climb down to Fleming Beach. But first she would go to the Kapalua Bay Hotel and look in the shops to find a special gift for Morgan.

She put on a pale blue split skirt and a matching shirt. Since her hair was sweeping her shirt collar, she found a piece of yarn in the kitchen and tied it back. Then she went out to the porch and locked the front door. A large mesh bag on the floor beside her held her camera and wallet.

"Where are you going?"

Sarita wheeled around. Patrice, clad in slacks and a black

leotard, stood with her arms akimbo, surveying Sarita. "Those don't look like work clothes you're wearing," Patrice remarked.

Sarita's response was cool. "They aren't."

"Life for you seems to be a series of days off."

"Not entirely, Patrice. I've turned in more than the quota expected of me. I'm not going to ask if you've been satisfied with the charts and reports, because I know they're exactly what you want."

"Very sure of yourself, aren't you?"

"Yes, I am. Aren't you sure of yourself, Patrice? Aren't you confident that your laboratory project is coming along well, that it will be accepted, that it will be successful?"

Patrice's dark eyes were cold. "I'm a bit bored with this ping-pong game of questions. Don't you think the two of us have had it, as they say?"

Sarita smiled. "Very definitely, I do. It's been nice and all that." Was she being fired right then? Yes, she was. "You know, Patrice, you and I have reached the same conclusion at the same time. I'm terminating myself. You just beat me to it by about half an hour."

Patrice smiled then too. *"Ciao,"* she said. And because Patrice prided herself on being an expert at public relations, she added diplomatically, "Let's hope the remainder of your stay will be pleasant." The tiny figure turned and started up the path, disappearing among the ferns.

Sarita stood staring after her. After that surprise, she wasn't even rattled when Nils stepped out of hiding behind the clump of bamboo. "Hi, wind surfer," he said. He waved an arm. "I heard it all. How does it feel to be out of a job and free?"

"I've always been free. But I have something much more important to talk to you about. Why didn't you tell me you're an artist? No one mentioned it, not even Maile. I saw your watercolor on exhibit in the Teahouse gallery. And you also did those lovely small paintings that are in the living room here. Why haven't I seen you sketching?"

"I've always painted. Everyone knows it. It's nothing unusual."

Sarita recalled that, last night at the Teahouse of the Maui Moon, it had been her impression that Morgan had rather casually dismissed Nils's very real talent. Sarita curved an arm around the porch pillar and leaned forward. "What do you plan to do with all that talent you have?"

"I came down to ask if you wanted breakfast—banana pancakes. But naturally I'd rather talk about myself." Nils was devilishly handsome. Sarita supposed there was an art patron in the background who sponsored him. His next words surprised her. "This is only between you and me, Sarita. I intend to go to California with Maile when she enters graduate school in September."

"She didn't tell me."

"She doesn't know it yet."

"Nils! She likes you a lot, and she hasn't been happy lately, stuck in that lab all the time and worrying about something—probably *you*, Nils. Why haven't you told her what you want to do?"

"There are certain—what d'you call it?—obstacles in the way. The need for folding money and . . . commitments I have to get out of."

Sarita held up her hand. "I can guess. There's a lady involved, and Maile knows it."

"Mmm . . . something like that. The money's not that much of a problem. I make gallery sales at Kaanapali. The lady . . . well, she *is* a problem. I won't say any more."

Sarita wondered who the "lady" was. It could hardly be Patrice, who appeared to keep herself free of physical entanglements for the sake of her career. Sarita became pensive. Did she really believe that story Patrice had handed out to Maile and herself during the first lab session? No drinks, no tobacco and certainly no high-test "Mowie-Wowie," the marijuana that was secretly grown among the sugar cane in some areas. Somehow Patrice didn't seem like the definitive "lily maid."

Nils apologized again for overhearing Patrice and Sarita. Sarita shrugged it off as they walked up the path toward her rented Toyota. The morning was practically unblemished. The polite confrontation with Patrice—as well as anything else about her—simply didn't matter. Now Sarita felt that nothing could go wrong after all. There was some easy explanation as to why Morgan had entered the main house at dawn instead of returning to his condo. She was certain of that.

Though she was starved for Nils's banana pancakes, Sarita didn't want to chance running into Patrice again. She slid into the car seat and leaned out of the window to pat Nils's cheek gently. "Please, Nils, tell Maile how you feel about her. It will mean a lot, to her and to you. I know."

Nils's response was laconic. "Not yet . . . later."

"Sometimes later can be too late."

Nils eyed Sarita sharply. "What d'you mean by that?"

"It just popped into my head."

"What they call . . . woman's intuition?"

Sarita nodded and turned the key in the ignition. The little car sprang into life. Nils stepped back and watched the Toyota disappear among the coco palms on the road to the highway.

From the lab window downstairs, wearing blue jeans and a smock, her lovely hair skinned back under a bandanna, Maile was watching Nils. And standing at the sink with rubber gloves on her hands, Patrice was watching Maile. She was almost certain now that it had been Maile on the cliff above the pool when she and Nils had made love there that afternoon. The way the younger woman was mooning around, she'd soon be making mistakes in the lab. If that happened, Patrice would have to get rid of her. The list of people who were no longer useful to Patrice was growing.

Chapter Nineteen

THE FIRST STOP SARITA MADE WAS AT THE Napili General Store, situated down a slope in a small grove of kiawe trees. The store area was stocked with swim fins, snorkeling masks and equipment, and bins of home-grown vegetables, papayas, guavas, local potatoes and Maui onions. Near the long shelf of canned goods, toothpaste and suntan oils stood a display of boogie boards. Sarita paused there, thinking she might come back later and pick one up. These mini-surfboards would be a better starting point for her than Nils's sailboards. Expertise, Sarita, she told herself—that's what you need!

Farther on was a refrigerator containing frozen foods, milk, yogurt, beer—all very expensive because they had to be shipped here by sea—and racks of T-shirts, current magazines and paperbacks. The General Store was a place where one could linger, sample some food items, meet people and exchange the news of the day. It also smelled wonderful.

Sarita bought film for her camera, a new pair of tennis shoes and several postcards. The clerk was a young girl who eyed Sarita's cropped-off split skirt with interest. Since most of the customers were in bikinis and T-shirts, Sarita guessed she might be considered dressed up.

On her way out she noticed the phone booth and remembered that she hadn't spoken to Peter Dome in days. She was really out of touch. This would have to change, especially if she accepted Morgan's offer of an executive position, which—for all her initial angry refusal of his suggestion—she was now beginning to consider. At least the possibility was there, and she could put it on the back burner and let it simmer. The night in Morgan's condo had made her less resolute. Was Pele, the fire goddess, working her magic? Sarita mused. Morgan had said these islands owned him. Could he leave Maui permanently? Sarita couldn't imagine Morgan striding through the crowds on New York's Park Avenue, for example, where the traffic signals and the maze of tall buildings would surely drive him wild.

The handsome Kapalua Bay Hotel was built high on a windy bluff and offered superb sea views. From the visitors' parking area Sarita crossed to a garden courtyard in which poinciana trees were ready to burst into masses of scarlet flowers tipped in orange and gold. Flowing bougainvillea vines, their sprays of varicolored blossoms vivid and dramatic, grew along a low wall beside flame and yellow hibiscuses. Sarita marveled at the sight. It was still winter gray in Chicago, yet here there was a brilliance of flowers everywhere.

Inside the arcade of the Kapalua's fine shops Sarita found a casually luxurious deli where three-tiered sandwiches were being made to order. The delectable fragrance of homemade pastries and pies vied with the aroma from the Kona coffee machine. Sarita carried a tray to one of the small tables in the courtyard. Over her selection—a slice of coconut-wrapped ham and a plate of the island's fresh fruit—she thought about a present for Morgan. It had to be unique.

Fortunately, with Morgan it wasn't a question of what she could buy this man who had everything. Sarita sensed that Morgan's life had been lived dashing from his executive offices to airplanes to board meetings, to private bank suites and to construction sites throughout the world. She strongly suspected he hadn't had time for the usual possessions—furniture, artifacts, houses—or even for the leisure of books, museum browsing, concerts or vacations. And yet he had taken the time to learn the history of the islands and about their peoples' early migrations from the Marquesas Islands and Polynesia, their legends and religious myths. Seemingly this was the extent of his culture and his relaxation. Strange man. She loved him.

Later, Sarita wandered through the attractive Kapalua shops, filled abundantly with gifts from every port in the world. There were enchanting handmade quilts, leaf and calabash bowls of rare native woods, Chinese silks, French clocks, German cameras. She finally chose an exquisitely carved tiny sea bird poised in flight. It was a small and perfect example of the early-day scrimshaw art practiced by anonymous American whalemen during long sea journeys. Morgan was certain to appreciate the historical background of her selection and, Sarita hoped, the implication of freedom that they both sought.

She was tucking the tissue-wrapped package into her mesh bag when a familiar voice called, "Ah . . . Miss Miller."

Surprised, Sarita looked up. "Mr. Mikimura!"

"Yes, indeed. It is pleasant meeting you. Will you join me for lunch on the Kapalua terrace?"

"I'd like to, but I've just had lunch here at the deli."

"Good, then we can go."

"Go where?" Sarita was baffled.

"To Hanalei in Kauai. I have business there and couldn't accompany Morgan to Kahana. He told me you might not be staying long in Maui, that you were planning an independent future. If this is so, you must see Kauai before you leave us. I'm fortunate to find you here. You can accompany me on my flight over." David Mikimura was smiling broadly.

Sarita was startled to learn she'd been the subject of conversation between Morgan and Mikimura. If she wanted to know why, she would have to ask straight out. "How did the subject of my . . . future come up, Mr. Mikimura?"

"David, please."

"David, then."

"That's better. I suppose it's because I'm Japanese-American that people think they have to be formal with me. It was my grandfather who did all that bowing. Oh, yes . . . it so happened that Morgan and I were discussing Patrice's project, and your association with her came up. That's when Morgan explained you'd finished your assignment very quickly and very efficiently. Shall we leave now?"

Sarita was hesitant. "I don't really . . ."

"Oh, come on, Sarita. Just pick up and run away with me. I'll show you Hawaii's dreamiest island. It has the old magic. The little grass shacks may be gone, and there's a lot of new development, but see it while it's still special. A short flight, that's all. My plane's waiting at the Kaanapali airstrip. I didn't know I'd be lucky enough to have company."

She wasn't sure where Kahana was, but it sounded as though Morgan would be there all day. She liked David Mikimura and had found him a good companion on the flight to Honolulu. She would go with him—why not? Also, there was the perplexing question of her "independent future." What exactly had Morgan meant by that? Was he casting her free, or was she supposed to be taking freedom on her own? She didn't understand.

She nodded. "I'll go with you," she told Mikimura.

Matters were quickly arranged. Sarita drove the Toyota the short distance back to Napili, saw no one around at the main house, parked the car and transferred herself into Mikimura's Datsun. After arriving at the private airstrip, Sarita adjusted her dark glasses, and they flew off into a bright blue, early afternoon sky.

Mikimura laughed at Sarita as she began scribbling in her notebook the details he was telling her about Kauai. It was the fourth largest Hawaiian island and was geologically and historically the oldest, having risen from the sea centuries earlier, born of violent volcanic eruptions below the ocean floor. It was also the last of Hawaii's independent kingdoms.

"What else?" she asked impatiently.

"Its lush green comes from the abundant rainfall, and therefore it's called the Garden Island. Got that?" Mikimura watched her with amusement. "There are mysterious legends there. Supposedly, a race of little people—two-foot gremlins known as the Menehunes—arrived long before the first Polynesians. How else can one explain the remarkable engineering feats whose remains have been uncovered? Were these people descendants of a lost colony? Could they have landed there by a flying saucer?" David's Oriental eyes glinted at Sarita's look of skepticism. "I believe in the Menehunes. Why don't you?"

A moment later they landed at Princeville. Mikimura hired a Subaru, ushered Sarita inside and drove off. When they stopped at a vantage point on the road above the incredibly beautiful Hanalei Valley, Sarita protested, "But you're taking time away from whomever you planned to see here."

David Mikimura waved a hand toward what he told her was the most glorious view on earth. "Forget time, Sarita. It only exists on calendars, which we don't have to look at today. And see?" He stripped off his wristwatch and slipped it into his pocket. "It's very simple. For us, time has stopped."

Sarita shook her head. "That's a perfectly lovely concept. All right, David, I agree." She took out her camera, laid the mesh bag aside and looked into the viewfinder.

Beneath them, like a reflection of the sky, a blue river ran through patches of rice and taro set out in squares of vivid green. Distant cliffs were spangled with shining waterfalls. At first Sarita saw one; then another and still another. They were like thin chains of molten silver gliding down the dark rock surface of the eroded mountain. Then Sarita and David crossed to the right side of the road to observe the mouth of the valley, which opened to the wide blue reaches of Hanalei Bay.

Once they were back in the car, the road wound down across a one-lane wooden bridge and led them on to tropical Lumahai Beach. There were no footsteps in the white sand, no bathers or trespassers; the tranquil beauty was lonely and untouched.

"Here serenity is protected by nature," David explained. "The undertow, the rocks and the current make this beautiful place unsafe for swimming. Pristine and nunlike, it cannot be ravished." He looked thoughtfully out to sea.

Sarita watched him curiously. Sometimes, she mused, one could never know the man. She had not expected sensitivity from this colleague of Morgan, but she should have remembered that his forebears came from a very ancient land where space and beauty were valued.

"David, I must come back here someday." Sarita did not add that it was with Morgan that she wanted to return.

Since David's business appointment was with one of the owners of a Hanalei Bay resort, a low-rise condominium grouping set on a plateau of cliffs that overlooked the turquoise sea below, Sarita waited for him on the terrace of the open-air Bali H'ai restaurant—a splendid place with an angled roof, colorful banners and bamboo and cane furnishings.

Sarita saw heavy mists suddenly appear from the island's interior, drifting and swirling above the dramatically serrated mountain peaks. Gray clouds, heavy with moisture, eerily obscured the land's jagged outlines. Finally, even the long, pure lines of distant waterfalls vanished in the mists. Sarita shivered at the sight, though sunlight continued to spill across the table at which she sat. For only a moment she thought of winter. Then she turned to face the sea, which still lay as bright as summer. This was not only another island but another world.

A waiter approached and Sarita ordered hot tea. She hoped David Mikimura would soon rejoin her. She wanted to get back to the private plane that was waiting for them in Princeville. She wanted to see Morgan again.

Two of her wishes were granted, and before long Sarita was sitting beside David as the plane circled Kauai's southwestern shore. She only half listened as he pointed out Poipu Beach with its white sand and spectacular surf.

"Sarita, there's the island of Niihau, where the beautiful shell necklaces are made."

Sarita peered down at a brown island lying low in the sea. It disappeared from sight as David told her about the private family that owned the island. Sarita was thoughtful. "The natives there lead a simple life, then, free from the problems of the modern world."

"Perhaps in a material sense, yes. But there are ancient problems that we all inherit, both spiritual and emotional. Would the heart of a Hawaiian woman dressed in an old-style muumuu beat differently from, say, your heart, Sarita?"

"Sometimes I think my heart is a mystery, too." Sarita smiled. "David, I will not be led into a self-indulgent discussion, though you tempt me. What's that jewel I see ahead of us down there?"

"Maui. Coming up fast."

It was dusk when David Mikimura let Sarita out of his car at the Napili estate. She thanked him for the day's outing and the generous amount of time he'd given to taking her sightseeing. As she walked in the direction of her parked Toyota, David glanced curiously toward the main house.

He had to get back to Kapalua, so there wasn't time to stop in and see Patrice, even if he'd wanted to. He wasn't too fond of Morgan's ex-wife, but he was glad she'd asked him to look up Sarita that morning and invite her to spend the day with him at Kauai. He had been lucky to run into her at the Kapalua Hotel shops. Yet he wondered why Patrice had been so insistent that he not reveal to Sarita that his invitation was at Patrice's suggestion. Some kind of surprise was brewing, he guessed, and the older woman had wanted Sarita to be out of the way during the arrangements.

Mikimura's impression of Patrice was not favorable. For all of her undoubted talent and early commercial success, which he respected, he considered her a rather artificial person, lacking in sensitivity and candor. He was surprised that Morgan Wycoff had been married to her as long as he had been. David had come to the conclusion that Wycoff's marriage must have been based on a European-style business partnership—and that he could well understand. On the other hand, Patrice and Morgan might have been too busy with their various enterprises to get around to dissolving their marriage earlier.

David Mikimura looked about him, measuring, as he usually did, the luxury of his surroundings. He was also estimating, as was also his habit, the current market value of the property, considering its extensive beach frontage, should Wycoff choose to sell. Mikimura had a Middle Eastern client who would definitely be interested.

Following the melodramatic flaring of the sunset, twilight was falling swiftly. Returning his thoughts to his coming dinner engagement with a group of Canadian investors, Mikimura switched on the Datsun's headlights and drove off toward the big hotel on the bluff.

Sarita reached into the glove compartment of her rental car to take out the tissue-wrapped gift for Morgan. Before going off to Kauai with David Mikimura, she'd placed the carved bird there for safekeeping and locked the car, not wanting to take the time to go to the guest house. As she started down the path to her own quarters, Maile called to her softly from the encroaching darkness. "Sarita . . ."

"Yes, where are you? It's about time you got out of that lab. Come on down to the cottage and talk to me."

Maile appeared from behind a cluster of traveler's-trees,

their odd, flattened foliage resembling a palm crossed with a bird of paradise plant. She was handsomely dressed in flowing white with a white headband tied around her forehead. The ebony sweep of her hair framed the dark ivory of her face, and her brown eyes seemed to glow in the evening light.

"I can't," she said. "I'm meeting Nils."

"That sounds promising." Sarita was pleased at the news. She was also curious as to whether Nils had told Maile of his plan to go to the mainland with her in September. But since Nils had spoken to Sarita in confidence, she couldn't question Maile about it.

"He made a big sale today and we're celebrating."

"That's great. By the way, Maile, I can't understand why no one told me that Nils is an artist, and a good one."

"He paints, he swims, he breathes, he is beautiful. Who talks about such things?"

Sarita chuckled and shifted the mesh bag she was carrying. "I don't know what to say to that, Maile. Anyway, have a wonderful time tonight. Did Patrice tell you to take off?"

"Individually, she did. She thinks Nils is going to the gallery at Kaanapali to get his check. She thinks I'm meeting two of my sisters in Lahaina."

"And where is our friend Alex Firman?"

"He is your friend?"

"Just a figure of speech. He's definitely not my friend, but I haven't seen him around."

"You can be sure he sees you around, and all the rest of us." Maile's reply was bitter.

"You don't like him either?"

"He is not one of my favorite people," Maile replied coolly.

"Nor mine."

Maile said good night and moved back into the shadows. Sarita hiked on down the path, wondering if the circumstances of Nils's "other woman" had been solved or

smoothed over. That was something else she couldn't ask
Maile.

She went up the porch steps, unlocked the door, turned
on the lights and swept on into her bedroom. She dumped
the contents of the mesh bag on the bed—camera, new
tennis shoes, postcards and wallet. Morgan's gift she carefully placed in a drawer.

Out in the living room, she started to pick up the phone,
then paused. There didn't seem to be an outside line on it
so that she could place a direct call to Morgan at his condo.
She'd taken his card out of her wallet to check the private
number he'd written on it. She supposed she could ring
through to the main house and ask to be connected to an
outside line, but whom would she speak to? None of the
other servants ever answered, and Nils and Maile had already left the house. She didn't want to speak to Patrice.
Or to Alex Firman.

Looking at Morgan's number, admiring the bold loops
of his handwriting, she began to laugh. They were intimates,
lovers, and yet here she was, holding his business card.

She wanted to dress up, meet Morgan, have dinner with
him, talk to him about Kauai, look at him, kiss him, love
him and go to bed with him. All in that order—or maybe
in reverse. She grinned knowingly.

The phone rang suddenly, startling her. Let it be Morgan,
was her instant hope.

"Hello?"

Patrice's voice purred, "You're finally back from Kauai."
She sounded friendly, as though nothing must interfere with
polite relations.

"How did you know I was there?"

"Oh! I—" Patrice continued hurriedly. "Listen Sarita, I
have a marvelous surprise. Come up to the house for a really
festive dinner party. Dressy time. I won't tell you any
more." The line went dead.

I'll be damned, Sarita thought. A festive dinner party?
No one social has been here at all. Patrice has never acted

as though she likes, or even knows, anyone else on Maui. Is the lady hermit finally breaking out of seclusion?

Sarita didn't want to go, but Patrice had sounded as if her presence were needed at a command performance. One more time wouldn't matter. And Morgan would probably be there. Patrice wouldn't miss a chance to have him act as host. Sarita smiled, a touch smugly. She'd wear her new pearl earrings and perhaps later—shameless thought—she would go to bed as promised, wearing one earring only and nothing else at all.

Chapter Twenty

DRESSED IN HER SLEEVELESS WHITE TUNIC AND green silk pants, Sarita started up the path. Not wanting to chance turning an ankle this time, she wore tennis shoes and carried her high-heeled sandals. She'd washed her hair, fluffy and curling almost to her shoulders. Morgan would like that, but Henri, the man who cut her hair in Chicago, would wince at her unshorn appearance. Too bad for Henri. He wasn't the one who was running his fingers through her hair these days—and nights. Morgan was the person to please.

The main house was brilliantly lighted, creating a real party effect. In the surrounding gardens tall torches blazed, their flames weaving dramatic light and shadow through the graceful growth of tropical planting. As Sarita came up the terrace steps she could hear music, and she glanced toward the driveway to see if Morgan's Jaguar was there. Surprisingly, there were no cars parked except the big station wagon that Alex drove.

She must be early for Patrice's gathering. Removing her tennis shoes, Sarita hid them near a railing post and stepped into the delicate sandals. Immediately she rose two inches in height. The green silk pants were now the desired length. She swished around, spinning on a stilt heel, feeling pert

and sassy and happy—and as fey as Tinker Bell. She recalled the sensation in the airport colonnade at Hilo when,
walking at the stranger's side, she'd seemed ready to take
off and fly. At that time she hadn't known the intriguing
man beside her was Morgan Wycoff.

Somewhere inside the house the stereo blared. Sarita
peered through the doorway leading to the formal white
salon. No one was there. As usual, the wooden paddle fan
revolved overhead, and Sarita knew she would always think
of this room as the Casablanca Room. The sound of music
muted a bit as she moved toward the bar and lanai on the
far side of the terrace, where she thought she had heard
voices and laughter. Now there was only silence. She
crossed the threshold to the darkened lanai—

Whispers, titters, then the lights leaped on.

"Surprise!"

Sarita stared in astonishment at what must have been a
rehearsed tableau of five faces turned simultaneously in her
direction.

Peter Dome. Meg Kirby. Ross Bailey.

From behind the bar Alex Firman wore a saturnine
expression. Sitting in the big peacock chair was an impassive
Patrice.

It was the kind of moment that could exist only once in
an eternity, where one juggled a shattering event with the
necessity of quickly recovering one's cool. In Sarita's case,
she felt like screaming and running, but she managed to
smile, make circles of delight with her mouth and appear
to be happily speechless.

The memento from her past, Ross Bailey—that handsome, prematurely graying, take-charge man—advanced
toward a seemingly paralyzed Sarita. He clasped her hand
possessively and led her forward.

Absolutely splitting with good humor, Meg put her arms
around Sarita and kissed her. "Am I overstating it if I say,
'Here we are, babe'?"

Peter Dome patted Sarita's shoulder, grinning the width

of his urbane face. "Good to see you, good to see you," he kept repeating. Then, rakishly, he began to hum a Bahamian calypso tune they were all familiar with called "Island Woman."

Meg applauded. "You're right, Peter. Look at that gorgeous tan she has! Look at that wild hair! She's gone native on us!"

Sarita ran her fingers through her sun-streaked hair. She was casting around for something marvelously warm and cheery to say that would express her pleasure at the sight of these dear, familiar faces. Weren't they dear? And if not, why not? The answer came immediately. It was because Ross Bailey was with Meg and Peter.

Yet Ross appeared to have a little more sense than the rest of them. Or perhaps he'd had fewer of the potent *mai tais* Alex was mixing. Bailey held up one hand, requesting silence. "Give Sarita a chance. We aren't exactly the nine wonders of the world to drop in on her like this." He glanced at Patrice. "Even if this super lady did arrange it."

Ah, yes, Sarita mused. It was as simple as that.

Meg's response was icily tart. "We love Sarita. Of course she's glad to see us. No one's implying otherwise. And Patrice was wonderfully kind to bring us together this way." Dome's senior vice-president sent their hostess one of her biggest and most tactful smiles.

Ross was still holding Sarita's hand. In fact, he was pressing it affectionately, starting with a squeeze at the tips of her fingers and working across the knuckles and into the palm. "We're your Chicago chums come all the way out here to take you back with us. Patrice says you've done a great job for her."

Sarita managed to release her fingers from Ross's clutch. She knew her palm must be sweating. She couldn't help the shock she felt. She had to be bright-minded in a hurry and start coping.

Everyone seemed to be looking at her, watching, waiting.

It was her turn. She gave them an urchin's grin. "I don't know what to say."

Peter ordered, "Say it anyway. Speech!"

She was fast getting hold of the situation. "It's wonderful to see you all. *Reahlly* it is." She mimicked a Hepburn intonation, her face alight as though they were lilies to be gathered. She put her arms around all of them at the same time. "I am just so darned surprised!"

At that moment Patrice took center stage. "I've been telling each of you that Sarita has worked very fast and expertly here. With the little time she's had in the lab, she's picked up the kind of information she needs, and her forecasts are most encouraging. Morgan and I are pleased. The next step is computer information—or whatever it's called. And that means back to Chicago. Peter?"

Peter nodded. "The best main-frame computer in the business is in our office, and Sarita's a wizard at dealing with it. We'll be glad to have her back."

Oho?! was Sarita's silent comment.

Patrice stood up, tiny and commanding. At the same time, she looked entrancingly youthful as well as regal in her white silk pajama costume, silver threads tracing across her dainty bosom. Three pairs of eyes turned away from Sarita as though mesmerized by their bewitching hostess. Only Alex Firman continued to stare at the younger woman, his avid though wary interest compelled by the trapped expression he hoped to observe in her blue eyes. This was the way he liked a woman to look—appealingly vulnerable and wavering on the precipice of panic.

But Alex was only seeing what he wanted to see. There was no panic in Sarita. After the first shock had worn off, she felt amused, then a flash of anger that was spreading fast. Patrice had arranged this get-together for her own purposes. The promising offer to Sarita of independent research under her own logo and the Wycoffs' patronage, which had been hinted at by Phoebe Adams in Los Angeles, was being

231

summarily wiped out. Sarita was being handed back in a very slick manner to Dome Advertising. If Patrice's project took flight, as everyone concerned hoped it would, Dome would still handle her account. But Patrice had made it plain that Sarita's usefulness here was finished. Sarita was practically on her way back to Chicago and her old friend, the main-frame computer.

Sarita half closed her eyes. What was to become of "The Night of the Rain Ginger"? She almost asked the question aloud and then decided not to. She couldn't bear it if that alluring label were shot down too.

Something was very wrong here. Patrice would hardly have brought Peter, Meg and Ross out to the islands on the Wycoff expense account merely to see that Sarita returned Had Patrice acted this way because she hoped to separate Sarita and Morgan Wycoff by both half an ocean and half a continent? Patrice didn't have that kind of clout. Morgan was his own man. So what was the missing piece that fitted the puzzle?

Ross Bailey was at his most charming as Sarita's dinner partner. Amazingly, he was behaving as though their engagement were still on. Sarita could barely keep her dislike of his manipulative deceptions under wraps.

During dinner Peter Dome and Alex were attentive to Patrice. Meg seemed fascinated by the native dishes she was being served by the two Polynesian girls who were the cook's assistants. A seventh place had been set at the oval table, but it had not been occupied. At a peremptory signal from Patrice, its Wedgwood-blue service plate and baroque silverware had been quickly cleared away and the other settings rearranged so that no trace of an empty presence would remain.

It was after ten o'clock when dinner ended with coffee and liqueurs. Alex was to drive the three guests to the Maui Regency at Kaanapali Beach, where they were staying in what Sarita guessed must be very plush surroundings. Cheerful, red-haired Meg Kirby looked overheated in her mainland clothes. She'd shed her Shetland wool jacket, but the hand-knit pullover and gray flannel skirt were not appropriate attire for a warm, tropical evening. Since she'd just arrived today, she hadn't had time to search out resort clothes in the Regency's luxurious boutiques.

Sarita wanted to get Meg alone for a good gossip. The two Dome executives and Ross had obviously made a quick decision to fly out to the islands. From everything that had been said so far, Patrice appeared to have been the instigator of the idea. Yet Sarita wasn't sure of that, and she didn't trust Ross Bailey either.

The others went ahead to the station wagon. Patrice, standing in the doorway, made a statement that astounded Sarita, who was getting a little tired of surprises. She knew that Patrice seldom left the estate, but now Patrice was saying, "I want you to go with them, Sarita, and I'll go too. It doesn't seem hospitable to turn our friends loose this way at the evening's end. It isn't all that late."

Not quite innocently, Sarita asked, "Couldn't they have been put up here instead of at a hotel?"

From beneath the veil of fine brown bangs, Patrice's eyes were cold, indicating that Sarita was being presumptuous to make suggestions to her. "Ross must have a suite in case he wants to conduct any business on the island. So must Peter. We don't have that kind of space in this house. I couldn't ask Meg Kirby to share your quarters with you, could I?"

Sarita tendered her sweetest smile. "Of course not. After you, Patrice." She followed Patrice Wycoff's size four figure as it moved down the steps to the station wagon.

Under the dim light of the moon's last quarter, the Maui Regency was fantastically impressive and beautiful as it sprawled across its twenty acres of beachfront property.

233

After Alex halted at the valet parking station, the strategy seemed to be that everyone had to come inside for a nightcap.

With Ross attentive at her side, Sarita moved through the enormous atrium lobby, whose floor was laid with Arizona flagstone, toward a seventy-foot-tall banyan tree, the lobby's centerpiece. From overhead, raucous cries signaled the balancing act of several handsome peacocks that were strutting across a second-floor balcony. Close at hand in the indoor, gardenlike setting were tropical plantings and vivid green and red parrots fluttering their wings, both inside and outside of cages. Stilt-legged pink flamingos minced delicately within a grassy enclosure.

In the Swan Court, graceful black and white swans glided along a shallow stream that flowed through the room to the lava banks outside. Penguins jostled for position on a bed of lava rock in the central stream. Peter shook his head as the group was led to a table. "Is that real? Maybe we don't need that drink. Patrice, how did you find this Arabian Nights extravaganza?"

"One can't very well miss it, dear Peter. I seldom travel beyond the bounds of our property, but I'm aware that this luxury inn exists."

Ross Bailey's smile flashed in agreement with Patrice. "How about calling it Maui's Disneyland for grown-ups?"

Sarita and Meg exchanged glances. It was as though they were back in the Chicago office, sitting in at a conference. Meg's gray eyes said, "Ross is playing politics." Sarita's blue gaze responded, "Do I have to say I told you so?"

Aloud, Meg said, "It was still light when we arrived, and we saw it all. It's a gorgeous place, with a golf course, tennis courts, health spa, Japanese gardens, lagoons. There's a swimming pool that has a whole acre of fresh water in which you can swim under waterfalls and bridges. It even has a sensational one-hundred-foot swimmers' slide I'm going to try out tomorrow."

Peter's smile flickered. "You're on your own, then. Tomorrow—all day—I'm staying at the grotto pool bar, the one with the great underwater view of all the bathers. See you around, Meg."

Patrice's scarlet lips curled in a faint show of distaste. It was Ross who was quick to observe their hostess's mood. He bent gallantly toward her. "Patrice, I did some exploring myself late this afternoon. Let me show you the original art displayed in the upper corridor. There are splendid works from the Far East and the South Pacific. There's also a nice little gallery that exhibits local artists. You might find it amusing. Coming, Sarita?"

Sarita could recognize a throwaway line when she heard one. She was not going to accept Ross's pretense that they were still a couple.

"I'll stay here at the table and talk to Peter and Meg. It's been weeks, and we've a lot of catching up to do. You and Patrice go ahead. We'll be along later."

Before Sarita had finished her sentence, Ross and Patrice were up and away. Half to herself, Sarita murmured, "What d'you know? So that's the way it is." She turned to the other two, who were looking at the list of after-dinner drinks.

Meg had put on her jacket. "Thank the good Lord for air conditioning. Why does Madame Patrice keep her house so warm?"

"The trade winds are supposed to air-condition it, and most of the time they do. Tonight they kind of subsided. Oh, Meg and Peter, it's so good to see you!" It would only be better if Morgan walked into the Swan Court. He was one surprise she could take.

Peter's smile crinkled with good humor. "You've missed us? We've missed you. That Patrice is a great-looking woman for a miniature. How old would you say she is? When they're tiny that way, do they look younger?"

"Where's your sensitivity?" Meg chided him. "You want to be charged with discrimination, asking a question like that?"

"The woman's a beauty. And a brain. I just wanted to know—"

"Don't ask. Come on, Sar, tell us all about everything before the others get back. Or before we catch up with them. Whichever comes first. And, Peter, if you promise not to make any more disgusting remarks, you can talk too."

They discussed Patrice's account and whether it was solid with Dome. When Sarita told her colleagues what she'd learned about Patrice's youth concept, Peter whistled softly. "'The Night of the Rain Ginger' . . . you thought that up? I don't know what it means, but it has a good fantasy sound to it. We could really work with that."

Meg was less sanguine. "First let's wait and see—make sure the rest of it isn't a fairy tale. It sounds a little sci-fi to me. I can't believe any chemical wand—or laboratory spritz—could make our faces young again. How I wish it were true! Tell me, Sar—what's Morgan Wycoff like? Do you get along with him, see much of him?" Meg watched Sarita intently. "You never seemed to mention him in your phone calls to Peter. I mean, is he a factor or isn't he?"

"I . . . see him."

"He's supposed to be hardheaded. Those rich guys aren't very much moved by impulse or goodwill, at least those I've come in contact with when I've had to work on their accounts. I assume he's a realist like Ross, so what's his attitude toward Patrice's achievements?"

"He's very supportive."

"What does that mean?"

All at once, and perhaps a little too obviously to her friend Meg, who was still interested in the subject at hand, Sarita asked, "What's happening in Chicago besides blizzards? We can talk about Morgan Wycoff another time. I want to know about the office. Does Coombs Corp still have its real estate holdings on the market? Was my projection correct?"

Meg was distracted, and she answered with enthusiasm. "The Coombs analysis you did before you left was fine.

Your research on them was on the button, and I'm glad we hung in there with them."

Sarita nodded, but she was really thinking about Morgan. Somehow she didn't want to discuss him with Meg and Peter—just yet. The subject was sensitive. There was his offer to her to mull over—should she or shouldn't she agree to join his Los Angeles office? What would that do to her independence? To her love for Morgan? To her own ambitions and future plans? Yet did anything in her future not include Morgan?

"What was that, Peter?" she asked.

Peter was leaning forward. "I said Coombs will hand their new accounts to us. The contract's signed on the frozen foods, and we've got commitments on a couple of other items. Ah, but let it go, girls. We're on Maui. Let's talk about . . . See those stunners!" His brown-eyed gaze followed a couple of beautiful women as they crossed the Swan Court to their own table of friends.

Meg's smile was polite and fierce. "Cut off his *mai tais*, somebody. Your eyes aren't focusing, Peter. Sarita and I are over here, please."

"Okay, you two women—what'll we have? You know what a Maui Moon Beam is?" He was again scanning the after-dinner liqueur list.

"Let's be conservative. A Rémy for me. What about you, Sarita?"

"Nothing, thanks. Except some information. Tell me the truth. What are you two doing here? I don't have to ask about Ross. He's onto something like a retriever, or he'd never have left Chicago."

"We thought you were the attraction for Ross." Meg twirled a curl of red hair around her little finger.

Sarita shook her head. "He may have been acting that way, but that's all it is—an act. I think he's headed in another direction."

"Gad, you're the suspicious one. By the way, where's that dragoon who drove us here in the station wagon? He

237

didn't say much during dinner, and I think we lost him in the lobby—or whatever that lush ballroom out there is called. I should say zoo. Have you ever seen so many animals walking around? Or birds? That would be an aviary, wouldn't it?"

"Is the subject Alex Firman? I don't think we've lost him. He's around. He denies it, but I think he's some kind of bodyguard."

"Oh, then he might be in that upper corridor looking at etchings with Ross and Patrice."

"Etchings? You just may have something there, Meg. I wonder . . ." Sarita wondered about something else. Should she tell Meg and Peter she was no longer on the Wycoff account?

Meg yawned. "Keep wondering, then. Jet lag is catching up with me. It's been a long, long day. We'll have a good talk tomorrow, Sarita. Excuse *moi*. I'm on my way for my room key. You can have my drink if you'd like."

Peter and Sarita watched Meg leave.

"You must be tired too, Peter."

"It's a helluva distance to come, but this place is beautiful and worth every mile to get here. Interesting to meet Patrice. She's a legend, isn't she?"

"Let's hope it's a legend that will come alive again."

"That's nice of you to say, because I don't think you really like her."

"Why do you say that?"

"Not that it shows. But, pet, she doesn't like you. I can see it, taste it, smell it—though it's all beneath the surface. Trust Peter Dome, the Merlin of Michigan Avenue. He knows."

Sarita was annoyed. "Is it your woman's intuition that tells you these crazy things?"

"Sure is. How do you think I made it so big if it weren't for my womanly intuition?"

"You finally admit it! Anyway, neither you nor Meg answered my question about the real reason you're here."

Peter tasted his drink. "Would you believe . . . I'm not sure myself. And it seems to me you were pretty elusive with Meg a while back when she was trying to pump you about Morgan Wycoff."

Sarita turned away from Peter and crooked a finger at a nearby waiter. When he bent solicitously over her, she slipped a bill from her wallet into his hand, reached up and quickly removed the purple orchid lei from around his neck. An unsuspecting Peter watched her action with interest. Sarita leaned across the table, and as Peter automatically tried to duck, she looped the flowery lei over his well-groomed head.

Sarita beamed. "There . . . that looks smashing with your tweed jacket. Just an old *aloha* custom. Peter, *aloha* means both welcome and goodbye. In this case, it's good-bye. It's time for me to go. Oh, what's your room number for the drinks chit?"

It was while Peter was signing the tab and they were both giggling at the incongruity of the enormous orchid lei decorating his city clothes that Alex Firman shot into the Swan Court and angled immediately toward their table.

Sarita caught sight of him and whispered, "Here comes the security force. He must have lost Patrice and Ross. Patrice and Ross," she repeated. "Now *that*, Peter, is certainly a twenty-four-carat combination."

"You trying to tell me something?"

"Maybe I am."

Just then Alex was beside them. "You're leaving," he said, almost in a whine.

"We are. Peter's tired, and I was going to walk out to the desk with him. If you have to go find Patrice, go. It's okay with us, Alex. I think Patrice and Ross went up to see some art exhibit on the second floor. I'll wait in the lobby for you."

Alex gave Sarita a venomous look. It certainly sounded as if she were giving him an order. "Go," she'd said, and he hated that. He decided that she and the ad man from

239

Chicago who was wearing that ludicrous lei around his neck had been drinking too much. Even though he'd never seen Sarita Miller take more than a sip or two of wine, he figured she probably drank on the sly. He had a good example of that in Patrice and her so-called vegetable tonic. He hadn't wanted to be a "guest" at dinner tonight, but Patrice had insisted . . . and then Morgan hadn't showed up as expected. What a selfish bastard. They all were bastards.

With an effort Alex spoke silkily. "I'll go look for Patrice. I won't be long. I'll see you in the lobby, Sarita. Good night, Dome." He walked off, his shoulders as straight as a drill instructor's in boot camp.

Peter yawned.

"Oh, Peter, I'm sorry. You're tired. We'll talk tomorrow."

"Tomorrow I'm going to retreat into silence. And sun. It's snowing in Chicago. I'm tired of all that. I have to spend my life on the phone . . . talk, talk, decisions, decisions, making deals, reading rate cards, budgets, being accountable for every damn thing that happens. Tomorrow I shall be a golden boy. You can some pay me homage if you want. But no talk."

They walked out of the Swan Court together. Peter got his key and disappeared under the banyan tree in the lobby. Sarita stared after him. She really owed it to Peter Dome and the agency to discuss with him Morgan's offer to her. But if she did that, Peter might think she was angling for a salary raise or a title on the door or a corner office—or all three at the same time. Better to say nothing for right now. She sat down in the lobby to wait, and to think about Morgan.

Chapter Twenty-one

SINCE THEY WERE THE ONLY OCCUPANTS IN THE
Maui Regency's elevator, Maile and Nils faced each other,
standing very close together and holding hands. Like everything else in the hotel, the sumptuously paneled elevator
was unusually large, with a cushioned bench running the
length of its rear wall. Maile saw none of this. Her attention
was concentrated on Nils as he raised her fingertips to his
lips and kissed each one lingeringly.

"I think I'm falling in love," Nils murmured, and ran the
back of his hand down the smooth ebony slide of Maile's
hair. He bent his head and kissed her moist, half-opened
lips. "Can't help it."

Maile whispered, "Don't ever try to help it. Give in to
our baser impulses any time you want to."

"How about right here? I could get really base." Nils
grinned, indicating the elevator's padded bench.

"I think not." Maile made a pretty face at him as the
elevator doors slid open. They stepped out into the elegant,
high-ceilinged reception area on the second floor. Maile
looked around. "Oh, wow—I had no idea!"

"Yep, this is where I hang out. And Fanné has kept the
gallery open so I can get my hands on that check. It's a big
one—five hundred dollars. It'll take us places."

To their right, a row of luxury shops extended along a wide corridor. It was nearly midnight, and only a few of the hotel's guests were wandering about, looking in the windows at cashmere sweaters, Gucci bags and Piaget watches.

Directly opposite Maile and Nils, a series of miniature Chinese sculptures was displayed behind heavy glass. The couple moved across and looked in at the magnificent gilt-bronze mythical flying beasts.

Maile tilted her head. "Someday, Nils, you'll have an exhibit right here, where everyone can see it."

"Nope."

"Why not?" Maile looked into the gray-green eyes that gleamed down at her.

"Why not in New York? Or maybe London . . . Paris?"

"You are an arrogant"—she reached up and kissed him— "kid!"

"You gotta have faith in me."

"I do. Five hundred dollars is a lot of money. For now. Don't rush too quickly toward your future—enjoy the flowers along the way. Oh, Nils." Maile leaned against him, intensely happy that Nils had explained to her—and was genuinely sorry for—his brief sexual episode with Patrice. Loving Nils, Maile was only too delighted to forgive.

"Come on. Fanné won't wait much longer." Nils pulled Maile after him down a narrow corridor that veered off at an angle from the main reception area. They rounded a corner and almost immediately entered a long, dim room, its overhead floodlights extinguished. Maile moved more slowly behind Nils as she scanned the partitioned exhibit areas.

Displayed against raw burlap sacking were pen-and-ink sketches, pastels, a few oils, and watercolors of local scenes that were familiar to her—the small boat harbor at Lahaina, the sailing ship anchored permanently near the breakwater, surf pounding over rocks into a secluded bathing cove, Lahaina's landmark Pioneer Inn. Maile stopped in front of two of Nils's watercolors. One showed clusters of sparkling shells lying on dark, wet sand. The other depicted rainbow cloud effects over the West Maui Mountains. It was this latter picture that wore a tiny red sticker, which meant it had been sold.

Nils called out, "Fanné?"

A tall, round woman in a chic black dress appeared. "You took your sweet time," she said grumpily, yet her tone revealed her fondness for the young man. She looked him up and down in a maternal fashion. "Still in blue jeans, I see. Even if they're pressed, couldn't you have dressed up a bit? And who's this? Molly McIntosh, isn't it. I know your sisters. You work at the Wycoffs'."

"Now she does, but she's going to school in California in September." Amused by Fanné's chatter, Nils glanced at Maile. "You can put up with my favorite Fanné, can't you? She knows everything there is to know about her business."

"I'm glad you've learned enough not to call my business an art. So, Molly, isn't the University of Hawaii good enough for you?"

"I'm going to graduate school at UCLA."

Fanné raised a pencil-thin eyebrow, then nodded toward Nils. "Taking him with you? You'd better not. He must build his reputation right here. Everyone important comes here from everywhere in the world. You know what they say: *Maui no ka oi*."

Maile laughed, her teeth very white, her eyes twinkling. "Not that old line again—'Maui is the best.'"

"Exactly that old line. You can't beat the truth. You want your check, Nils—I took out the commission. I love you like a mother, but still you have to pay me."

"It's okay, I'll pay—any way you want." Nils kissed the tip of Fanné's nose. "And, Fanné, thanks for keeping the gallery open and waiting for us this late. I took Maile over to Pukalani to meet my folks."

"That serious, is it? Then I forgive you." Fanné looked

over Nils's shoulder. "Ah, we have customers. Probably lookers, rich lookers. I can tell. Sign for this, will you, Nils? I'll be back in a minute. Have to tell these people we're closed." Fanné rustled off, all black taffeta and clicking high heels.

Half curious, Maile turned to gaze after her. "Oh, no! Nils!"

"What is it?" Nils glanced up from the paper he was signing and glanced at Maile's face. Then he also turned. His face blanked. "Jeez . . ."

Slowly he looked back at the paper that showed his obligation to Fanné. He finished writing his signature, added the date, folded the check, put it into the breast pocket of his pale blue flowered shirt, sighed and turned once more— to face Patrice Wycoff and the distinguished-looking man who accompanied her.

Fanné sensed there was a complication. Her eyes shifted from the tiny woman with the pert bangs and the big, sad eyes to the well-dressed man beside her. Quickly Fanné's gaze went back to the woman, whom she had thought looked familiar. She knew she recognized that face, but only from fabulous pictures in magazines of a few years ago. Fanné had a trained memory. "Mrs. Wycoff . . ." she said soothingly.

Patrice brushed aside the gallery's proprietor by merely raising the palm of one small, authoritative hand. Fanné, with artistic acumen, immediately and accurately judged the tensile strength of those fingers. But what was going on here? And then she remembered what she should not have forgotten. Nils, as well as Maile, worked at the Wycoffs'. She made a swift and accurate connection: Nils, the sexy young man, and this dominant, dark-haired beauty who was old enough to know better. But one was never too old when someone who looked like Nils was concerned. Oh, Lordy, Fanné thought.

She spoke firmly. "The gallery is closed." The ineffective phrase filled up the stormy silence.

The man said, "Let's go, Patrice. There's nothing here anyway."

Fanné glared at him. Had he intended to insult her small gallery?

Patrice's red mouth pursed. "Ross, you haven't met these two people, who work for me."

"Oh?" Interested now, Ross moved forward. He took the measure of the young man and dismissed him as too good-looking in an uncommonly strange and foreign manner. The girl was an exotic, probably one of those intriguing island blends of Polynesia and the Occident.

"Molly McIntosh—her native name is Maile—works in my laboratory. Morgan and I have subsidized her education."

Maile wanted to correct Patrice, but she refrained from doing so. The Wycoffs had helped out only during Maile's last year at the university. Maile's assistance in the lab and her domestic duties had more than repaid them.

"And this is our houseboy, Nils," Patrice continued. "By the way, did you get your little check for the thing you did? That was your reason for asking for time off tonight, wasn't it? Maile, I thought you were spending the evening with your sisters. Since we had guests, I could have used you to serve at table."

The gallery owner well understood the mistake of insulting resident wealth on the island. Even though she was fairly sure she understood the reason, Fanné couldn't stand by and see these two young people bullied by Patrice Wycoff. So she decided not to speak, but to act.

Maile's face had paled. Before Nils could respond explosively, as he had seemed about to do, Fanné's instinctive sense of drama intervened. Besides, she was on her own turf. The protective overhead tubing panels had been removed in this section of the studio, which made it easier to study the canvases. Fanné raised her hand and placed it flat against the electric switch on the wall. Immediately there was a flood of harsh neon lights.

Under the merciless brilliance, Patrice's full-lipped mouth and mysterious eyes became tired artifacts imposed upon tight, frail-looking skin. Ross's bold nose appeared to extend into a predatory beak, shadows deepened into grooves surrounding a thin mouth, his chin diminished.

What could be seen now of those two faces presented a startling contradiction. Their presumed strength and maturity vanished under an electric eye of truth. In Ross's case, power and suave good looks disappeared, replaced by a speculative craftiness. As for Patrice, style and seemingly youthful allure surrendered irrevocably.

It was war declared without pain, except to vanity, and Fanné was fascinated. She was as clever a judge of the interior of people as she was of her canvases and water colors.

Furious because she knew what it had done to her, Patrice wheeled away from the glare. An unaware Ross Bailey had not seen the lovely Patrice stripped bare. Instead, he stood riveted by the clear deliciousness of Maile's face bathed in light. In that instant Patrice made a decision about Maile and Nils, both of whom she considered ungrateful and disloyal. She even thought of a better word for them—ingrates. She still needed Maile in her lab, but she did not need Nils in her bed.

Patrice spoke sharply. "Ross!" The lawyer followed her quickly. Safe in the dim far end of the gallery, she turned and addressed Maile coldly. "You lied to me about what you were doing tonight, and I'm disappointed in you, Maile. Nils, I'll speak to you tomorrow." Of course she wouldn't. She would have Alex Firman terminate Nils and hand him his last check. Actually, she felt a bit relieved. This was a neat solution to a rather slovenly sexual situation which she'd allowed to develop. Momentarily her breath tightened as the thought of possible blackmail crossed her mind. No, it couldn't happen. The boy was probably wild about Maile, and he did have a special talent. He couldn't risk his be ginning career as an artist. Patrice knew he was damn good, though she'd never admit it.

Again she spoke in a commanding tone. "Coming, Ross?" Ross Bailey followed her out of Fanné's small gallery.

It was at that moment that Alex Firman stepped out of the elevator and found them.

Having no clue to the drama taking place upstairs in Fanné's studio gallery, Sarita settled back to wait for Alex and his charge, Patrice—and, of course, for Ross Bailey. Ross. She wondered how he could con so many people so many times. He hadn't been able to fool her for very long, nor perhaps even the good people of Chicago. As rich and politically powerful as he was, he hadn't yet had himself appointed to the influential city office he craved.

What a pair he and Patrice would make! Sarita was beginning to suspect Ross was onto something regarding Patrice's project. He always liked to be in on the ground floor so that he could rise to the top with the cream. It was a mixed metaphor, but Sarita was too sleepy to think of a better one. Sometimes the truth was a bit mixed up anyway.

Through half-closed eyes Sarita watched the guests going into and coming out of the nearby lively disco that opened off the lobby. They formed a glossy parade of winter people enjoying the island's year-round summer—the women in flounced necklines and a swirl of tropical colors, the men in summer-weight slacks and racy shirts. It didn't matter that the hour was very late. They all were spending time, every one of the twenty-four hours in a day, as though time were made up of golden coins.

And there was really only one person in all of time that Sarita wanted to see, and that person was Morgan.

The big station wagon sped up the coast from Kaanapali with Alex at the wheel, a silent Patrice beside him and Sarita in the back seat. No one spoke, except for Sarita's polite comment that dinner and the evening and the island of Maui seemed to have been a rousing success with Patrice's guests. Sarita suspected that something unusual must have happened during Patrice and Ross's visit to the upper corridors of the Maui Regency. Patrice had a pinched, contentious and angry look about her.

Whatever it was, it probably had nothing to do with Ross, because he'd been effusive in saying good night. Kissing Patrice's hand, he'd also tried to hold Sarita's. But at least he had stopped acting as though he and Sarita were an engaged couple. Sarita had been amused to see him showing Patrice his best side—aggressive, self-confident, quick and dominant. All of which meant he was up to something.

Patrice's own thoughts in the Maui night were rambling. She was sure she'd put Sarita Miller on the defensive as she'd intended to do by unexpectedly producing two of the Dome executives as well as Ross Bailey. It would be no problem to arrange for Sarita to make a speedy return to Chicago. Patrice wanted her out of Morgan's sight and reach. She'd decided that Morgan was definitely the man she wanted to keep, though a week ago she might have had some hesitation about this, thinking he'd outlived his usefulness to her.

Now Patrice was firm. It never occurred to her that she could fail with Morgan. With Ross she could crack the whip whenever she desired. It was Ross Bailey who worshipped "connections." That was her hold over him. And she did have connections—in New York, Chicago and a few other high places that counted, in this country and in Europe. When she was again established in the arena of action with her extraordinary "youth" discovery, there would be no stopping her. She knew her accounts had been settled with the people in Belgium. Emotionally and professionally, she was as tight as a drum. No loose flaps anywhere.

Patrice settled back, her face smoothing itself. She

breathed deeply as they swung into the short access road leading from the highway to the main house. The air was divine with its scent of ginger . . . enough moisture in the earth to make that fragrance rise. She'd sleep tonight.

As the station wagon stopped in the driveway, the only car the three of them observed besides the jeep was Sarita's rental, standing underneath a traveler's palm. Sarita slipped out of the back seat, mumbled good night and said she had to pick up her tennis shoes from the veranda. She slid away from them on her way to the darkened terrace.

Patrice opened the car door, stepped out and marched ahead of Alex. The pattern was working for her. She'd gotten rid of Nils, though she was still furious at him. If he hadn't exactly cuckolded her, his actions—as Patrice viewed them through her special vision—were very nearly that. It would probably be unwise to keep Maile around too. Her dismissal of McIntosh's daughter wouldn't cause dissension between herself and the chemist. He was a mercenary man with a big family to support, and she'd promised him a percentage deal, which, she'd discovered long ago, was the best way to bind anyone to her service. For the little time left, she could do without Maile in the lab. It was better this way. Tomorrow Alex could terminate both Nils and Maile. She would come up with a good reason to give Morgan for what she had done.

"Patrice, you okay?"

"Why shouldn't I be?" Patrice halted and looked back at Alex's lean profile.

"I thought you seemed a little . . . disturbed when I saw you and Bailey in the upper corridor."

"It was nothing much. I'll tell you later."

Patrice swung the big entrance door shut behind her and crossed the large living room to the stairs. Alex! Morgan had hired him, but she could fire him! No, she'd never do that. Too dangerous. Instead, she'd sic him on Ross. The Chicago lawyer would be happy to take a man with Alex

Firman's qualifications off her hands. Conveniently, Patrice temporarily forgot that Alex served another master besides herself. Morgan would require another explanation.

All of them were accounted for. Nils, Maile, Alex. Each knew too much about Patrice. But she was clever enough to rid herself of them. Nils and Maile would have each other, so they couldn't hold a grudge against her. And Alex would have his secure position with Ross Bailey. All settled, then. Yes, she would sleep tonight.

Patrice walked to her window and looked out over the driveway. It was nearly one-thirty in the morning. The waning moon had left the night an empty blackness. The surf was high, its plunging roar in the distance. The trade winds sighed, then began to blow steadily. When she was free of the island, ready to move on, would she miss the hollow sound of the sea, the vividness of the sky, her dolphin pool? Probably not. Her life here held only a small circumference. She had not explored the island as others had done. She had never gone to the Haleakala ranch, Morgan's retreat.

Even with the night so strangely black, a curious, micalike glitter settled within her vision. She narrowed her eyes in order to pick it up again, a phantom sheen. The winds increased, tossing the flat leaves of the tropical plants to expose anything hidden within. There . . . with the wild movement of pliant branches, she saw it again . . . a dark shape, the gleam of metal. It was too late to investigate. She was tired. She wouldn't call Alex to tell him she thought there might be a car hidden among the leaf shadows in the grove below. Alex took himself and his duties too seriously. He tried to run her life, insinuating himself into it—but he was no longer a part of it. Of course there was no car there. The wind was fooling her. Nature and imagination could play sly tricks.

Sarita, wearing her tennis shoes and carrying her high-heeled sandals, walked down the dusky path toward the guest house. The pale spirals of ferns growing alongside guided her by their fine, feathery feel. It almost seemed to Sarita that the night was like a black butterfly that had settled for this brief span of time at a place where she could touch its tenderness. She wandered slowly, letting serenity creep through her body. She was too superstitious to admit that this—her youth, her living breath and beating heart, her contentment with things as they were—was a perfect moment to be savored. If she did it might be taken away from her.

She came up on the porch of the cottage. The shallow steps, the wooden columns, the siding, were white. The key was already in her hand when she halted. The shadow next to the door did not belong there. It was the height of a tall man, the rugged width of a strong man.

Then she knew.

This *was* the perfect moment, it could not be taken away from her. Next she was in Morgan's arms, his kiss hot on her mouth. All of her stirred wildly beneath the pressure of his body. She heard him murmur, "I've been waiting for you, Sarita."

One arm holding her close, he took the key from her, unlocked the door and drew her inside. The room had a lovely darkness, and they left it that way.

Chapter Twenty-two

IT WAS NEARLY DAWN, WITH THIN STREAKINGS of rosy light pushing through the slatted wood of the shutters. In sleep, Morgan shifted from back to side, heavy limbs and wide shoulders indenting the surface of the mattress until Sarita rolled down into the space beside him. Half awakening, she could feel the tips of her breasts touch the circle of Morgan's arm. Sleepily she lowered her head, tucking it against the column of his neck so that her tongue could explore the pulsebeat at the base of his throat. As memory returned of their night just past, the slow, reckless summoning of desire courted her once more. She raised her face until her lips lightly swept his brow and drifted up into the bronzy thickness of his tumbled hair.

She was aware that his hand—was he still asleep, was he still within his own dream?—was beginning to move up her body. Sensually, and without haste, he tenderly stroked her breasts, seeking their velvety points, finding her quivering throat. His fingers next touched the insolence of that one white pearl ear stud she wore. She knew then that he was awake, or partially so, and teasing her.

"Morgan?" she whispered.

"Mmmm . . . don't talk . . . " And raising himself up,

252

he covered her body with his own. Sarita felt herself shivering with a desire to be taken, but first she needed to challenge. She held her legs tight together between his. He attempted to force her limbs apart with his knee, but she tensed. Groaning at her lack of submission, he dipped his head to punish and caress her shoulders and breasts with the hard thrust of his whisker-roughened chin and the curling stab of his tongue, an act both tantalizing and erotic.

His arms tightened around her until she threw back her head and cried out. Quick to seize the advantage, he plunged his mouth into hers, deeply, with a great thirsting sweetness.

There was no need for either to give in. Swiftly, and together, each clasped the other. Their joined bodies moved tenderly, then fiercely, to climax. Love, hastened by passion, prolonged their magical journey.

Full sunlight splashed into the room and across the bed before they released each other. Morgan threw the riotously colored spread across his love, kissed her bosom through the covering's sensuous shades of red, garnet and violet, then picked her up and strode to the window. He pulled open the shutters with one hand and, quite naked himself, stood there holding her in his arms. Beyond the window were the leaning coco palms and the wildly blooming flowers and the sea. "Now tell me that Pele hasn't granted my wish!" he cried.

Like a replay of words gone before, Sarita heard herself murmuring, "And that is?"

"That you will remain here in the islands as long as your heart desires. How long, Sarita?" He kissed her lingeringly before he would allow her to reply.

"Unfair, unfair . . ." she muttered. And then she said what he wanted to hear, what she wanted to shout. "Forever . . . if it's with you, Morgan."

Satisfied, he set her down, gave her a light paddle on her rear and sent her along to get dressed.

She halted in the doorway of the bathroom. She was curious. "Morgan, where's your car? I didn't see it when we drove up last night. I can't understand how I didn't know I'd find you here."

"I parked the car in the kiawe grove below the main house, where no one could see it," he explained a bit smugly. "I wanted to surprise you, and I wanted to avoid having to talk to anyone else. It's privacy with you I want— not another neurotic discussion with either Patrice or Alex. *Did* I surprise you?"

"Oh, you are a fine, big, vain surprise package! But I was very glad to find you on my doorstep last night." Sarita's face grew serious. "What about the others . . . up at the house? Suppose someone did see you?"

"Believe me, dearest one, if it's Patrice you're concerned about, she knows the facts of life. Now hurry up so we can go somewhere and eat breakfast. I'm starved!"

"Well, you can't go that way, Morgan!"

She regarded him with a mischievous gleam in her eyes, thoroughly enjoying the sight of his beautiful body.

He looked down at himself and grinned. "Thanks for reminding me. Listen, I'll pull on a pair of pants and go out to the car and wait for you."

"Morgan, you're sweet." Sarita showed him the tip of her tongue and vanished.

Firman was the first to see the Jaguar. He wondered at its owner's boldness in half hiding it in the kiawe grove. His eyes narrowed thoughtfully. Morgan could at least have gotten out of Sarita's bed and been on his way back to his own condo before daylight. Alex hardly had to guess that Wycoff had spent the night in the guest house. Or what was left of the night after they all had returned from Kaanapali.

He glanced up at Patrice's second-story window. The shutters were closed. She must still be asleep. He doubted that she'd seen Morgan's car, since it was fairly well hidden from her view. Would she have cared if she had seen it? He wondered.

Neither Nils nor Maile had shown up at the house last

night. Something out of the ordinary must have happened at the hotel. Alex was sure of it. He'd observed them coming out of the elevator just as he was entering it to look for Patrice and Bailey. Both Nils and Maile had brushed by him without a word or a glance. They'd appeared upset, yet, at the same time, they'd looked happy. A funny combination. He couldn't figure it out.

Alex Firman walked around the Jaguar. Out of habit he kicked its tires a couple of times, then started toward where the jeep was parked. He was also wondering what Morgan's reaction had been to that obscene note he'd scribbled on the back of the match cover and stuck in the steering wheel. Alex would probably never know. He didn't seem to be in anyone's confidence these days—except Patrice's—and he wasn't sure of her any more. Firman sensed it was time to start moving on. He'd been useful to Morgan in the beginning while settling Patrice in at Napili and watching over her. But Patrice seemed to be doing all right for herself now. She looked as if she was ready to tear right back into the big time and score again.

Firman got into the jeep, checked the gun he kept in the glove compartment and sped off to his private target range beyond Fleming Beach. He always liked to do a little early-morning practice shooting. He chuckled as he swung onto the highway heading north, thinking about Morgan and Patrice running into one other when Morgan came up the path from the guest house. That might not happen, but then again, it might. The sight would have pleased Alex.

The trade winds were blowing in his face. Softly he let out the weird Bedouin howl he'd learned during his tour of duty in the Middle East. Recently he'd received an offer to go to Australia. Now he would seriously consider it.

Morgan strolled up the pathway, experiencing that extraordinary exhilaration that seemed to be conferred on him by Sarita Miller. She invigorated him, both in the quality of his mind and in his physical energies. Right now he was mentally reasoning, sorting out, planning. The Kahana deal had been advantageously concluded—for his company as well as for the Hawaiian family with whom he'd made a leasehold arrangement. He'd agreed that the old grandmother could remain in the house she'd lived in for seventy years. The company would simply build the new development around it. She could have her yard, her fruit trees, her beach frontage, and her sons and grandsons could continue to store and repair their fishing nets there. Everyone was satisfied. Whoever was willing to pay an excessive amount for a handsome townhouse condominium would regard the ancient house and its fishing nets as local color, part of the tropical ambience he was buying.

Morgan halted and looked around him. It was one of those incredible island days when the sky was cloudless and turquoise in color, the sea a bright blue-green, the flowers magical. Maui was the best, no doubt about it. He said the words to himself in the Hawaiian language: *Maui no ka oi*.

Morgan continued up the path. He was wearing lightweight twill pants, cinched with a canvas belt. His brown upper torso was bare, and he carried a red and white flowered shirt over one shoulder. His bare feet were thrust into a pair of old sneakers.

"You look like a beachcomber." Patrice stood, hands on her hips, surveying Morgan from the end of the veranda.

Morgan felt so good this morning, she didn't bother him. "I can't say the same for you, Patrice. There's nothing of the beachcomber about you. You look kind of gorgeous. What are you all gotten up for?"

Patrice was wearing some sort of beige-colored, shimmery costume intended for warm weather, yet it had a pulled-together city look to it. A necklace of brown, lacquered wood beads, clasped with a gold and topaz pendant, adorned her neck. Her dark hair was exquisitely groomed, her skin like porcelain, her eyes unreadable beneath the fine fringe of bangs. The perfume she wore reached Morgan despite the competition from the surrounding flowers.

"What scent is that you're wearing?" She'd trained him to use the proper words, at least. He made a guess, knowing he was wrong. "Is it ginger?"

Patrice's reply was sweetly whimsical as she sidled in his direction. "It's Rochas' Femme, and if you can smell it from this distance, I'm a bit too evocative."

"It *is* a little early in the morning for that." Morgan stopped and let whatever else he was going to say hang there. He realized he didn't want to sound critical since Patrice was obviously trying to be pleasant now, after she'd got that "beachcomber" remark out of her system.

"It *is* early. You led right into that one," Patrice countered. She stared meaningfully toward the cottage. "In the past, at least you used to be discreet."

"I've outgrown discretion. You reach a certain age and you can do what you want."

"Thirty-seven? That's hardly a reachable age." Patrice's lips tightened. Age was a subject she didn't care to pursue this morning.

Morgan slid both arms into his shirt sleeves and slowly began buttoning the shirt. He glanced again toward the sea as he climbed the terrace steps. "Where are you going, Patrice?"

"I too am off for a little dallying. But with me, Morgan, it's business. Always. I wouldn't neglect my branch offices in L.A. or Houston or New York." She said this last pointedly.

Morgan's smile was wide and innocent. "Then you must be having breakfast with Ross Bailey."

"How do you know that?" Patrice's mouth dropped open a little.

"You're not the only one around here with a sixth sense." Morgan attempted to brush by her.

"If you have a sixth sense, I taught you that. And you're very cocky today," Patrice said heatedly, then paused, remembering that Morgan was the man she wanted to keep.

Or did she? It might not be as easy as she'd thought.

There was a difference in Morgan. He was suave and polite and though he'd just been close enough for her to touch he still seemed a remote distance away. Patrice's mind worked rapidly. She could always give it a try now and change her strategy later, if necessary. Imperiously she called, "Morgan!"

His back to Patrice, Morgan halted in the doorway to the salon. He knew that tone. Very slowly he turned, waiting "Yes, Patrice?" He could almost see her mental wheels nipping along.

She moved toward him, a small woman with a panther's tread. Her strong fingers clasped his arm. He tensed, looking down at her, then repeated, too politely this time, "Yes Patrice?"

Patrice again glanced toward the guest house. "I sent for a cab to take me to Kaanapali," she whispered. "Before it gets here, let's have this out. Let's let bygones . . ." She paused, knowing very well that he was ahead of her, that he understood her. But only because she had taught him—savvy and intuition. Conveniently Patrice could forget Morgan's contributions to their life together.

In his turn, Morgan was thinking that only a woman with supreme self-confidence would—in brilliant sunlight, the first thing in the morning, with the knowledge that he'd just left another woman's warm bed—proposition him to forget the past divorce, start over and make it Patrice and Morgan once more.

He bent toward her. Patrice made her mouth soft. He raised his free hand and released her fingers from his other arm. Her mouth hardened slightly. He touched her chin, held it in a firm grip and turned her face into what he considered to be the realistic light of day. "It's over between us, Patrice. I admire your nerve and your talent, but I've simply had enough of my dealings with you. I won't be here for you, Patrice—ever! I think you've got yourself another stepladder, and if that's the case, stick with him.

258

Because I won't be around, thank God I won't! You're a bitch goddess. I don't know what that means, exactly, but it certainly suits you."

Shock collided with sensuality behind Patrice's dark, veiled eyes. For an instant more she and Morgan regarded each other. Then she threw back her head, exploding with laughter.

"How did I stand living with you, Morgan—or rather, near you—for almost ten years?" She was thinking fast. She had to be the one to let go first. Or at least she had to make it seem that way. Actually, Morgan had shown her how. He had made a guess about Ross Bailey. So Ross had to be the man of choice, then. "I'm leaving here myself. I have an appointment in Kaanapali." Morgan knew that, of course, but she was merely giving herself time.

"Keep your appointment in Kaanapali," Morgan said gravely. "Make it pay off, Patrice. I think you and Ross will pair up to great advantage. I've known him as a business associate for a long time too, don't forget. I was never as close to him as you were. He's richer now, even more politically powerful than he used to be. And you can give him the East Coast connection he believes he needs. You've still got it all, you know. No heart, maybe." He tapped her forehead. "But you have it up here—that's what counts. At least with your kind of people."

"Morgan, stop telling me what I already know." Stop getting ahead of me, Morgan, was what she really wanted to say. There was something else. "By the way, Maile and Nils are leaving. As a matter of fact, they've already left." Patrice knew they hadn't shown up at the compound.

Morgan's glance was cryptic. "Okay. I take it you've straightened out the bookkeeping with them, what we owe them. It's all right with Maile's father?"

Patrice shrugged. After a split second, she asked, "Will you keep Alex Firman on? I won't be here, you know." It would be impossible now for Patrice to settle Firman with

Ross Bailey. She was settling herself with Ross. She wanted Firman out of her life.

Morgan was still expressionless. "Alex will land on his feet, as they say. He's had offers."

"I didn't know that." Patrice waited for an explanation. But Morgan wasn't going to say any more. He was supposed to be at the car, waiting for Sarita. He was beginning to be concerned that his love would appear at any minute.

"I'm going now . . . I think I hear the cab. It's not up to me to write a letter of recommendation for our research analyst, though I have been pleased with her work, I'll admit that. And I'm sure you've been delighted, Morgan— with her expertise."

Morgan said nothing. He was thinking that Patrice had better go quickly, before he lost his temper.

Patrice picked up a beige silk handbag lying on a nearby chair. "Cheerio, Morgan." She walked rapidly past him and through the living room, then out the door on the other side, where the cab was waiting. She'd never left the estate by herself before, but today would begin her reentry into the world of Patrice. Ross Bailey would be a good future partner. She'd make him one. Recalling his attentiveness last night at the Maui Regency, she didn't think her task would be too difficult. What she wanted was what he wanted. More power, more money, more celebrity status—more of everything!

Morgan came out of the house and stood by the Jaguar, watching the gray taxi scoot off among the coco palms. He heard footsteps and turned. Sarita was hurrying toward him, tying the ends of a scarf around her waist as she hastened along. Breathless, she stopped beside him and took an object out of her pocket, holding it up for him to see. It was a tiny, carved bird, exquisite in its detail, looking almost ready to float out of Sarita's hand into the air.

"What have we here?"

"It's for you, Morgan. Do you like it, darling?"

He took the small carving out of her hand, his face awash with emotion. "It's beautiful, and it's about to take off." His voice trembled slightly.

Sarita nodded. "That's the idea. It's ready to soar."

"Like us?"

"Like us."

He kissed her. "Nobody ever gave me anything like this before. I love the gift, I love the giver." Sarita flushed with pleasure. Morgan thought, My God, I don't want to cry in front of her. But she's the loveliest, the kindest, the sweetest . . . He said, somewhat gruffly, "Look, you and I have things to do. Breakfast first, of course."

"Of course. At the Lahaina Broiler?"

"Where else? Then, after breakfast, we're going to that gallery I told you about and find my artist friend who designs very special rings for very special people." Morgan raised Sarita's left hand and kissed her fingers. "A ring for Sarita's fourth finger—does that suit you?"

"Oh, Morgan! Yes!" Sarita quivered with happiness. She had it all. The best in the world . . . a truly golden moment. She breathed deeply of the island air and looked around her. This was paradise, this Maui. Yet she felt it could hardly contain the two of them. They *were* ready to soar.

"What are you thinking?"

"That I love you. That I'm happy. That I want to do something absolutely wonderful for everyone else. I want everyone in the world to be happy and healthy and secure and well loved."

"A tall order, Sarita." Again he kissed her fondly. "We'll see what we can do about it. But think about this first. Do you want to be married here and move into the condo for your honeymoon?"

"That sounds perfect. And it's wonderful that Peter and Meg are here. They can be with us at the ceremony, and afterward we'll celebrate and talk and laugh and . . ." A little shadow crossed Sarita's face. "I forgot . . ." She paused.

Morgan opened the car door for her. "Don't worry about Bailey, Sarita love. He and Madam are off to conquer the East Coast of the United States."

"You don't mean that Patrice and Ross . . . ?"

"Why not? As the saying goes, they were made for each other. It's surprising they haven't gotten together sooner. Come on, let's go eat and talk about what you and I are going to do. I can't run Houston and L.A. and New York without you, you know. You're the one who writes everything down in that little book and understands figures and computers and such. I'm going to depend on you, Sarita. You think I'm kidding, but I'm not."

He slid in behind the steering wheel and placed his gift on the dash. He knew that before he started the motor, he had to put his arms around her once more. But when he did, when he gathered Sarita close to him, her warmth, her softness, her scent, drove him crazy. He bent his head down to her. Their lips parted and met. It was as though they had to devour life, have it all—now! There was no confusion of the senses. Their passion was direct, swift and sweet.

The familiar longing that he always evoked in Sarita raced through her body as, with eyes closed, she felt the strong pressure of his coaxing mouth. She responded to him with mischief and desire. She was aware that if they weren't careful, in a few moments they would find themselves back in her bedroom. Morgan knew this too. He looked at her questioningly. She shook her head. "Why not?" he asked.

"Breakfast," she reminded him.

"Then later?"

"Sooner than later," she murmured.

Morgan grinned. "We'll be back. But first we're going to go out and tilt the world on its axis." He glanced at the little, carved bird and put it into his shirt pocket. "You know what? We're going to fly."

She kissed him once more, nuzzling close. "Look out, now," he cautioned her as he started the motor. "Don't get fresh."

"We'll fly, Morgan. I believe it. Take off."

The Jaguar went spinning down the road. The coco palms were swaying. The trade winds were blowing. It was really a perfect day.

About the Author

Muriel Bradley was born and raised in Los Angeles. However, she has also lived in Chicago, San Francisco, and New York City. She currently resides in Encino, California, with her husband, who is an advertising executive, her daughter, and several pets.

She embarked on a literary career several years ago and has had seven suspense novels published. In addition, she has worked as a research analyst in the major film studios. Her latest assignment was as an associate producer on a picture filmed in Nova Scotia.

One of her major passions is traveling. She has been to Hawaii several times and was delighted to have been able to use it as the setting for *Flowers in Winter*.

CAREER AND LOVE COLLIDED IN THE MAGIC OF A HAWAIIAN ISLAND PARADISE

Ambitious marketing analyst Sarita Miller
had the brains and beauty to reach the top
of Chicago's advertising empire.
And, researching a new miracle youth cream
on the lush Maui estate of developer
Patrice Wycoff, a once-famous cosmetics
queen, was a plum assignment.

But when Sarita met handsome industrialist
Morgan Wycoff—Patrice's ex-husband
and financial backer—she felt a deep sensual
attraction that challenged her
more than her career.

Soon they were caught up in a passionate
love—a love now threatened by the
scheming intrigues of the selfish and devious
Patrice. But Sarita endured, fighting for
her honor, her beliefs—and the only man
who had claimed her heart.

LOOK FOR THE SILKEN WEB BY LAURA JORDAN COMING FROM RICHARD GALLEN BOOKS NEXT MONTH

ISBN 0-671-45142-1